"So you said you had a proposition for me?"

Ethan gulped as J.C.'s words and his thoughts got tangled up in one vivid, erotic image. Her naked... sitting in front of him. "I didn't mean it that way."

"What way is that?" She smiled at him across the table.

"You know, like..." Did he really have to spell it out for her? He pictured her left breast. The right one. What color were the tips? How would they taste? Her butt. He'd already grabbed a handful of that, but his fingers itched to feel skin, not denim. "Like I was asking to have sex with you."

There. He'd said it. Out loud.

"Do you want to have sex with me?"

Oh, yeah. Practicality answered before lust could. "No, of course not."

Her eyebrow arched at the unintended insult.

Ethan flushed. He'd give a month's pay to get himself out of this mess right now. "I mean, I'm not against the idea. I would love to have sex with you." *Later. Now.*

Her amusement was tempered by the downward focus of her eyes. Her fingers circled the rim of her cup. It didn't take much for Ethan to picture those *same* fingers touching the shell of his ear or trailing along the length of his arousal. As if right on cue, the little major popped to

Uh, now what?

Dear Reader,

Back when I was teaching, our school always celebrated Veterans Day by inviting local veterans and active duty personnel to a school assembly. Our high school band would play a medley of hymns from each branch of the service— and as each tune was played, we invited the marines, soldiers, sailors, airmen and coastguardsmen to stand and be saluted. I always cried.

You see, I'm the daughter of a marine. I'm the big sister of a marine who's served in the Gulf. I have some idea of what these men are about—they've always been heroes to me. And I always knew that one day I wanted to write a story about a marine, one with my dad's character, my brother's devotion—and okay, yeah, with one of those hard warrior bodies they keep in such tip-top shape!

I wanted my heroine to take a journey and discover, like me, all the wonderful things that make that military man more than a hunk—they make him a hero. Please visit my Web site at juliemiller.org.

Enjoy,

Julie Miller

Books by Julie Miller

HARLEQUIN BLAZE
45—INTIMATE KNOWLEDGE
77—CARNAL INNOCENCE

HARLEQUIN INTRIGUE
699—THE ROOKIE*
719—KANSAS CITY'S BRAVEST*
748—UNSANCTIONED MEMORIES *
779—LAST MAN STANDING
*The Taylor Clan

MAJOR ATTRACTION

Julie Miller

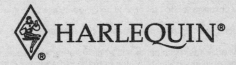

HARLEQUIN®

TORONTO • NEW YORK • LONDON
AMSTERDAM • PARIS • SYDNEY • HAMBURG
STOCKHOLM • ATHENS • TOKYO • MILAN • MADRID
PRAGUE • WARSAW • BUDAPEST • AUCKLAND

For the Pageturners reading group—
Linda W., Amy, Mel, Linda S.

Thanks for introducing me to iced coffee drinks,
expanding my literary horizons,
sharing my love for books
and letting me be one of the bunch.

And for the real Marines in my life—
Dad, George, Uncle Ed
and students over the years.
Time and again you've shown me it's
the man or woman who makes the uniform.
Thank you.

ISBN 0-373-79154-2

MAJOR ATTRACTION

1

"I NEED A MAN?"

Josephine Cynthia Gardner repeated the statement her editor had just expressed and sank into the chair on the opposite side of the newspaper editor's cluttered desk. She could tell this wasn't going to be good.

"Isn't that a sort of old-fashioned view for you?" J.C. questioned.

"Oh, honey. We could all use a man in our lives every now and then." Her editor, Lee Whiteley, dug into the sleeve of the turquoise silk caftan she was wearing, fishing for a tissue to dab her nose. Her garish outfit matched her personality. She'd never been shy about voicing her opinion. "Don't you miss sex?"

J.C.'s eloquent splutter betrayed her unattached, career-obsessed, too-long-without-sex status.

"Just as I thought."

"I don't have to test every position for myself before writing about it or recommending it."

"Oh," Lee tutted, "poor thing."

J.C. bristled at what sounded like genuine sympathy. She didn't need it. She tugged down the hem of her royal-blue blouse and sat forward to correct the misconception. "Not poor thing. Professional. I read, I research, I interview people. I can find what works and doesn't work in a relationship without muddying up my own life with a man I don't need right now."

"But you do." Lee leaned forward. With at least one ring on each finger, she braced her hands on top of her desk. "I have a topic for your next series of articles that simply cries out for firsthand experience."

This definitely did not sound good. "Firsthand experience?"

"It came to me in a dream last night, J.C." Lee splayed her bejeweled fingers like the grand *ta-da* of a cut-rate magic act. "American heroes. It's a hot topic right now, and I think you should jump on it."

J.C. twisted her lips into a skeptical frown. "You want me to jump on an American hero?"

Lee shot her fingers through the hair at her temple, leaving the carrot-red strands sticking up straight from their gray roots. "Listen to me, Dr. Smart Mouth. It's a plum assignment. I'm asking you to surround yourself with some of the most gorgeous men in the country and tell me what's to love or not about them."

J.C. threw up her hands in surrender. "Maybe you'd better explain this dream of yours in more detail before I start to think you're asking me to prostitute myself for the paper."

"Fine." At last Lee sat back in her chair and assumed as businesslike a pose as a woman wearing turquoise and glitz with carrot-red hair could manage. "I look for all the news that's fit to print, not just your column. You might be earning a pretty penny in syndication, but it's still headlines that sell my papers. Heroes are in. Men in uniform—cops, firefighters, soldiers. Readers want to read about them. They want to know how to find a hero of their own."

J.C. definitely didn't like this idea.

"Men are more heroic when it comes to serving their

country than they are when it comes to serving their families. That civilian adoration is a power trip.''

J.C. had grown up in the empty shadow of such a supposed military hero. Her father had used his uniform as an excuse to stay away from his wife and daughter. He'd used it as a calling card to seduce women all over the world. He'd even worn it to marry a gullible woman when he'd been stationed in the Philippines, conveniently forgetting to notify—or divorce—J.C.'s American mother.

She knew the truth behind the myth Lee wanted her to profile. She waved her hand aside. ''The creature you're talking about—a dependable uniformed lover—doesn't exist. You might not like the tone of my columns.''

Lee harrumphed in her chair. ''Well, that's damn cynical of you. You don't turn thirty until December, and yet you already sound like an old crone.''

''I sound realistic. I'm not knocking the institutions of law enforcement and the military—I know we need them, and I appreciate that they're here to defend me.'' Lee wanted firsthand experience? She was an expert on busted relationships and martyred hopes and fruitless dreams—and how to steer clear of them. ''But I am not going to recommend to my readers that they can solve their loneliness by dating a man they have to salute and call 'sir.'''

J.C.'s bitter diatribe didn't seem to dissuade Lee from the idea. In fact, judging by the twinkle in her hazel eyes, Lee liked her star columnist's opposing point of view.

''Why don't you approach the articles from that perspective?'' Lee challenged. ''Infiltrate the military. Get to know some of those hunky scoundrels and find out what makes them so darn irresistible to women when—as you say—we should know better. Is it the broad shoulders? The shoot-from-the-hip attitude? The ribbons and shiny brass trim on their uniforms? The way they pop to attention so easily…''

Lee's voice trailed off, and her eyes fixed in a dreamy stare behind the rhinestone-studded half-glasses perched atop her nose.

J.C. quirked an eyebrow, wondering just what kind of fantasy her editor was conjuring—or remembering—right now. She leaned forward and snapped her fingers. ''Hello? Earth to Lee.'' The editor's gaze blinked back into focus. ''What were you thinking about just now?''

''Not *what*,'' came her devilish reply. *''Who.''*

Despite her love for flash over fashion, Lee Whiteley was a brilliant, insightful woman. Besides sharing a feminist streak, J.C. had always appreciated the way Lee's mind worked, and how her unique blend of creative energy and business savvy had helped produce some of the best writing of J.C.'s career. Lee's cutting-edge topics, penned with J.C.'s professional expertise and frank, witty style, had been picked up over the wire from Lee's weekly newspaper, *Woman's Word*. J.C. credited her editor almost single-handedly with conceiving the idea for her Dr. Cyn advice and editorial articles, saving her from the need to sign on to dull university research projects to supplement her dream of becoming a full-time writer.

But this was a distinctly soft side to Lee she hadn't seen before. Curious. And suspicious. This meeting to discuss her next series of columns had been a setup from the moment she walked through the door. A shameless matchmaking ploy to get her sex-and-relationship columnist back into some sex and relationships.

''Okay, I'll bite.'' J.C. suppressed a wary groan. *''Who* were you thinking about? And why is this going to change my mind?''

The older woman's eyes twinkled with mischief. ''PFC

Robert Tortelli. Now there was a soldier for you. I sent him off to Vietnam with a smile.''

Was this a story about great sex back in high school? Or of a lost first love? J.C. shook her head and brushed a lock of short, chestnut hair behind her ear. ''But you've never been married. Private Tortelli apparently didn't come back. At least not to you.''

''Oh, he came back, all right.'' Lee sighed and twirled the giant turquoise and silver ring around the index finger of her left hand. ''I welcomed him home with a big smile, too.''

''So the sex was good?''

''The sex was great.''

''But he didn't stay, did he?'' Relieved the memory hadn't had a tragic outcome, yet pleased that she'd predicted the man's love-'em-and-leave-'em behavior accurately, J.C. pushed to her feet, seeing the opportunity to make her point. ''I never said a soldier couldn't make great sex. I said he doesn't make a good long-term partner.''

''The reason Bobby and I went our separate ways had nothing to do with his career in the army.'' Lee was still smiling as she stood and crossed to the microwave in her office to zap some heat into her herbal tea. J.C. planted her fists on her hips, controlling the urge to reach out and shake some sense into yet another woman who seemed willing to forgive a sexy male brute for not sticking by her. ''I saw him again at our fortieth high-school reunion. He's been married almost thirty years and has two boys in college now.''

''His wife must be a saint.'' She struggled to control it, but sarcasm still managed to work its way into her voice. ''Or a fool.''

"Neither. They're very much in love from what I can see."

"Then they're the exception to the rule." J.C. wasn't going to concede without making her point. "But he still hurt you. He probably sweet-talked you into bed. Gave you some kind of 'this is my last night in the country, I'm going off to face who knows what—make it memorable for me' speech."

Lee shrugged as she turned, dismissing the argument with a sexy grandma smirk on her face. "It was the sixties. Free love was everywhere. He had a tight butt and silky, dark hair, and he was great in the sack. I got what I wanted as much as he did. And that was long before he met his wife. They seem very happy together."

"But—"

"But nothing. You're too young to be this jaded about men. And until you have sex with a man in uniform, you can't really argue that they're not a good catch."

What? "You *do* want me to prostitute myself."

"I want you to get out and practice a little of what you preach to your readers." The microwave dinged and she pulled out her tea, ignoring the accusation. "You're the one who's advised a number of women in your column that it's okay to enjoy sex just for sex's sake. As long as you protect yourself and both partners understand the expectations. I wasn't hurt. I was ahead of my time." She toasted J.C. with her mug. "I think you're behind your time."

J.C. was going to lose this argument and get stuck mingling with the type of man she hated most if she couldn't think of something, fast. "Maybe men in uniform just aren't my style. You know I prefer men who are more cultured. Well educated. My Ph.D. seems to intimidate a lot of guys."

Was Lee clicking her tongue? "Haven't you ever heard of Westpoint? Annapolis? Some of the finest minds in history have graduated from military schools."

She was grasping at straws now. "What about the short haircuts?" She fingered the soft strands that hugged her nape. "I hate dating men with hair shorter than mine."

"Expand your horizons. A good crew cut shows off the shape of those intelligent heads." Lee peered over the top of her glasses, clearly seeing something that J.C. could not. "They don't have those studly reputations for nothing, dear."

J.C.'s stubborn streak was still looking for a way out. "How can I do in-depth research on military relationships with the deadlines you expect from me?"

Lee carried her tea to the desk. "You once told me you were a Navy brat. Surely you still have some connections you could draw upon."

Her family's past was the one place she absolutely refused to go. Lee was her boss, not her best friend. And though she'd become a pal and mentor in the months they'd worked together, J.C. had never told her much about the man who'd fathered her. She'd never told anyone about the hurt and humiliation she'd lived with for so long. She was protecting her mother's feelings, she'd always reasoned.

Her mother, Mary Jo Gardner, had been reduced to a fragile shell of the vibrant beauty J.C. remembered from her earliest childhood. Believing the best of an absent, philandering husband had a way of sucking the life out of a woman. And J.C. had been there for years to witness the deterioration of her mother's soul firsthand. She'd vowed time and again never to be swayed by a man in uniform. And now that her mother had remarried a safe, sedate, reliable homebody and found happiness again, there was even more reason to keep the truth about the swashbuckling sailor who'd knocked her up and ruined her life a family secret.

"I've lost touch with my family connections," was all J.C. said. Like she'd ever been connected to her father in the first place. J.C. circled the desk and leaned her hips against the edge right beside Lee. She had to make her understand her reservations about this project. "I just have a bad feeling about this. I don't want anyone to think the armed forces is this gourmet smorgasbord of men waiting for some lonely heart to have her pick. There's a false hope implied there I don't want to be responsible for."

"You're the lonely heart I'm worried about." Lee reached out and clasped her hand around one of J.C.'s tension-radiating fists. She was frowning. "You don't have a romantic bone in your body, do you? You have degrees in counseling and sex therapy, and you're an insightful observer and a dynamite writer. But you don't believe in happily-ever-after's yourself, do you?"

J.C. stared down at the supportive clasp of hands, wondering if Lee sensed how fraudulent she now felt about dispensing advice on long-term relationships. "Not with a military man."

Of course, she hadn't made it work with a botany professor, a stockbroker, or a meteorologist, either. But she'd helped countless other couples find and maintain the happiness she couldn't find for herself. She'd rescued stale sex lives and coached readers and clients to find a fulfillment she could not. That had to count for something, didn't it?

Lee patted her hand. "Think of it as a cautionary piece, then. What to look for. What to be wary of. How far is safe to go with a man in uniform? Are they good in bed or is that macho facade all for show?"

"You said you wanted heroes for your headlines." J.C. hugged her arms around her waist, already accepting that the assignment was a done deal. "What if my research supports *my* theory and I don't find knights in shining armor among all those eligible men?"

"Readers are hungry for relationship advice of any kind. They're not all necessarily looking for marriage. Some simply want to meet someone. Share some laughs. Have fun. Maybe you could find out which branch of the service is the best in bed. Or who has the worst pickup lines." No matter how painful the proposition might be, Lee's ideas sold papers. J.C. could see the potential popularity of a series of columns focusing on the available man market. "Maybe you could offer practical tips on keeping a long-distance relationship strong. Surely you'll be able to find something to recommend about a man in uniform."

"And if I can't?" Navy Seaman Earl Gardner had made a strong impression on his abandoned daughter and left a devastating lack of trust in his wake. "What if I do my research and prove that men in uniform are selfish in bed, and cads in the relationship department?"

Lee smiled with as much satisfaction as a cat who had just discovered where the cream was stored. "I'll bet you fifty bucks you're wrong. I say there are more men like Bobby Tortelli, with thirty years of a happy marriage beneath their belts than there are randy young bucks who are just using the uniform to get laid."

Her editor had finally pushed the right button. A challenge. J.C.'s weary sigh ended with a cautious smile. "Fifty bucks that a soldier makes a good lover?"

"Fifty bucks."

"You're giving me carte blanche to write whatever I want to say?"

Lee grinned. "As long as it's interesting."

J.C. straightened. She had to write these articles, anyway. She could make them very interesting. And finally expose the truth about men like her father. "You're on."

She extended her hand and the two women shook on it. Then J.C. gathered up her red canvas attaché and slung the long strap over her shoulder.

"Oh, and J.C.?"

"Yes?"

"We don't call you Dr. Josephine. Keep some of the sin in Dr. Cyn. It's what readers want."

J.C. nodded. She was charged and ready to do this right. "I'll give readers something to talk about. Don't worry."

Lee's eyes narrowed above the rhinestones. "I want fair reporting. Study a wide sample. Give me in-depth observations. I can run several articles on the topic."

"Of course. My research ethics have never been questioned." Now *she* was the one smiling. She fully intended to back up every word of truth she wrote. "I promise to be honest with my findings. But fifty bucks says I'll prove you wrong."

2

————————

"I NEED A WOMAN."

Major Ethan McCormick paced across his Pentagon office, needlessly adjusting the gold oak leaf on the impeccably pressed epaulet of his khaki shirt. He attacked the imaginary speck of lint on his sky blue slacks next. Nervousness was a whole new experience for him.

He'd graduated at the top of his class from Annapolis. He'd traveled the globe and protected presidents and prime ministers and ambassadors. He'd trained the finest troops in the world. He'd even foiled an attempted embassy takeover by a local terrorist faction.

But his newest assignment left him flustered.

He crossed to his desk and picked up the memo from General Craddock again. Damn. He hadn't misread the message. He tossed the paper onto the desk and sank down into his chair, tapping his fist against his chin and striking a thoughtful pose. "The general wants to use tomorrow's Cherry Blossom Embassy Ball as an opportunity to meet my wife or significant other."

"Um, I know I'm not the smart one of the family, but I see a slight problem here." A younger, badder version of Ethan leaned back in the chair across from him, grinning his wiseass face off. His brother, Travis. "Does Craddock know you're not married? Not engaged? Not seeing anyone—significant or otherwise?"

"Ergo, my problem." Ethan dropped his fist and

counted off the competition on his fingers. "Doug Sampson is married with two kids. Ty Richards is a newlywed. Regina Moffat has been engaged to that doctor of hers for almost three years now. I have to at least show up with a date if I want to stay in contention for the lieutenant colonel promotion."

"You really want a Quantico training school assignment?" Travis, a captain with a covert special forces unit, still possessed the wanderlust that had once driven Ethan to apply for transfers to embassies on nearly every continent. Travis loved the action of serving in the military, while Ethan thrived on the discipline.

"I want to *run* that program," Ethan clarified. And since Quantico, Virginia was the Corps' main training base, it was no small-potatoes assignment. "I'm thirty-five years old. I've seen enough of the world. Now that Dad's retired and Caitie's married and living in Virginia, I want to stay close to home and see something of my family for a change. And the idea of heading up a task force to train embassy protection units really appeals to me. Plus, it would put me in line to eventually lead a regiment of my own."

He drummed his fingers on the arm of his chair, letting his gaze slide across to that damned memo. "But they won't put me in charge of anything on any base unless I can provide a suitable hostess. All this time I thought I'd joined the Marines to protect my country and my people. Now I find out I should have joined the country club, instead."

Travis smoothed his palm over the top of his closely cropped dark blond, almost brown, hair. Ethan's hair was equally short and a shade lighter. He outranked his younger brother, stood an inch taller and outweighed him by twenty pounds. But Travis had the looks and the charm. And the women.

Ethan had, well, he had his career. A damn fine, exemplary one, at that.

"So what, exactly, are you asking me?" Travis was enjoying this way too much for Ethan's peace of mind. "You need me to hook you up?"

Hook him up? He wanted to hire him a hooker? Surely not. Hell. Ethan had been out of circulation for so long, he didn't even know relationship terminology anymore. He had a real situation here. And it required a well thought-out plan of action in order to be resolved. "I've been stateside for what, all of five months? That's hardly enough time to meet somebody, much less marry her."

"Uh, hello? Speak for yourself, big brother. Five months? If all you need is a date, I can line one up for you in five minutes." Damn, but little brothers could be annoying sometimes. Why had Ethan thought asking Travis for help with his nonexistent love life would be a good idea?

"Thanks for rubbing it in." Ethan stood and resumed his pacing. Travis was the poster boy for the Marine Corps' lean, mean fighting machine image. He was equally adept at being a love machine, if his reputation was even halfway accurate. But Ethan had developed other skills at the expense of learning how to finesse a woman. Self-discipline. Multilingual communication. Razor-sharp strategy. Diplomacy.

Travis could build a bomb out of gum wrappers and coffee grounds. He could infiltrate an enemy post and knock out their communication system before the guards even blinked. He could sweet-talk a woman and have her in his bed faster than most men could even get her phone number.

Ethan could talk to a world leader and command his respect. He could placate local authorities who thought U.S. troops were taking over their jurisdiction and defiling their culture. He'd safeguarded princesses and sheikhs and the men under his command. He could direct massive security missions behind the scenes without a party guest ever seeing anyone but the uniformed M.P. at the door.

But sweet-talk a woman?

Bed her?

Propose marriage—even a fake one—to her?

The last time Ethan had sex with a woman had been New Year's Eve—one year, four months, two weeks and a handful of days ago—in Cairo, Egypt. Of course, Bethany Mead had turned out to be *Mrs.* Mead, the junior ambassador's young trophy wife, not his daughter as she'd claimed. Ethan thought he'd been navigating a tricky point in his career, getting involved with a woman he'd been assigned to protect. But he'd been willing to take the risk for love.

The sex between them had been great. Frequent. Naughty. Fun. But that's all Bethany had wanted.

Mrs. Mead had traveled to Egypt two months ahead of Mr. Mead to have an affair with someone—anyone—lots of anyones—to retaliate against her philandering husband. She'd targeted Ethan before they'd even finished the limo ride from the airport to the embassy. He'd fallen for the lonely, vulnerable daughter act. Fallen hard. But when he uncovered her masquerade, the bitter, vindictive wife gave him a new understanding and appreciation for the Corps' focus on rules and discipline.

He'd salvaged his career without a black mark on his record. But he hadn't salvaged his heart. Or his trust.

Self-discipline was like breathing for Ethan. The whole experience had prompted him to make a vow to avoid all serious relationships—to avoid the temptations of sex—until he could find the right woman to commit to and guarantee that she was his alone.

It had been almost a year and a half and counting...he hadn't found her yet.

No wife. No fiancée. No bedmate. Not even an old gal pal he could call in a favor from.

"I need more than a date," Ethan reasoned, seeing the words of that memo playing over and over in his head as a sorry reminder of his personal life. Or lack thereof. "I can't show up at one function with a blonde, and the next one with a brunette. General Craddock and the review board are looking for stability. I need a cultured, classy lady who's willing to donate a few weeks of her time to me."

"Donate?" Travis's expression was doubtful as he rose and scooted aside a file on the top of Ethan's desk to lean his hip there. "Didn't you inherit *any* of the McCormick charm?"

Ethan splayed his hands at his waist and puffed out a frustrated sigh. "I think it all bypassed me and got dumped on you." He couldn't resist a dig. "Lord knows, you're full of it."

The double entendre earned a fake laugh. "You're too clever for your own good, big brother. But I'm sure you have some raw materials in there somewhere we can work with. Good bone structure. Respectable bank account. Power."

Ethan groaned at the compliments that sounded more like teasing than flattery. "I see you neglected wit, intelligence, sex appeal. You don't think I can pull this off, do you?"

Travis shrugged. "You called me for help. That makes me think you're the one with the doubts." He pointed his cap at the newspaper lying on Ethan's desk. "Maybe you should have written that relationship columnist, Dr. Cyn. She can tell you what a woman wants and needs in order to go to bed with a man." He spread his arms wide and made a pity face. "Or commit to a two-week engagement."

"I'm not about to lower myself to asking advice from some tabloid columnist." Ethan snapped his opinion with the succinct force of a commander dressing down a non-com.

But Travis had known him for thirty-two years. He didn't bat an eye at the righteous bluster in his voice. "She's more than a tabloid sensation. I've read some of her stuff. The woman, whoever she really is, is a licensed therapist with several college degrees. One of the guys in my unit joined an online chat with her—he says it saved his marriage. Hell, I even picked up a few pointers."

"*You* need pointers?" Was it freezing over somewhere?

"Well, it was more of a validation that I was doing things the right way." Travis grinned one of those what-was-good-for-the-cat-must-be-good-for-the-cat's-big-brother grins. "Sounds like she's got the answer to all your dating woes."

"I doubt it."

Travis picked up the newspaper and started thumbing through it. Good God, he was actually going to quote the woman. Travis located the column and folded the paper to highlight the suggestive heart and fig-leaf logo that marked the *sin*ful play of words in the headline. "Have you ever actually read Dr. Cyn? She's insightful. Honest. Funny. She knows what she's talking about."

Ethan questioned Travis's defense of the anonymous woman who had the entire East Coast talking about her views on men and dating and sex. The woman probably wasn't getting any of her own. Otherwise, she wouldn't have time to write so much tripe and create such a stir.

Okay, so technically, he hadn't actually read any of her columns beyond their teasers, like, Boy Toy or Manly Man? Which Do You Have? and Pleasure All Night Long—How To Give It, How To Get It. But he'd overheard enough gossip to know this Dr. Cyn pushed the boundaries with her sex and relationship advice. She was hardly the type of woman who could understand conservative values or the appeal of old-fashioned romance and honor.

Ethan snatched the paper, rolled it up and swatted the air in lieu of his brother. "I don't need advice. Not from this Dr. Cyn and not from you. What I need is a woman willing to act a part for a couple of weeks. She needs to take direction, and she needs to deliver."

"Boy, you *didn't* get any charm, did you?" Travis grabbed the paper back and tossed it onto the desk. "This isn't a military exercise, Ethan. You can't just command a woman to be yours. You have to seduce her."

"I don't want to have sex with her." Travis raised a skeptical eyebrow. Ethan clarified that it wasn't sex he objected to, just the casualness of it. And how sex for lust's sake could muddy up a man's thinking, keep him from seeing the truth about the woman he was with. "It wouldn't be right. I'll save that kind of attention for a real relationship. I'm talking a strictly business proposition here."

Either he'd just said something very profound, or something very amusing, judging by the way Travis kept shaking his head. "I'm not even going to ask you the last time you made love to a woman. I'm not talking about sexually seducing her, numbskull, though that's always an option if you find someone you click with. I'm talking about luring her into your plan. Enticing her into being your steady for a couple of weeks.'' Travis raised his hand and curled his fingers as if he was holding an imaginary apple, symbolically cupping the idea in the palm of his hand in a way Ethan understood in theory, though not in practice. ''You have to make her believe she wants to spend time with you.''

''You think I need to arrange some kind of cash reimbursement?''

Travis crushed the imaginary apple in his fist. ''God, bro—you need more work than I thought. When was the last time you even went out on a date?''

Ethan circled his desk and thumbed through the catalog of engagements on his desk calendar. ''April 18. General and Mrs. Schuck hosted a dinner party. I took Colonel Hoffner's wife because he was overseas on assignment.''

Travis turned to face him. ''No, you *escorted* Mrs. Hoffner. You did your duty.'' He shook his head again. ''When was the last time you took a woman to someplace intimate or fun? A movie? Dinner? A walk on the beach? Where it was just about the two of you?''

''Well—'' Ethan reached for his calendar again.

Travis reached across the desk and stilled his hand. ''If you have to look it up, it wasn't a date. You should be able to give me a name. Either you had a nice time and you want to remember the lady, or you had a lousy time and she made a lasting impression you wish you could forget.''

Ethan jerked his hand away and thumped the desktop with his index finger. ''I'm a damn fine Marine. I've earned that promotion. It shouldn't hinge on whether or not I can dig up a fiancée on short notice.''

''I won't argue with you there.'' At least he'd concede

that point "But the fact remains it does hinge on that. Now I can dress you down in casual clothes and take you someplace where the women are nice and willing. Where they have a particular fondness for picking up men in uniform."

"Picking up?" Ethan had his doubts about this plan already. "That sounds trashy. I need a first-class lady who can pass muster with the brass."

"If this ball is tomorrow night, and you called me instead of some sweet thing in your Rolodex, then I'm thinking you can't be too choosy right now." Travis had him there. He hated when his pesky little brother was right. "I can guarantee you someone attractive, and I can guarantee you someone willing to consider your proposition. They might not be the same girl, though. To be honest, I don't know that I can guarantee you this paragon of dream-girl virtue you want on such short notice."

Ethan had been prepared to make concessions. Calling Travis had been the first one. "Looks are optional. If she's female and her age is compatible with mine, I'll consider her. I just need someone reliable. Someone convincing."

"All right." Travis checked his watch and strode to the door. "I'll be at your place at eighteen-thirty hours. We'll scruff up your hair, take the shine off your shoes and find something denim for you to wear." He paused with his hand on the doorknob and glanced over his shoulder. "But I tell you what, big brother. I can get you in the door and introduce you. But, ultimately, it's going to be up to you to get the girl to say yes."

Ethan nodded. "Understood."

Travis rolled his eyes as if that answer revealed just how hopeless this whole find-a-fiancée-for-the-major project was.

After Travis left, Ethan stared at the closed door for

several moments, trying to ignore the symbolism. The man in him who hadn't been with a woman for over a year wondered if this mission *was* hopeless.

But the Marine in him refused to say die.

3

DR. CYN IS IN...

Hey out there all you lovers and wannabe lovers—
Holding out for a hero?

Dr. Cyn is always on the lookout to help you find where
you can meet that special someone—and, of course, tell
you the places to avoid at all costs.

My editor posed an interesting question to me this
morning. She challenged me to find a marketplace loaded
with eligible men—one where you could blindfold yourself, spin around, point—and voilà—come up with a guaranteed catch. Let me give it to you straight, ladies. There
is no such wonderland.

Aha, she said. What about the military? Thousands of
gorgeous guys in uniforms—all sizes, shapes and colors.

I'll let you in on a little secret—a stud in uniform is a
guaranteed heartbreaker. So, sure, if all you're looking
for is a little fun for a night or two—find yourself a soldier
or a sailor or an airman. But if you want a real relationship—commitment, support, showing up in your bed and
no one else's!—then look elsewhere. There's a reason
they coined the term "ship out." Because they'll leave
you. They have wars to fight, nations to defend, conquests
to make in other towns, in other countries, in other ports.

Am I painting a clear picture? Stud is as stud does.

Have your fling. But don't count on a Marine.

I know some of you are out there thinking that with

hundreds of thousands of men serving in all the branches of the military, that that studly playboy image must be the exception rather than the rule.

Don't you believe it!

Now you know I'm one to back up what I say with solid evidence—four years of graduate school taught me that. So I accepted my editor's challenge. Yes, I'll grant that there are a few dedicated family men in the armed forces. But I'll bet I can find a greater number of men in uniform who play on their hero status to a) pick up women, b) seduce women and c) leave a trail of women in their wake.

There's a fifty-dollar bet riding on this, readers.

So watch for upcoming columns as I explore the perks, perils and pitfalls of loving a military man. If you're looking for a longtime lover, forget that hunky soldier.

You'll have better luck in the produce aisle.

"There." J.C. typed her signature sign-off into her laptop and e-mailed the introductory column to her editor. She leaned back into the overstuffed pillows of her eggplant-colored chaise lounge and sighed with satisfaction. "There's the 'cyn'-ful style. That should stir up a few readers and sell a few papers."

The springtime sunlight was beginning to lose its afternoon heat as it filtered through the eyelet curtains at her windows. But J.C. had already warmed up to the idea of "infiltrating the military," as Lee had suggested. She loved a challenge. Loved how it made her mind come alive, loved the energy it ignited inside her.

Her plan was simple. There were several nightspots, right here in the Washington, D.C. area, that she knew were frequented by soldiers and sailors from all branches of the service on their off-duty hours. She would find herself a comfortable seat at the bar, order a lemon-lime soda, and wait for the boys to hit on her. She would ask a few questions, flirt a little, let them buy her as many nonalcoholic drinks as they wanted, and listen to their weak pickup lines. If one of them did actually come up with something clever or meaningful to say, she would take her research to the next level.

She'd done enough dating studies to know how to weed out sincere interest from a line geared toward a romp in bed. She would make a few observations and record some informal statistics to use in her column. She would even let a few of them get to first base, just so she could evaluate them fairly in the physical prowess department.

Of course, none of it would mean anything personal to her, despite Lee's not-so-subtle hints that she needed to spice up her real love life to match Dr. Cyn's standards. This was all in the name of research. Of promoting her column. Of winning that bet.

Thoughts of getting back a little of what her father had taken from her never even crossed her mind.

"You go, girl," she laughed at herself. If she could save one woman from the heartache and humiliation her mother had endured, then Lee's ridiculous challenge to get involved with a military man would be worth it.

But her anticipation of the challenge at hand wavered on a lonesome sigh.

She longed for a sparring partner to debate the risky goals of her investigation—and to break the silence of her tiny A-list apartment overlooking the Potomac River. Success had landed her a prime location and a big picture window, but there was still no one to answer back besides the giant stuffed polar bear sitting in the corner, and he wasn't talking. Tucking her laptop and notepad into her attaché she set them on the floor, rose and crossed to the window. She pushed aside the curtain and stared into the sunset's silvery glint off the Potomac. The bustle of crowded sight-seeing boats and sleek racing skulls on the water seemed to mock her carefully cultivated independence.

J.C. let the curtain close and headed toward the bathroom to shower before her night on the town. Her bare feet made no sound as she padded across the carpeted floor. Her apartment suddenly felt uncomfortably quiet and embarrassingly empty, despite the eclectic collection of treasures she'd filled it with.

Her mother had suggested she might try filling her life with people instead of things. But things didn't leave. Things didn't run out on you.

Things didn't fill the loneliness. And though technically she'd slept with a heating pad during the coldest part of the D.C. winter, things didn't warm her bed at night.

Expert knowledge didn't warm her bed, either. Not like a man could.

And her bed had been cold for a lot of nights.

Very cold.

Maybe she'd let one of her military guinea pigs get a little further than first base.

All in the name of research, of course.

GROUCHO'S PUB wouldn't have been Ethan's first choice of places to pick out a potential fake fiancée. He wasn't sure if the quirky name of the place referred to the relics of movie memorabilia nailed to the walls, or to the grumpy old fart serving drinks behind the polished walnut-and-white-tile bar.

The place didn't even boast the small, intimate feel of the pubs he'd frequented when he'd been stationed in Great Britain and Berlin. It was a huge, cavernous warehouse of a place with a mile of booths on two levels, a dinky dance floor and a D.J. whose music was too loud to talk and too fast to make it worth the effort of asking a girl to dance.

But the first two bars Travis had taken him to hadn't been any better. If he just wanted to get laid for the night, fine. He'd had one solid offer and two more women who'd been willing to consider it as long as Travis was included in the deal.

But any mention of the words commitment or courtship had earned him a handful of *huh*'s and one definite no.

"I tell you, bro, you're too serious to pull this thing off." Travis's ribbing had turned into sage-sounding advice. He raised two fingers to order a second round of beers and nodded to the group of chatty, energetic women who just walked through the door.

Ethan studiously ignored making direct eye contact with any of the new candidates. "You don't think I should take my future career seriously?"

"You know that's not what I mean. The closest thing to a come-on line I've heard out of you all night is, 'Yeah, you can sit.'" He talked as if Ethan was some kind of dating dinosaur. "What is that about? You've never once commented on anyone's hair or eyes or smile or bod—or whatever it is that turns you on. There *is* something about women that turns you on, right?"

The bottles of beer arrived with a splash and a scowl. "Five bucks, sirs," the bartender grumbled.

Ethan pulled out a five-dollar bill before Travis could so he could get rid of the testy bartender and show his brother what a real scowl looked like. "I'm not looking for sex. I'm looking for a suitable fiancée. I need more than a pair of boobs and a vacant-eyed gush about touching my hair to see if it's as stiff as it looks." He quoted one short-lived conversation from earlier in the evening, then picked up his beer and took a long drink, chilling the frustration that burned in his throat. He set down the bottle, ready to move on to a new topic. "And why the hell did he just call us *sirs?*"

Travis shook his head and savored his first swallow. "Probably because you even sit at attention. I swear to God if you yelled 'ten-hut' right now, half the customers in this joint would fall into line." He reached over and tugged loose the top button of Ethan's pale yellow polo shirt. "Now relax and try to look as if you're at least willing to have fun. And smile, for Pete's sake. If you didn't look so damn mad at the world, those three babes who just came in might have come over."

Ethan hadn't really considered an evening trolling for make-believe mates as fun. It was a mission. An unpleasant one, but one he was determined to complete successfully.

Mentally gearing up for another foray into Travis's world of easy, willing women, Ethan began a routine reconnaissance of the establishment and its patrons. He ticked off his list as he surveyed the place. Too young. Too blond. Too loud. Too drunk. Not one genteel, sophisticated, colonel's wife candidate anywhere.

The only thing that Groucho's did have going for it was the leanly curved brunette holding court at the opposite end of the bar. Her blue eyes, dark and intense as cobalt, sparkled with an intelligence that gave Ethan the impression she knew things that no one else even had a clue about. Her hair was cut short and sexy, falling in a touchable disorder around her face, with all the careless wisps and spiky bangs seeming to point straight to her mouth.

And that mouth—wow. Ethan hadn't ever really considered what it was he liked best about women. When he *had* looked just for the pure pleasure of looking, he'd always seen the whole package. Not just the size of the breasts. Or the length of the legs. Or the roundness of the hips. But right now, judging by the response stirring behind the zipper of his jeans, he was very definitely a mouth man.

Covered in a slick shine of copper color, her lips were full, but not fake. And they were tilted with just enough invitation that Ethan found himself licking the rim of his own lips, tasting more than the tang of beer there. In his lustful imagination, the taste of her kiss was much more potent. They'd give, just like a ripe peach, teasing him with their softness, surrendering their strength to his.

A dormant desire awakened inside him, speeding his blood with a determined pulse through his veins, making his lips tingle with the need for action. To taste. To take. He could imagine the sensuous curve of those lips pressed elsewhere, and shifted his position on the barstool to give his imagination room to expand.

If she'd been alone, Ethan would have considered her his best bet for fiancée material. Hell, he would have considered her enough temptation to break his vow of self-imposed celibacy. Not that he would engage in a relationship that was only about sex. Not after the Bethany debacle. But he would consider it. He would go back to his apartment and consider that blue-eyed brunette's lush lips all night long.

But she wasn't alone. Ethan buzzed his throbbing lips with a reality-check sigh and wrapped them around his beer bottle again for another cold drink. His fantasies had to take a back seat to his career goals. He'd seen at least three different men sitting on the stool beside her.

Kissing her was not an option. Not for show in front of General Craddock. Not for real to assuage his own lusty urges.

The third man who'd joined her, black-haired and sporting the distinct eagle, earth and anchor logo of the Corps on his tattooed bicep, got up from his stool, shaking his head at the woman he was leaving behind. With his back turned toward him, Ethan couldn't make out the words he was saying, but he could read the upturned contempt of her eyes that indicated he was challenging something she'd said.

A vague sense of potential danger kindled in Ethan's veins, igniting something far different than his libido. It was probably all those years of training to stop a threat before it started that had him interpreting the other man's jerky movements as signs of a brewing temper.

But it wasn't his business. If Miss Temptation wanted to play games, let her. There was a bouncer at the door to step in in case she got herself into trouble.

Yet when the man slipped his arm around her shoulders and she stiffened in the moment before he forced her chin up, Ethan's protective radar blazed into full, territorial alert. He was kissing her! That jackass was kissing those lips that had sparked the first sexual hunger Ethan had felt in months. He would bet a round of beers for the whole house that the jerk didn't appreciate the sensuous artistry of her slightly crooked mouth the way he did.

And obviously she hadn't wanted that kiss. Ethan's social skills might be rusty, but when a woman had to brace herself before a man touched her...

His feet were on the floor ready to move when the kiss ended abruptly and she pushed the man away. Ethan froze. She was smiling. Not a full-blown, *take me I'm yours* smile, but a smug sort of Mona Lisa smile. Crazy.

With one last remark that couldn't be overheard, the man moved away and joined a buddy of his at one of the pool tables. Ethan's hand fisted around his beer bottle, but he held his ground. The woman watched the discarded suitor until his focus shifted to the game at hand. Only then did her posture relax. Her mouth twisted into a grimace and she looked away. Intriguing.

As her eyes swept past Ethan, she hesitated. They sat too far away to talk, but for several charged moments, their gazes locked. Her pupils dilated, turning her eyes to twin pools of midnight blue. Something secret and hot passed between them, loaded with questions, begging for answers. He'd been unabashedly staring, with the motive of defending her. But now that protective rush of testosterone became something much more basic as it thickened like hot honey through his blood.

Ethan lost himself in the unguarded depths of those haunting eyes. On some level, he must have imagined losing himself inside her because, rationality aside, he had the most amazing hard-on of his adult life. And he hadn't done a damn thing beyond look at the woman and fantasize about kissing her.

"Yo, Major." It took a thump on his shoulder for Ethan to finally realize that Travis had been talking to him.

For a brief second, Ethan tore his gaze from his blue-eyed fantasy and concisely communicated that his little brother's interruption was unwelcome. But by the time he glanced to the opposite end of the bar once more, the spell had been broken.

The woman's eyes were lighter in color and shuttered now. She spared him a graceful nod of her head, then flipped open a page in the notebook that sat on the bar in front of her, effectively tuning him out and turning down an unspoken opportunity to get acquainted. She jotted something down, closed the notebook, then scanned the bar, looking almost everywhere else except at Ethan. Weird.

Travis's breath rasped against Ethan's ear in an amused whisper. "Are you gonna go for it?"

Ethan bristled at the challenge. She was older than most of the coed types he'd met tonight. She had the looks. But no way would that eccentric flirt make a suitable impression on the top brass. "What do you suppose she's writing over there?"

Travis settled back onto his seat and shrugged. "Phone numbers? Maybe she's a modern woman and wants to call the man instead of waiting for him to call her."

"That's an awful lot of phone numbers."

"She's got nice hooters. Not very big. But perky in all the right places. And her eyes are about as blue as—"

Ethan slowly turned and glared him into silence. "Do I want to have this conversation with you?"

"Defensive, huh?" Travis let the attack slide off his back. "So, we finally found your type. Cheeky brunette. What are you going to do about it? Are you going to go over and ask her to be yours for the next two weeks?"

Technically she wasn't a true brunette. As she shifted to pack her pen and notepad inside a large tote, the lights from the mirror behind the bar caught in her hair, revealing subtle auburn highlights. But that was hardly the point of Travis's comments. Ethan shook his head. "She looks the part—classy, smart." *Sexy.* "But she's a little too free with her affection for my taste."

"Isn't that the type of woman you want for a two-week relationship?"

Ethan watched her get up, drape her bag over her shoulder and head for the exit. She was average in height, but there was a leanness about her long legs and narrow waist that made her seem taller. There was also an earthy sway to her backside that had Ethan's hormones firing up again. Of all the women he'd seen tonight, she was the only one whose effect on him had lasted beyond his initial observations.

He checked his watch. Zero-fifteen hours. After midnight by civilian standards. By dinner tonight, he needed an escort with an engagement ring on her finger to take to the Cherry Blossom Ball. He was out of options.

Ethan faced the dare that lurked in Travis's expression. "Damn, I hate when you're right." Ethan stood and tossed a couple of bills onto the bar for a tip. "I'd better suck it up and go introduce myself."

"Better move fast," Travis warned him. "She just went out the door."

"I'm moving." Ethan straightened the tuck of his shirt at the waistband of his jeans and smoothed his palm over the top of his hair. Hell. He was more nervous than he'd been when he'd asked Amy Bartlett to the senior prom.

"Hey, if you're not back here in fifteen minutes—" Travis slapped him on the back, taking on the tone of experience "—I'll expect you to call me in the morning to fill me in on how it went. Not too early, though. I intend to see some action myself."

"Shit." But it wasn't Travis's teasing that hardened his nerves into something closer to anger.

The tattooed man who'd kissed Ethan's soon-to-be-asked-fake-fiancée-for-two-weeks had nudged his buddy at the pool table, and now they were both hurrying out the door. They turned the same way the woman had gone.

Ethan's suspicions revved into gear, his instinct to detect danger canceling out any trepidation he felt at asking this woman a huge favor. His long strides quickly ate up the distance to the exit. With his shoulders thrown back, his senses on keen alert, he shoved open the door and trailed the men outside. Beyond them, he spotted the woman in the parking lot, strolling across the pavement at a confident pace, oblivious to the danger that pursued her.

Cajoling each other, the two men quickened their steps to a slow jog and headed straight for her. Ethan's hands fisted at his sides. He was unarmed and out of uniform. But he was still a Marine. It was his duty to protect.

And whether it came down to his rank or his clear-thinking or his big, badass self, the blue-eyed brunette was going to be safe.

And she was going to be his.

J.C. ADDED THICKHEADED to her list of all the undesirable qualities to be found in a military man.

The Marine who'd kissed her in the bar had destroyed the last of her patience. He couldn't seem to quite grasp the concepts of *no. You're not my type. Thank you, but I'm not interested.*

As if that gorillaesque, wet tongue thing he'd done with his mouth would change her mind about his Neanderthal charm!

"Oooh." She shivered with revulsion, remembering that lip-lock assault with the same fondness of her last trip to the dentist. "Of all the nerve."

She dug her keys from her tote as she hurried to her car, anxious to get home and start her next column. The patrons of Groucho's Pub had given her plenty of raw material to work with. Already she could generate columns about awkward pickup lines made all the less endearing when uttered in the form of a command or wishing for substance behind dashing good looks.

J.C. halted a few feet from the rear of her Camaro and routinely checked underneath her car and the one parked beside it before sliding between them. At the very least, she could write a paragraph about not needing to primp to pick up a soldier. She'd worn nothing more provocative than jeans and a gray knit shirt with three-quarter sleeves. Yet she'd received no fewer than seven compliments about how nice she looked.

"Hey, baby."

J.C. froze with her key in the lock at the inebriated drawl behind her. Her evening had just gone from mildly amusing and mostly annoying to downright awful. Gorilla-boy had followed her to her car.

She fixed a superior sneer on her face and turned to face him. She froze. Forget awful. Make that scary. Gorilla-boy had brought a friend with him. Both were drunk, both were ogling her breasts and parts south. And she was trapped.

Panic flared in her chest and tried to strangle her throat, but she fought back the urge to scream and opted for sarcasm instead. "If I'm not interested in one of you, I'm not going to be interested in two."

"I know you want me." The black-haired man who'd introduced himself as Juan—make that Don Juan—Guerro entered the slot between the cars and backed her up against the concrete parking barrier. "I saw you write down my name after I left."

"No. I—" He snatched her bag off her shoulder, and though she struggled to hang on to it, he pinched her wrist in a way that shot pain up her arm and made her fingers refuse to work. "Ow. Jeez."

He easily pried the bag from her limp grasp and tossed it to his sidekick. "Check it out."

"That's stealing." But her argument fell on amused ears.

While Juan's buddy dumped out her bag on her trunk and rifled through her things, Juan himself kept hold of her wrist and turned her so that she butted against the hood of her car. He moved forward, sliding one of his legs between hers and leaning over her in such a way that she could smell beer and cigarettes on his stale breath.

"Find the book, Manuel. See what fine thing she said about me."

Oh, God. If he could decipher shorthand, seeing *prick* next to his name would hardly endear her to him. She was in trouble. J.C. flattened her hands against his chest and shoved. "I told you no, and I meant no." He stumbled back into the neighboring car, giving her a chance to go after her bag. She waved an accusatory finger at the sidekick who was rudely touching her things and tossing them aside. "I will call the cops and have you arrested for purse snatching."

But Juan was a trained Marine. Drunk or not, he was still physically stronger and swifter than she would ever be cold sober. He grabbed her arm and jerked her back against the car. Her elbow smacked against the sideview mirror.

"Ow!"

He thrust his groin against her hips and pressed his cold gorilla lips to her ear. "I'm saving you from your shyness."

Shy? Her?

"Stop it!" J.C. twisted and aimed with her knee, but she was pinned beneath his hips and hands and that awful tongue. She curled her fingers into claws and scratched at his forearm, but it was hardly enough damage to free herself. If he angled his head just a little farther, she would chomp down on his ear.

"Hey, Juan." His sidekick must have found her notebook. "This don't make no sense. It's all numbers and scribbles. If your name's here—"

The sidekick fell silent with a startled *oof.* The car

shook behind her as he slammed into the trunk of her car and then collapsed to the ground.

"What the—?" Juan muttered and lifted his head.

"Get your hands off her. Now."

If Gorilla-boy wasn't intimidated by the deep-pitched precision of that order, she was.

She shoved him as he turned to the commanding voice, and scuttled back against the wall, away from the unwelcome contact with his body. Juan looked stunned to see his buddy curled up in a ball on the asphalt, holding his bloody nose. "Manny? What the hell?"

J.C. saw him before Juan did. A tall, broad, golden hunk of hero materialized at the back of her car. He was gathering up her things and dropping them into her bag, all without looking away from Juan or even blinking his battleship-gray eyes. "Your ears work?" he challenged.

Juan bristled. "You mind your own business, old-timer. I saw the lady first."

Old-timer? J.C. recognized the broad-shouldered man from the bar. She'd caught him staring at her with such intensity that she'd forgotten the military shave of his head and the stiff carriage of his shoulders and responded to the hungry appreciation in his eyes. He was fit and strong and might even be handsome if he ever relaxed the rugged lines of his face and smiled.

But there was no mistaking him for old. Serious, yes. Authoritative, definitely. He was a mature man in the prime of his life. And he'd wanted her.

"What unit are you two with?" he demanded.

The terse trade-off of information continued as J.C. relived those few tension-fraught moments at the bar when she realized she'd lusted after a man who made her forget her purpose for being there. Those few charged moments had been about sex and desire and long-denied need.

The tips of her breasts had tingled and her panties had gotten damp. All because he'd looked as if he'd wanted to bed her on the spot. Without saying a word, it had been the most straightforward invitation of the evening. And the most flattering. The raw desire flooding his expression had caught her off guard. First base and beyond had been a real possibility for a moment.

But a split second later, she'd wondered if that was the same kind of inexplicable attraction her mother had felt when she'd met her father for the first time. Remembering her mother's pain, she'd finally found the strength to look away.

"If you want to stay a corporal, you'll move aside." That clipped, low-pitched voice brought her instantly back to the here and now. "Honey?"

The blond man's gaze slid beyond Juan's stunned posture and swept over her. He extended a large, trim-fingered hand toward her and urged her to come out from between the cars and join him. *Honey?*

She'd just mentally complimented the man on his honesty. What game was he playing now? Had she missed something important? She bought herself a moment by playing along. "Sweetie?"

"Come out of there," he urged her again.

This time, with Juan's dark-eyed scowl over his shoulder to remind her of the danger she'd been in, she scooted around Gorilla-boy and reached for her rescuer's outstretched hand. She fixed a smile on her face. "I'm glad you showed up."

That much was true. But the charade was going to be more than just verbal. He handed her her bag and slipped an arm behind her back, claiming her as his own, carefully angling her away from the moaning man with the bloody nose and Juan's cautious advance.

"Are you telling me she's yours?" Juan challenged.

"You questioning my word?" Her *sweetie's* hand settled with a possessive grip on her hip and he pulled her snug against the mile of hard, muscular lines that formed his thigh, waist and chest. *Yowza.* J.C.'s sex drive kicked in, remembering everything he had promised in that long, heated stare earlier.

"No, sir." Juan took another, more hesitant step forward. "But you two weren't together inside. And I wasn't the first guy to hit on her."

Setting aside her libido, J.C. understood the game plan now. "So we had a little fight and I wanted to make him jealous. I'd still rather go home with him than with you."

She wrapped her arms around *sweetie's* flat waist and sidled impossibly closer. Was that a tremor she felt go through him? Or her own body's involuntary response?

"What'd you say about me in that notebook?" Now Juan was addressing her. "It ain't cool to lead a man on like that."

"Lead you on?" J.C. puffed up. "I told you I wasn't interested and you planted a kiss on me like that was going to change my mind."

"That's when I decided I'd had enough." Her rescuer had the most deliciously possessive timbre in his voice. "I'm the only man who gets to kiss her. Now beat it while you still can."

"I'm sorry, honey."

Sorry? What was Mr. Tall, Blond and Built apologizing for?

Oh. *Honey.* The lovers quarrel charade. "I'm sorry, t—"

Without any explanation, without any fanfare—without giving her a chance to play her part—he turned her in his arms, tucked a finger beneath her chin and tilted her mouth up to receive his kiss.

Alarm bells dinged inside J.C.'s head at the instant spark of raw, pulsing energy that cascaded through her at the touch of his lips on hers. Sheer, masculine power, bathed in untempered desire, assaulted her senses down to her most feminine core.

This was no polite, cover-story kiss. No make-believe apology. This was the physical expression of everything that had passed between them in those silent, heated moments at the bar.

Her breasts crushed against the rock-hard foundation of his chest as his big hands skimmed with needy roughness along everything they could touch. From a sifting tangle through her hair down over the flare of her hips where his long fingers dipped down to squeeze her bottom and lift her inexorably closer to his burgeoning male heat.

J.C. was on fire, crazy with the carnal madness he'd ignited in her passion-starved body. A feverish pressure pushed the tips of her aching breasts to rigid attention. The juncture between her thighs wept with unleashed need.

His lips were firm and demanding, seducing her mouth from corner to corner, and deeper inside. Stroking. Nipping. Asking. Taking.

J.C. clung to his shoulders and wrapped an arm behind his neck, running her sensitized palm back and forth across the erotic prickle of his short, soft hair. Her knees weakened at the unadulterated desire of their embrace. He wanted her. She wanted him. It was as if they'd been destined to share this kiss from the moment they'd been born. If she could crawl inside him right now, she would do it. Nothing less would quench the craving she had to possess him. To complete herself in the raging wildfire of this kiss.

The deep-pitched moan in his throat was the first reminder that this was insane. As he slowly lowered her and her feet touched the ground, she twisted her body in a last, pulsing bid for orgasmic release. But the fire was cooling.

By the time she came up for air, Juan and his sidekick were long gone. *Sweetie*'s hands were scorching the skin on her back inside her shirt. And she was ready to take her research into an intensely personal direction.

"Thank you," she managed to eke out between swollen, unsatisfied lips that foolishly wanted more. "I guess I got in over my head."

"You're not the only one." He touched his forehead to hers, his husky, breathy voice a potent echo of her own.

J.C. smoothed her palms over the sculpted enticement of his chest and pushed some much-needed breathing room between them. "One question."

"Yes?" His gray eyes opened, revealing beautiful irises dappled with shades of silver and steel and charcoal.

"Who are you?"

4

SON OF A BITCH. Son…of…a…bitch.

Ethan swiped a hand across his mouth and flexed his jaw, trying to ease the white-hot fever that ravaged every cell in his body, leaving him feeling raw and unguarded.

Where the hell had that come from? That kiss? That sensual assault? That complete abandonment of purpose and control?

Instinct more than conscious thought had him scanning the parking lot and street beyond to verify that the woman's two assailants had been smart enough to scramble for cover. Not that there'd been anything terrifically smart about what he'd just done.

All clear except for a couple strolling toward a pickup truck. Even the shadows seemed deserted, and the steady stream of traffic on the street running in front of Groucho's Pub indicated no particular interest or threat.

He should be feeling relief that he'd cleared the scene without further incident. But he was still wound tighter than a coil. He *was* the only danger lurking beyond the flash of the neon signs now. He'd been ready to get inside this woman's pants in a public parking lot because her body had proved to be every bit as lush as those lips. Ripe. Soft. Hot. Responsive.

Even now, as she realigned her clothing, her breasts rose and fell with her sharp, sweeping gasps for air. They weren't big, but man, they had attitude, thrusting tips that were still at attention against the thin cotton of her sweater, begging him to touch. Her lips were a deep, rosy pink, stamped with the evidence of his need. They'd parted to reveal the sweet, soft interior he'd already feasted upon. She was a walking, talking seduction who disrupted every rational train of thought and standard course of action.

He'd just wanted her to be safe. He'd done the possessive tough-guy routine to get those wasted noncoms away from her. But he'd taken it too far. And, damn, if she hadn't gone every step of the way with him.

There'd been nothing tentative in the way she'd opened her mouth beneath his and dug her fingers into his flesh and rubbed herself against him, waking every dormant male hormone he possessed. He'd taken everything she'd offered and demanded more, just like a greedy man who hadn't had sex for one year, four months, two weeks and a handful of days. He hadn't realized how much he missed it. He hadn't been aware how successfully he'd shut down that part of himself to focus on solidifying his career. He hadn't known how much he needed, craved, wanted....

Criminy. Ethan scraped his palm across the short crop of his hair and inhaled a deep, cleansing breath. He wanted to shove his hands into his pockets to stifle the urge to reach for her again, but there just wasn't any extra room in his jeans at the moment. He'd have to do this through sheer willpower. He needed to reestablish control of the situation. Control of himself.

Gritting his teeth to keep anything stupid from flying out of his mouth, he bent his head to evaluate the turbulent shadows in her wide blue eyes.

"Are you okay?" The words snapped out with the efficiency of a dressing-down. He cursed his ineptitude at conveying patience and concern and tried again. "They didn't hurt you, did they?"

She shook her head, smoothing those reddish brown wisps of hair he'd so thoroughly mussed back behind her ears. "I'm fine."

Ethan ran his gaze up and down the trim curves of her body, inspecting her for any sign of injury. As she smoothed her sweater down over the waistband of her jeans, he noted that everything looked to be in exactly the right place. And that sure, sexy voice had claimed she was fine, but the tiny line marking the frown between her eyes could be an indication of emotional trauma. Trauma he might very well be responsible for. He wanted to touch that little line—kiss it, soothe it. But he clenched his hand into a fist at his side instead. "I'm sorry."

She arched one eyebrow at him, replacing the frown with a question. "Our audience is gone. You don't have to keep apologizing."

"I'm not doing it for show." He reached around her and picked up her carry-everything-size shoulder bag from the trunk of the car. Shaking loose the kinks from the canvas strap, he stepped back and held it out to her. "I just meant to help. Those two looked like trouble from the get-go. When a man traps a woman, and she's pushing him away…" He briefly considered one of the sick games Bethany had tried to play on him once. Charging to her rescue had nearly held deadly consequences for the sap she'd used to provoke Ethan's protective instincts back then. His fingers tightened around the strap. "You didn't want them around, did you?"

She snatched the bag from his hand and hugged it to her stomach. "God, no. I mean, I can take care of myself nine times out of ten. But they were drunk and this isn't the best-lit parking lot and…'' The sassy bravado in her voice faded. ''I'll admit I was a little scared.''

Great. She'd been scared, and he'd shown all the sensitivity of a tank. ''I didn't mean to take advantage of your predicament. That kiss got way out of hand.''

''Do you hear me complaining?'' There was something reassuring in her teasing tone and gentle smile that curled through Ethan's veins and made him consider launching an assault on those lips all over again. ''But I would feel a little more comfortable if I knew your name before we tried anything like that a second time.''

Ethan's simmering libido slammed into his conscience and came to an abrupt halt. *Smooth move, McCormick.* How the hell did he ever think he could pull off a fake engagement if he couldn't even get the basics of dating etiquette right?

Meet the girl first. Find out what they had in common, if anything. Share some drinks, some food, maybe even a movie or, God forbid, a dance. *Then* kiss her. Lips only. Groping and mussing and tongues down throats came way later in a relationship.

He wasn't looking for a woman to get naked in the sheets with, anyway. He needed one who could play classy, ladylike—*engaged*—for a couple of weeks. But Ethan suspected he wasn't scoring any points that would encourage her to say yes to his unorthodox proposition.

Who are you? She'd been standing there for several minutes, waiting for him to answer her question. Yep, McCormick, ultrasmooth.

''My apologies.'' He retreated a step and extended his hand the way he should have in the first place. ''I'm Major Ethan McCormick. USMC.''

"I'M…" J.C.'S WORDS choked on an uncharacteristic stutter of incoherent shock.

Uh-oh.

If her fingers weren't locked up in Ethan's firm grip, she would be jumping into her car, gunning the engine and putting distance between them as fast as her little red Camaro could take her.

She absolutely could not like this guy.

But she'd gotten so…distracted.

Major?

What rotten luck!

The best damn kiss of her life had to come from a die-hard, career-driven Marine.

Processing the introduction as if he'd just announced he had trenchfoot, she withdrew her hand and hugged her arms around her bag. She made a conscious effort to close her mouth and hide her stunned expression. Disappointment cascaded through her, knocking aside the silly fantasy she'd conjured about unzipping her jeans and doing it right here on the trunk of her car with the big, bronze hero hunk who'd rescued her.

Of course, he was military. Common sense ridiculed her frustrated hormones. What did she expect in a place like this? With a crew cut like his? With that commanding voice?

But that kiss. *Ay-yi-yi.*

Those eyes.

God, if he could make her horny just by looking at her across a noisy room, imagine what…

J.C. sighed. What a waste.

"You're a major?" Maybe she'd heard wrong. She tilted her chin and searched the square jut of his jaw, the buzz cut at his temples, that sexy, sexy mouth, clinging to an impossible shred of hope.

He folded his sturdy arms across that sturdier chest and nodded. "Twelve years of service, not counting my Annapolis training. Combat, peacetime, foreign, stateside. I'm currently stationed at DoD, Department of Defense. The Pentagon."

Impressive.

Awful.

J.C. nodded, politely acknowledging his achievements while secretly cursing the irony of their intense hormonal chemistry. "So you're a career soldier?"

"Career Marine, ma'am," he corrected. "A soldier fights in the Army."

Ma'am? She'd liked *honey* better. Oh, hell. She shouldn't care one way or the other.

"I see. Sorry." Her father had been a career seaman, a sailor. A career jerk. Plenty of years to fool around on her mother before his dalliances caught up with him. "I guess there is a distinction in terminology among the different branches."

The major grinned. Or at least, she gathered that was what the shift in the creases beside his mouth meant. "It's a pride thing. I'm sure the other branches are just as gung ho about their nicknames and traditions."

Ah yes, pride. One of those questionable virtues her father had possessed in such abundance. But extreme pride in the job didn't often translate well into a relationship. She bristled at an old memory of her father jumping her case for leaving sticky finger marks on his white uniform when she'd hugged him goodbye once. *"I can't set sail looking like a bum."* He'd lambasted her and handed her over to her mother without giving either of them a kiss. *"What were you thinking, Josie?"*

At five years of age, she'd been thinking her daddy was

leaving for another six months and that she would miss him.

She'd finally learned to move beyond such juvenile sentimentality.

Breathing deeply to squelch any lingering resentment, J.C. challenged this modern-day warrior on his pride. "Do you always correct people when they make a mistake about the Corps? I'm using the proper term now, right?"

"Right. Marines, the Corps, USMC—they're all pretty interchangeable. Different bases, divisions, units and teams have various nicknames and numerical titles—including a few I wouldn't use in mixed company."

Though he didn't expound, she dutifully smiled at his effort to make a joke. She had a few names for men like her father she didn't care to share, either.

The major tapped his chest as the lesson continued. "I'm a commissioned officer, meaning I have a college degree and I'm specially trained for command. I go by Major or sir. Those two boneheads who were here earlier were noncoms—noncommissioned officers. Enlisted men. But we're all Marines and we're all necessary elements of the Corps."

"Wow." Fount of information that he was, she noted that he'd made no effort to deny the *correction* part. She arched the brow above her right eye, subtly expressing her sarcasm. "Ask a simple question…"

His jaw tightened beneath a rueful frown. "Sorry. I tend to get carried away. *Semper Fi* and all that."

The Marine Corps motto. *Semper Fidelis.* Always Faithful. To the Corps, that is.

He was quickly sliding back into the ultraserious, all-work/no-play personality she'd observed in the bar. This guy was so career focused that he might not have the time or energy to cheat on his woman. But then, think of that poor woman who did get involved with him. Work, work, work. From the sound of things, she'd always come in second to his real mistress—the Corps.

Not a stellar recommendation for relationship material.

J.C.'s infatuation with Ethan's kiss began to fade. It surely must have been a fluke. Or maybe it hadn't been that great in the first place. Maybe the quality of Major McCormick's kiss had been enhanced by the danger of the situation she'd been in and her own man-starved libido. This guy didn't have any moves, no clue about flirting.

Ethan shifted in his dark brown loafers, diverting her attention back to the present conversation. Or, more pointedly, the awkward silence her thoughts had put between them. He smoothed one of those big hands across the top of his head, but the wave of dark golden stubble snapped right back into place.

"We never finished introductions. I'm assuming you have a name?" he asked.

"Oh, duh. Sorry." Disappointment was justifiable. But rudeness she wouldn't tolerate, especially in herself. After all, the major *had* saved her from a potentially threatening and definitely uncomfortable run-in with Juan and Manny. "My turn to backtrack. I'm J. C. Gardner."

"What does the J.C. stand for?"

"Josephine C…" Her voice trailed off in a hiss of sound as her analytical mind finally burst through the blockade of hormones and emotions inside her.

Ding. Ding. Ding. Ding. Ding.

Golden opportunity.

Lee Whiteley and her readers would eat this up.

J.C. had a living, breathing, dysfunctional research specimen for her column standing right in front of her.

A major could give her a whole new perspective on the

upper echelon of military men. Did a commission make a man a better catch? Make him more honorable, trustworthy, reliable than an enlisted man? Or was the rank just a better cover for his infidelities? Were officers like Major McCormick a bunch of old farts who spouted military rhetoric instead of *I love you's?* Who were more devoted to the Corps than to their women? Did a man accustomed to being saluted make a good lover? Or would he expect that same kind of deference in the bedroom?

Oh, yeah.

Fifty bucks to prove a point.

Making it with a Major: The Inside Story

There was definitely a column here. Or two. Or more.

J.C.'s heart pumped a little faster, quickening her pulse. She bowed her head to hide the smug smile of satisfaction that threatened to erupt, and rifled through the contents of her purse. Her fingers tingled with anticipation as they brushed against her notebook. She breathed in deeply, her nostrils flaring as she schooled her patience and organized her thoughts.

She would have to approach Ethan McCormick differently than she'd played Juan and the other men in the bar. That had been an anecdotal study on the superficialities of pickup lines, a casual observation of how little it took to generate a military man's interest in a woman and how far he would go to pursue a potential conquest. J.C. wanted in-depth responses from the major. Long-term evaluations. Hidden truths.

He was interested in her, judging by the way he'd made love to her with his eyes across the bar earlier. He was interested enough to follow her outside and rescue her from a couple of pesky drunks. He was interested enough to kiss her.

J.C. squeezed her eyes shut as her hormones reawakened with an involuntary flutter. An adjunct research project would be to see if she could get him to kiss her again—to find out if he was really that good with his lips or if he'd just gotten lucky. *Liar.* She was the one who wanted to get lucky again.

"Josephine what?"

J.C. opened her eyes and found her focus aimed directly at the lingering bulge in his jeans. He was definitely interested in her. If she played this right, Major Ethan McCormick would make a very engaging case study. And she could maybe get a few jollies of her own—all in the pursuit of science and healthy recommendations for her readers, of course.

Adjusting her smile from amused to apologetic, she lifted her gaze to those ever-changing gray eyes. "I'm sorry. My brain jumped ahead of the conversation. I'm Josephine Gardner." Better keep the *Dr. Cyn* part of Cynthia a secret if she wanted to get honest, unfiltered responses from her test subject. "But my friends all call me J.C."

"J.C.," he repeated, as if testing whether or not the nickname met with his approval. "Sounds like a tomboy."

"I can be. Mostly, I'm a modern woman who—as much as I loved my grandmother—doesn't especially care to share the old-fashioned name. And it's *Dr.* J. C. Gardner, if that helps. I'm a clinical psychologist."

His silver eyes suddenly sparkled—if she could believe a rock-solid, nuts-'n-bolts kind of guy like Ethan McCormick ever could sparkle. "Do you prefer *Dr.?*"

"Do you prefer *Major?*"

Her challenge earned a reluctant smile which revealed straight, white teeth. The effect softened the rugged lines of his face and rendered him almost handsome. "My friends call me Ethan."

"Could I buy you a cup of coffee, Ethan? To thank you?" She pulled her wallet from her bag and held it up to appeal to his practical side, in case charm alone couldn't intrigue him. "My treat. There's a coffee shop just around the corner that's still open."

Silhouetted against the green glare of the bar's neon sign, his broad shoulders shrugged with a heavy sigh, then settled back to near attention. She dropped the wallet back into her bag, feeling instantly on guard.

"Dr. Gardner." Had he missed the *friends* part? Or was distance and formality typical of what a woman could expect from him? She'd be sure to write that one down. Later. Right now she cocked an eyebrow and waited for him to continue. "I don't know how to ask this any other way but to come out and say it."

"What is it?"

"Are you married?"

J.C. scrutinized the fine web of lines that appeared beside Ethan's narrowed eyes. Any flash of silver in the irises had disappeared into gunmetal depths. He propped his hands at his waist and leaned ever so slightly forward to observe her equally intently. My God, he was serious!

Would she be in a bar, letting men hit on her if she was married? Would she be asking him to join her for coffee? She wasn't like her father. J.C. stiffened defensively, her fists clenched around the strap of her bag. "No." Her gaze instinctively dropped to his left hand. Naked. But that was no guarantee. She looked up and demanded the same truth from him. "Are *you* married?"

"Never have been." She retreated half a step when he moved toward her and she realized just how far she had to tilt her head to maintain eye contact. Jeez, Louise, this was important to him. "Are you engaged? Living with someone? Seeing anybody?"

J.C. automatically put up her hand to block his advance and silence the inquisition. Her palm flattened against a wall of chest. *Mistake!* Her defensive anger got twisted up with a flare of instant desire. And both were tempered by a curious need to understand his concern with her personal status.

Ethan halted as if she'd cast some spell to keep him at bay. She wasn't pushing, neither was he. Yet a magnetic force kept them bound, hand to chest. He stood close enough for her to detect the faint, cool scent of the soap or aftershave he used.

His nostrils flared as he breathed in deeply. But he came no closer. He was waiting. Holding back. Brimming with energy as if it required a great deal of willpower to stand so still, to maintain such control. Her palm buzzed with the intensity of the strength and emotion he was keeping in check. The tension shimmered through her, tingling in the tips of her breasts and fingers, making her breath catch in soundless, shallow gasps.

What would it take to break that control?

Is that what had made his kiss so soul shattering? Had he temporarily lost his grip on that considerable restraint?

J.C.'s hips butted against the cool metal frame of the car, but she was consumed with Ethan's encompassing heat. Telling him to *lighten up* didn't feel like an option right now. She wasn't even sure this guy could do that. And she was pretty sure that was half of the crazy reason she was so insanely attracted to him. She liked his intensity. Focused on her and her safety, it had been devastating.

Her voice came out hushed and husky with her emotions. "I thought I was sending out plenty of I'm *single* signals."

"Please. I'd appreciate a simple yes or no."

The pale cotton of his shirt was soft to the touch, but everything was solid, warm and pulsing with unleashed energy beneath it. J.C. was tempted to break the spell of sensual overload by clutching a handful of that material and dragging him down for another kiss. But she sensed her research and any further contact with Major McCormick hinged on giving him the answer he needed to hear right now. Intellectually and physically, she didn't want this to be her last encounter with Ethan, either.

"The answer is no. I'm completely unattached. No husband, no fiancé, no boyfriend, no lover." *Unless you'd like to change that last one?*

His deep sigh mingled with her own and he smiled—a wide, tooth-flashing grin that made her think he'd just won some kind of prize.

J.C. didn't know whether to be alarmed or flattered by his obvious relief. It took everything she had not to snatch at his shirt when he straightened and pulled away, breaking the connection between them.

"Then I'd love to have coffee with you."

He didn't leave her standing weak-kneed against the car for long. He turned and held out his arm like a formal escort. When she stared at it a moment without moving, he reached for her right hand and pulled it into the crook of his elbow. Muscle and skin and springy, golden hair created a sizzle of awareness at even that impersonal contact. If he was feeling any of the same sexual attraction she was feeling, he wasn't acting on it.

Still, frustration aside, there was something earnest and sincere in the old-fashioned gesture that left her smiling and looking forward to whatever time she would get to spend with this man. J.C. smiled and strolled beside him onto the sidewalk.

Interesting research, indeed.

5

ETHAN'S EYES WERE TRANSFIXED by the dollop of creamy froth that clung to the bow of J.C.'s top lip. He wiggled his finger against his own mug of black coffee, combatting the urge to reach across the narrow booth and wipe it off, just for the excuse to touch her again.

And his taste buds were suddenly developing a craving for mocha latte. He could sweep it aside with a kiss and reward himself with the flavor of something sweeter and more potent than chocolate or coffee. But, forcibly reminding himself of his shrinking time frame, he put his depraved desires on hold and simply pointed to his own mouth. "You've got something there."

"What? Oh."

Oh, no. No, no. Ethan's grip tightened around his ceramic mug as he watched in helpless fascination. *Don't do it!*

She did it. The tip of her pink tongue darted out to lick the rim of her lips. Ethan's crotch lurched in response beneath the laminate tabletop. His imagination skipped flirtatious innuendo and jumped straight to the idea of what else that sweet, flexible tongue might be willing to lick. *Jerk!*

She smiled. "Thanks."

No, thank you were the words he wanted to say as he eased his legs farther apart on the vinyl bench seat, giving his randy instincts room to maneuver. He lifted his mug and sipped at the tepid brew, wishing it was hot enough to burn some sense into him.

Had he been dead for the past year and a half? Had Bethany's betrayal tainted the allure of every other woman until now? Maybe Dr. J. C. Gardner was transmitting some secret pheromone weapon that had completely brainwashed him. This was crazy! This instant, intense, graphic desire to take this woman he barely knew and touch, taste—mate with—made him question his sanity. His cool, calm and collected persona seemed a distant memory. He was crawling inside his skin with the need to run a personal reconnaissance mission to acquaint himself with each one of her hidden feminine attributes.

Her left breast. The right one. What color were the tips? How did they taste? Her belly button. Was it an innie or an outie? Her butt. He'd already grabbed a handful of that, but his palms and fingertips itched to feel skin, not denim. And, oh, he most definitely wanted to acquaint himself with her—

"So you said you had a proposition for me?"

Ethan gulped as her words and his thoughts got tangled up in one vivid, erotic image. The dregs of his coffee ate a bitter path down his throat and he coughed in his hurry to choke down the acidic aftertaste and explain himself. He set down the mug before he did further damage to himself and held up both hands in apologetic surrender. "I didn't mean it that way."

"What way is that?"

"You know, like…" Damn. Did he really have to spell this out for her? Though the booth's high-backed seats sequestered them from the chatty line of patrons waiting to order their last drinks before closing, Ethan still glanced over his shoulder to ensure their privacy. He braced his forearms on the table and leaned in, dropping his voice to a whisper. "Like I was asking to have sex with you."

There. He'd said it. Out loud.

"Do you want to have sex with me?"

Oh, yeah.

Practicality answered before lust could.

"No. Of course, not." Her eyebrow arched at the unintended insult in his quick response.

Ethan flattened his palms against the cool tabletop in a placating gesture. He would give a month's pay for one smooth line to get himself out of this mess right now. "I mean, I'm not against the idea. I would love to have sex with you."

Damn. That flush of heat flaring up his neck and into his cheeks better have something to do with faulty wiring in the coffee shop's air-conditioning system. Ethan fisted his hands as he took a deep, calming breath. "Forget I just said that. That's not what I'm asking."

She was actually smiling at his fish-out-of-water lack of charm. "I wouldn't be offended if you did."

Now how the hell was he supposed to respond to that? *Okay, then get over here and do a lap dance for me?* He was trying to do the right thing here. He was failing miserably.

Where was Travis when he needed him? A little advice on how to steer this conversation back to a safer, saner topic would be appreciated right about now. Of course, Travis would probably tell him to go for it. If the woman was willing…

"This isn't about sex," Ethan stated firmly, needing to hear the words out loud as much as she did.

Her amusement was tempered by the downward focus of her eyes. Under studious scrutiny, she circled her index finger around the rim of her cup with such methodical precision that Ethan was soon mesmerized by the slow, repetitive motion himself.

It didn't take much imagination to picture that finger tracing the same circles across the back of his hand or around the shell of his ear or along the length of something else that seemed to have a mind of its own tonight. Right on cue, the little major popped to attention, completely oblivious to the more important agenda of finding a fiancée and nabbing that promotion.

Too late, Ethan realized the hypnotic display had been a stalling tactic. With her face still downcast, she lifted her gaze, giving her an expression of drowsy innocence that was pure seduction. But he was quickly learning there was little coy or innocent about this woman, an observation which put him on guard even while it intrigued him. "Are you embarrassed to talk about sex, Ethan?"

"No." But he was so far out of practice, apparently he'd forgotten how. With a rueful smile, he shook his head. "I just don't believe it's something a gentleman discusses with a lady, especially on a first date. And this isn't even really a date."

She tipped her chin and looked him straight in the eye. Bang. She had him. So much for guarding himself. "But you're thinking about it, aren't you?" He'd been thinking about it from the moment he'd spotted her across the bar at Groucho's—and she didn't need a Ph.D. to figure that out. "What if I told you I was, too?"

Ethan leaned back in his seat, letting that nugget of information sink in—giving himself room to breathe without inhaling her warm, inviting scent and scattering his concentration. "I'd say I'm flattered. I'm interested. But that doesn't mean we're gonna do it. I'm a workaholic. *Thinking* about sex is all I have time for these days."

"That's a shame." Was that disbelief or disappointment in her voice? J.C. pushed back from the table, too, matching his stiff-backed posture. "Well, it can't be that important because you've talked all around it. And every time I force the issue, you politely change the subject. As if it's something civilized ladies and gentlemen wouldn't normally talk about."

Civilized people didn't hunt down women in bars to ask complete strangers to save their professional butts. "This *is* important. To me. To my future. And if I hesitate, it's just that…I need to ask you a huge favor. But I'm afraid you'll say no and I'll be S-O-L."

J.C. paused to consider his words. She took a sip of her latte and dabbed the froth from her lip before he got any more stupid ideas. That tiny frown line reappeared on her forehead as she turned her attention from the mug cradled between her hands up to him. "Do you want me to bear your love child?"

"No."

"Do you want me to kill someone for you?"

"Of course not."

"Betray a national secret?"

"No, nothing like that."

"Then try me." She set down the mug and reached across the table to lay her hand over his tightly bunched fist. The warmth of her drink was instantly transmitted to his skin and Ethan nearly flinched at the gentle familiarity of her touch. But he held himself still and tuned in to that hushed voice and those searching eyes. "And don't worry about sweet-talking your way around it. The direct approach seems to work best for you. I'm a big girl, I can take it. What do you need from me?"

Ethan decided to state it just as plainly as she'd requested. "I need you to be my fiancée for the next two weeks."

Her laughter was loud enough to turn a few heads in the dwindling line of customers. "I thought this was all some elaborate pickup line. You aren't trying to get me into bed, are you? I thought you were just too shy to come out and say it."

"Shy?" He commanded men. Gave orders. Saved lives. He snatched his hand free and sat at attention.

She wisely shut her mouth and contained her laughter. "Old-fashioned, then. A fiancée for two weeks, huh?" She sat back, tucking both hands well out of reach beneath the table. Humor still shook through her shoulders. "You don't believe in long-term relationships?"

"I don't have time to find one."

"You're not dying, are you?"

"This isn't some damn game. I'm trying to get promoted to lieutenant colonel!" The natural authority in his voice bounced off the hardwood walls.

Her grin flatlined. At last she saw that this was no joke to him. "I'm sorry. I wasn't making fun of you. Your request surprised me, that's all. It certainly wasn't what I expected."

The apology soothed his wounded pride and made him regret the outburst. He'd probably been broadcasting his attraction to her with all the subtlety of a rutting elephant. And after those two bozos in the parking lot had made an aggressive play for her... No wonder she'd misread his intentions.

Ethan dropped his voice to a more sociable level. "I'm the one who should apologize. Obviously I'm not much good at communication. If I had other options, I'd use them. But I don't. This promotion means a lot to me. I already have a strike against me because I'm the youngest candidate. My chances of getting that promotion improve tenfold if my superiors think I'm a guy intent on settling down. The Corps prefers their base officers to be leaders both professionally and socially.''

"I see." J.C. shrugged. "Is there some reason why you're not intent on settling down?''

"I just haven't gotten around to it. Like I said, I'm a workaholic." And a blind-assed loser who would never trust his heart to a deceiving woman again. "I'm not asking you to marry me. We just need to pretend we're engaged for a couple of weeks.''

She gestured down at her sweater and jeans. "You think I could pull off something like that? The corporate wife-to-be or whatever the military equivalent is?''

"I think you're perfect for it.''

"Me? But you don't know..." Gray eyes locked on blue, and for a few seconds Ethan thought he saw something raw and vulnerable in her sarcastic expression. But the notion was quickly dispelled by a blink and a crooked smile. "You know, I've never pulled off a dinner party for more than two or three close friends. And I'd rather run barefoot than wear panty hose any day of the week.''

"You don't have to throw any parties," he reassured her. "You just have to attend a few functions with me. A ball, a dinner, some luncheons, a family weekend. We'd need to make up a story of how we met, hold hands, do enough familiar looks and touches so that our relationship would be believable.''

She huffed a derisive sigh. "Is that all?''

Ethan checked his watch. It was nearly 0-200 hours. Only half a day away from the Cherry Blossom Ball. He pleaded his case. "I know I'm asking for a lot of your time, but it won't cost you a penny. I'll pay for any expenses you incur. A ball gown, transportation, missed time at work, whatever.''

The arch of her right brow reflected curiosity *and* skepticism. "You'd buy me a ball gown?"

"You pick it out. I'll just pay the bill. Choose whatever suits your tastes. I'm not asking you to become a different person, I just need you to take on an extra job. Socialize with the other officers and candidates and their spouses or significant others."

"And say good things about you? Act like my world revolves around you? Make them believe I'm as much of an asset to the Corps as you are?"

"Exactly."

For a moment he hoped. But then she raked her fingers through the fringe of hair at her temple and shook her head. "I don't know, Ethan. I tend to be pretty opinionated, and high heels absolutely wreck my feet. I might be more of a hindrance than an asset to your promotion."

"Nonsense." He crossed his arms and braced his elbows on the table, leaning closer. "You're mature. Attractive. Intelligent. You can carry on an interesting conversation. You think on your feet and you're not afraid to take risks."

A hint of pink colored her cheeks and her mouth curved into a teasing smile. "Careful. That sounded dangerously close to sweet talk if you ask me."

"It's not false flattery. Believe me, I looked at a lot of women tonight." He gestured as he spoke. "Some of them had bigger boobs or longer hair. Some were dressed more seductively—"

J.C. reached out and captured his flailing hand. "Quit while you're ahead, Major."

Ethan turned his hand to hold on to hers. Palm touching palm, he savored that fiery energy that seemed to burn inside her and pulse between them. "Sorry. Honesty has always been a curse of mine."

"A curse?"

"I'm not good at sugarcoating things." He lacked the words to express what he felt. But his body seemed to have no problem expressing what it wanted. The world around them shrank down to the frictive heat of skin against skin as he massaged his thumb across the back of her hand, teasing her the same way she'd teased the rim of her cup earlier. Her pupils dilated with subtle arousal, turning her bright eyes into hazy pools of deep, midnight blue. "What I'm trying to say is, you're the only woman tonight who...clicked."

"Clicked?"

Her fingers splayed, inviting the stroke of his thumb along their delicate lengths and the soft places in between. Ethan obliged.

"You're the only woman I wanted to ask to do this for me."

More silence. More strokes. More lazy heat. Then a crooked, beautiful smile. "I don't think honesty is such a curse. That's a very sweet thing to say."

He groaned. "Sweet's good, right?"

J.C. nodded, tightening her grip around his when he would have pulled away. Ethan had never understood the whole *sweet* appeal that women seemed to crave. But when she rewarded him by turning over his hand and starting a slow massage of her own, he decided the concept might be worth investigating. She traced each line of his palm with a touch so light it was almost a tickle. But every nerve ending awoke and eagerly awaited the next caress. And as the touches deepened, his blood turned into warm, thick molasses and drizzled a lazy heat into every part of him.

Sweet was very good.

His breath hitched. He was dying to have those mesmerizing hands work their magic on other, more neglected, parts of his body.

Her fingers trailed up to the pounding pulse point on his wrist and he began to consider doing more than simply fake a relationship with this woman. Maybe celibacy was an unnecessary safeguard against women messing with his life. As long as he kept his heart out of the picture and didn't lose his head over any promises she might make or break, there was no sensible reason to deny his body the pleasure of her company.

If she was willing.

"To be honest..." She was using both hands now, watching her own work, and the thoroughness with which she studied and stroked him stirred his fantasies. This was nothing more than a hand massage, yet he was completely under her spell. "You were the only man tonight who...clicked...with me."

"Yeah?"

"Yeah."

Nice. No declaration of love. No pressure. Just an admission of...*clicking*. Admitting a mutual attraction. Safe enough.

"So, will you help me?" he asked. Her hands stilled on his. Her downcast eyes were unreadable. Edgy anticipation quickly vanquished Ethan's mellow mood. "J.C.?"

"Well, I suppose I do owe you for defending me against those perverts tonight."

"I'd have done the same whether you say yes or no."

"I believe you would." She pulled away entirely, and he had to grab the table to keep from snatching back her hands and demanding an answer. After taking a moment to rifle through her cavernous bag without retrieving anything, she closed the top and hugged it to her chest. She lifted her gaze to a point barely above his chin. Uh-oh. "I'll do this fiancée act for you on one condition."

"Name it."

Ethan held his breath. Short of committing a felony, he would do whatever she asked to make this happen.

Her eyes finally met his. "We seal the deal with another kiss."

"Sir?" Ethan figuratively picked his jaw up from the table and dragged his attention to the college boy who had summoned him from behind the counter. The thrills of unexpected success and sexual anticipation pounding through his veins had momentarily deafened him to the world outside this booth. "We're getting ready to close down the machines for cleaning. Can I get you anything else before you go?"

Ethan got the hint. He doffed the kid a two-fingered salute. "We're good. Thanks." J.C. was still clutching her purse to her chest as if it afforded her some kind of security, but her sensuous smile radiated the same hunger that twitched along every nerve ending in his body. She wanted another kiss, huh? He stood and held his hand out to her. "Shall we?"

Arm in arm, they double-timed it back to the bar.

THE NUMBER OF VEHICLES in the lot at Groucho's Pub had thinned enough to offer them virtual privacy in the shadows where J.C. had parked her jazzy little Camaro coupe. While she dug out her keys to unlock her car, Ethan took note of the broken light in the street lamp nearest to her car.

Like the guard he'd been trained to be, he hovered close behind her, taking stock of their surroundings. He spotted the homeless guy settling in for the night in the alley behind the bar. Two teens drove past, their ground-thumping music at two in the morning begging for a call to the D.C. police. In the silence that followed their departure, one of the cocktail waitresses came out the door, tucking a respectable wad of bills into her purse and hurrying over to a beat-up truck. Ethan scowled at the open invitation to a mugging. He followed her all the way with his gaze, easing his conscience once she started the engine and drove safely away.

When he finally heard J.C.'s key sliding into the lock, his focus shifted from the potential dangers to the all too vulnerable woman beside him. He reached around her to hold open the door, creating a triangle with the car and his body that shielded her in the center. "You should have your keys out before you get to your car, and try to park closer to the door and under a light when you know you're going to be out late like this."

J.C. shook her head and turned. The glimpse of a smile seemed to make light of his concerns. "Enough with the lecture, Mr. Marine. One, I know the standard safety rules. If I was alone, I'd have used them. Two, there were no spots available near any of the streetlights or the door. And three, you're the one who kept me out so late."

"Then it's a good thing I'm here to watch your back." And my, what a tempting backside that was.

She turned and leaned into the car to toss her bag onto the floorboard in front of the passenger seat. Her butt rounded before his eyes, and his crotch roused at the tempting target she presented. Her sweater rode up to reveal a stripe of smooth, pale skin above the waistband of her jeans. His fingers burned with the sudden desire to release the car's cold metal and touch that hot, secret peek of naked woman.

A kiss. A *kiss,* he reminded himself as she straightened and the skin disappeared. All the lady had asked for was a kiss. And he still had a point to make. "You walked out here on your own earlier. You should have asked the bouncer to walk you to your car."

J.C. turned. "That's not his job."

"It's dark, it's late and you were alone. No wonder those goons thought they could accost you. You shouldn't take chances like that."

She reached up and flipped his collar into place. "Don't fret, Major. I was taking care of myself long before you came into the picture."

He seized her wrists to pull away her distracting hands and force her to listen. "Well, I am in the picture now. Either have somebody walk you out or call me."

That tiny frown line dimpled between her brows. "Right, like you'll show up just to see me safely from that door to this car if I call."

"I'll be there."

She jerked her hands free. "Not after two weeks, you won't."

Ethan didn't know how to respond to that comment, especially since, despite her teasing tone, it felt like an accusation. Unsure of what his guilt might be, worried that she would change her mind about posing as his bride-to-be, Ethan retreated a step and racheted back his emotions. "The Cherry Blossom Ball is tonight. Formal attire. I'll pick you up at nineteen hundred hours. That's seven o'clock civvie time. I'm free later this morning if you need to do some shopping."

"*You* want to go shopping?" She arched an eyebrow that indicated sarcastic humor, but that tiny dent which spoke of thoughts he couldn't know or understand was still in place.

"To be honest, I'd rather be lined up in front of a firing squad. But I said I'd pay for everything. You find the dress and then call me.'' He pulled out his wallet and handed her a business card. ''That's got my office and cell number on it.''

''If you insist.'' She tucked the card into her pocket.

With that much of a plan in place, J.C. climbed into the car. Ethan shut the door as she started the engine. She hadn't gotten that kiss she'd asked for, but then maybe she'd changed her mind. He might still be simmering with newly awakened, long-denied lust, but her jets had cooled considerably since he'd voiced his concerns about her safety. So when she rolled down her window, he leaned down close enough to see and hear yet maintain a polite distance.

''Aren't you forgetting something?'' she asked.

''Sure.'' He pushed the button to lock her door.

She pursed her lips and sighed, stirring those wisps of mahogany hair against her forehead. She turned in her seat, crossed her arms and rested them on the open window frame. ''We still haven't sealed our bargain. A two-week, all expenses paid trip to fake fiancée-ville?''

So she hadn't forgotten the kiss. Something warm and grateful eased his frustrations and doubts. ''Anything I can do to make this up to you, you let me know.''

''We'll see.''

''Good night.'' He lowered his head to her upturned face and dropped a quick, no-hands kiss on her lips. They were soft, sweet and delicious, but he allowed himself only a taste.

J.C. grabbed his wrist as he pulled away. ''Ethan. We're sealing a rather important agreement, not playing tag. We have to do better than that to be a convincing couple.''

''I suppose. We should get used to those familiar touches.''

"Then try again. Convince me."

Maybe he wasn't supposed to understand this modern, complicated fireball of a woman. Maybe he shouldn't even try. Whatever her hang-ups might be, and despite the fact he was better trained to serve his country than to court a lady, there was no denying the physical chemistry between them.

Besides, he was a man who knew how to take an order. And if the woman demanded convincing that they could pull this off, he was the go-to man to deliver.

Ethan cupped her jaw and slid his fingers into the silky fringe of hair beside her ear. When he kissed her this time, it was a slow, reverent, get-acquainted activity. Her lips parted beneath his and a whisper of warm air and chocolaty coffee teased his tongue. He closed his eyes and inhaled with lazy satisfaction as he explored every dip and curve, drawing the rich, enticing scent of the woman herself deep into his senses.

With her willing response, Ethan moved the kiss beyond acquaintance status and made himself a welcome friend. The good doctor's sensuous, offset mouth might well be the tastiest damn thing on the planet. It was like eating ambrosia. He felt godlike. He couldn't get enough.

He nipped and she pressed. He suckled and she teased. He licked the rim and she reached out and captured his tongue with hers. And all the while he felt his powers growing—his senses sharpening to every nuance of taste, every mew of sound, every grasp of needy pressure as she wound her fingers behind his neck and scraped her palm across the sandpapery stubble of his ultrashort hair.

His pores opened to release heat, his nostrils flared to suck in oxygen, his blood thickened and traveled straight to his groin. But when Ethan instinctively thrust forward, all he got was unbending contact with the car's steel chassis. He wanted something warm against his body, something responsive. He wanted her.

Leaning farther inside, Ethan sifted his fingers through the sassy spikes of her hair, then skimmed along the soft velvet of her nape and length of her back. Without breaking the feast on her mouth, he used his hands to admire the strength of her muscles, the delicacy of her bone structure, the soft swellings of shape that made her decidedly all woman.

But he was a man on a mission. He was searching for that strip of skin he'd seen in the moonlight. J.C. wrapped her arms around his neck, pulling herself off the seat and into the kiss as he dipped his fingertips into the waistband of her jeans. He tried to work the sweater out of the way with his thumbs, but her mouth distracted him. She'd sucked his bottom lip between her teeth. He tried again and lost contact with the flare of her bottom. Impatiently he tugged up the hem of the nubby cotton material and flattened both palms against the smooth expanse of skin along her spine. She might be cool to the touch, but there was something scorchingly hot about her incendiary response.

J.C. gasped against his mouth, calling his name in a throaty whisper and pushing her breasts against his chest. Her soft mounds pillowed and spread, increasing the contact. The hard tips branded him through their clothes.

"Ah, Doc… Darlin'…" Ethan ground his hips against the car as a nearly overwhelming bombardment of sensations surged through him. *The hell with this.*

Strengthened by their passion, crazed by the fever of it, Ethan reached farther into the car. He slipped his hands beneath her bottom and lifted her right out of her seat. J.C. tucked her head and held on as he set her in the open window frame and wedged her hip against his aching shaft.

He felt right at home by the time he'd taken the sweater off over her head and wrapped her up in his arms. Rubbing himself shamelessly against her, Ethan proceeded to touch every exposed inch of skin his hands could find. He rewarded her with a kiss each time he discovered something he liked, so he was touching her everywhere, kissing her constantly, consuming her.

"Ethan?"

He loved when she said his name like that. A rush of breath, a husky plea. He rewarded her for that, too.

"J.C." He wasn't much more articulate as she untucked his shirt and skimmed it up past his pecs. She rolled his own tender buds between her fingers and he groaned at the prickly shots of lightning that arced into his swollen dick. He wanted her hands on him, every part of him. He thrust against her hip, wanting it to be her hand there, wanting to be inside her.

He slipped one thumb beneath the lacy cup of her bra and flicked it across her hardened tip. "Ethan!" she gasped. Her fingers dug into the hair on his chest.

"Ow." He kissed her on the mouth. Kissed her again. "Watch it, baby."

While he stroked her breast, while she fed his hungry lips, he unsnapped her jeans. Her thighs eased apart as he lowered the zipper. He cupped her through the denim and whatever she wore underneath, accustoming her to his more intimate touch. She was nothing but sweet, sweet heat as she pushed against his hand. She moaned into his mouth, reached behind him and clung to his shoulders.

Ethan pleasured her that way until she bucked against his touch. Then he slipped inside her panties and zeroed in on her hidden, feminine crevice. She was slick and tight and dripping on his fingers.

"Is this okay?" he managed to ask on a stuttered, feverish gasp beside her ear.

In answer, she squeezed his shoulders and lifted herself, granting him access to the very heart of her. Ethan dipped one, then two fingers inside and did to her what he wanted her to do for him.

He found that secret nub, thrust his tongue into her mouth. Her thighs clenched and tiny muscles fluttered all around his fingers. The delicate contractions intensified. J.C.'s breath rushed out. She threw back her head and Ethan gloried in her lusty response to his wicked touch. He twisted his fingers and she buried her face in the juncture of his neck and shoulder. She dug her teeth into his shirt and caught a bit of the skin underneath, stifling her cry of release as she—

Honk!

J.C. jumped in his embrace as her foot hit the car's horn a second time. "Aagh!"

Ethan quickly removed his hand from her pants and caught her before she fell to the ground. But, startled from the climax of passion, his movements were jerky and uncoordinated. He ended up smacking his head against the car roof and dumping her in on the seat.

"I'm sorry. Damn." Ethan threw his hands up into the air and stepped away. "I'm sorry."

"What am I doing?" J.C. huddled behind the steering wheel, her arms wrapped in protective cover across her chest. Her bra strap had slipped off her shoulder and caught in the crook of her elbow. Even in little more than moonlight, he could see she was red from the swell of that barely revealed breast all the way up her neck. What the hell had just happened? How did he make this right?

She flipped on the interior light, then just as quickly turned it off. Her focus darted around the interior of the car. "Where's my sweater?"

"Hell!" One quick glance and Ethan spotted the top on the asphalt beneath the car. Swearing at the pain behind his zipped-up jeans, he bent down and retrieved it. "If it's ruined, I'll replace it," he promised, handing over the wrinkled mess.

"Forget it." She snatched the sweater from his hand. He pulled the strap back onto her shoulder, trying to help, but she swatted him away. "I said forget it!"

Ultimately, Ethan backed off. He braced his hands at his waist and tipped his head to the moon, feeling the frustrated hormones rage through his body as his conscience and common sense kicked in way, way too late.

Public place. Possible audience.

And though they were masked by shadows, and the drunk across the way was snoring on a pile of newspapers, Ethan wasn't too far gone to realize the horrible blunder he'd just made.

What had happened to rational thought? Planning? Purpose?

Self-control had vanished as if it had never existed. And if that damn horn hadn't have honked, he would still be making a spectacle of himself—and of J.C.—for God, the spring night, and anyone else in the world to see. So much for discretion. So much for keeping his distance or treating her like a lady.

So much for thinking he could be as casual about sex as his brother Travis seemed to be.

Ethan's lust for Bethany Mead had nearly destroyed his career. It had certainly done irreparable damage to his heart. Josephine C.—whatever her middle name was—Gardner was supposed to be his professional salvation.

But until he got to know her better, until they had the details of their arrangement ironed out, until he could firmly remember that he'd only asked for two weeks out of her life—he couldn't afford to lose his focus or anything else.

Sexual frustration he could live with—if he could get to a cold shower fast enough. But a guilty conscience, professional regrets and blown chances were more than he could stand.

With his manhood still pointing due north, Ethan's brain was finally fully functioning again. Sometime during his self-damning version of a pep talk, J.C. had slipped back into her sweater. Her lips were swollen, her skin red with the depth of his need.

"I'm sorry." His instinct was to touch her, hug her. But he suspected that was the last thing she wanted right now. "I didn't mean for that kiss to get so far out of hand. Certainly not here. Certainly not on our first night... together." He swallowed hard and asked the tough question. "We are still together, aren't we?"

She nodded. "I promised you two weeks. And stop apologizing. We're both adults. I wanted all of that...*kiss*. I just didn't realize I'd want it all so soon." She gripped the steering wheel in both hands and looked at his reflection in her sideview mirror as she spoke. "Apparently that familiar touching thing you mentioned won't be a problem for us."

Ethan groaned. No problem at all.

And that could prove to be a huge problem if he let this woman and his attraction to her become more important than his future with the Corps.

6

BLISS IS THAT oft-elusive nirvana where conscious thought ends and one is left simply feeling the joy, the passion, the pleasure of the moment. Sure, there's a physiological element to it—increased blood flow, a slight rise in body temp, the release of hormones. But there's no analytical reasoning to explain the rapture that consumes your body; it just is. That's what an orgasm is all about, ladies.

Pure feeling. Pure heat. What a rush.

Bliss. Bliss. Bliss.

J.C.'s fingers froze on the keyboard. She opened her eyes and read the words on her laptop screen. "Oh, God, I can't publish this."

She highlighted the last three paragraphs of her article and hit Delete.

Leaning back against the pillows of her purple chaise lounge, she scrolled through her laptop screen, trying to find where stream of consciousness had taken over from clinical opinion and common sense. She'd intended to write a cautionary piece, advising her readers to be wary of a military man's dogged determination to accomplish his goal—in the relationship arena as well as against the enemy. She'd included humor with some direct quotes—*"I'll show you my tattoo"* and *"Women love to see my sword. You wanna?"*

She'd balanced her stats about the number of men who'd approached her—including the one who'd worn a wedding ring, the one who'd offered her a hotel key but couldn't get her name right, the one who wouldn't take *no* for an answer—with a genuine compliment about how fit and healthy each man had been. She'd even admitted that some of them knew a few amazing kissing techniques.

Right there. She pointed to the traitorous, all too personal words on the screen. *Don't misread me here. If all you want is a night of sex, fine. Take precautions and have fun. You'll find plenty of able volunteers to choose from.*

But I'm still holding off on recommending these guys for the long-term, ladies. In port, off base, on leave—time is a precious commodity to these guys. When their bulging biceps and overeager efforts to seduce didn't pique my interest, they quickly took their act on to the next available female. It wasn't ME they were interested in. It was the conquest. The chance to get laid. Any woman would have met their need. And we deserve better than being a matter of convenience, don't we?

And, hey, let's be honest, there was really only one kiss out of several offers and a couple of samples that made me want to come back for more.

And come and come...

"Ho, boy." J.C. shoved her fingers into her mop of toss-and-turn hair and cursed her talent for remembering details.

Vividly.

She'd found the problem. *Kissing in the Major Leagues* had evolved into a testament to Ethan McCormick's sex appeal. Her article had taken a sharp left turn from chatty advice column to true confession, sharing all the juicy details about the way Ethan had made her feel. Safe. Hot. Raw. Orgasmic.

Bliss.

"Idiot." With a heavy, restless sigh, J.C. closed her laptop. She swung her legs over the side of the chaise and walked to the window to inspect the view, reorienting herself to the real, waking, rosy spring morning. The world was alive outside and warm with the sun that couldn't yet penetrate her glass. There were already rowing crews training out on the river, joggers and walkers exercising on the pathway beside it, cars and their occupants starting their Friday commutes.

She still had on the T-shirt and flannel pants she wore for jammies. Her cooling coffee sat untouched on the table behind her and her usual instinct to rise early and dive into work had abandoned her this morning. After four hours of fitful sleep, she'd finally left the uncomfortable tangle of sheets on her bed and come out into the living room to write.

But her words sounded more like some starry-eyed lover's diary about her first date with destiny than a savvy journalist's perceptive take on the real world of men and women. Instead of warning her readers about grabbing the pleasure of the moment without considering the consequences of the future, she'd gone on and on about her body's wanton, wild response to the major's wicked hands.

J.C. flattened her palms against the cool pane of glass, trying to ease the heat that flushed her skin and mocked her resolve. Her research last night had lacked a definite scientific detachment.

Instead of disproving Lee Whiteley's claim, she'd confirmed the myth that a man in uniform made a great lover. He was ultramale. Potent. Strong in both need and physical abilities.

J.C. was no flyweight. Her love for dancing and long

walks had given her a muscular set of thighs and some generous hips. She liked her chocolate, too. But Ethan had lifted her right out of the car. He'd given her an anchor to cling to while he...while he kissed...while his hand...

Her thighs clenched and her fingertips dug into the windowpane as her mind conjured a jumble of erotic images—some, vivid memories—others, untested fantasies. The desire she'd felt last night instantly rekindled, leaving her feeling all prickly and unsettled, inside and out.

She stroked her cool fingertips across her sensitized mouth, recalling the tactile memory of Ethan's lips. She let her fingers slide down her throat to the neckline of her shirt. Did he have any idea how good he was? She'd had full-blown intercourse with former lovers that hadn't yielded as explosive a climax as the major's hands and mouth had given her.

The big lug had been distant and polite—awkward even—sitting in the coffee shop and getting acquainted. But then he pulled out that kiss, those hands, that magic— as if he was brandishing some sort of secret weapon. And she'd fallen prey to it. Boom. Just like that.

Boom?

"Oh, God." J.C. backed away from the edge of the windowsill where she'd been rubbing herself. She clutched her hands into fists and hugged them around her middle, praying no one had been watching the unintentional show in the third-floor window.

How pathetic could she get? *Lonely woman fondles self in weak effort to recreate the best sex since*—ever. "You need to get laid, girl," she advised herself. She needed to get that man out of her system and off that virtual pedestal her hormones had placed him on. She massaged the guilty tension gathering between her eyes. "I need to at least get a life. No wonder Lee worries about me."

J.C. forced her brain to concentrate on watching the bustle of activity outside. An elderly couple strolled hand in hand down the river's walkway. A family of tourists clumped together, then ran apart, switching positions as they tried to take a photograph with the domed Jefferson Memorial in the background. She looked closer to home, taking note of her building's daytime security guard arguing with a black-haired man over the way he'd parked his car on the curb outside the parking lot gate.

Norman Flynn was a grouchy old codger who would bend the rules for a friendly smile and some home-baked cookies. The dark-haired man could shake his fists all he wanted. If he didn't say *please* and *thank-you* and grease the retired M.P.'s palm with some oatmeal scotchies, there was no way he was getting through that gate.

J.C.'s whole body relaxed into a smile as the first ray of hopeful sunshine broke through her brooding mood. She propped her hands on her hips and breathed in deeply, as if taking in her first breath of fresh, morning air.

Of course. A life. She had one. She just needed to get out of here and get on with it. A couple of miles of power walking should do the trick to get her started.

She dumped her coffee in the sink, packed her laptop in her bag and headed for the bedroom to change. She needed to talk to people. Say hi to Norm. Interact. Reassert her power over her own thoughts and actions. She needed to get back into the moment and get out of the past. The future would take care of itself.

She quickly made up the antique four-poster bed and changed into a pair of running pants and matching jacket. She grabbed her weights and headphones, tucked her keys into one jacket pocket and pepper spray into the other.

J.C. locked her door and jogged down the stairs. Ethan McCormick was just a man. A man who wouldn't commit to more than two weeks with a woman. Needing her help on his promotion was just a built-in excuse to say goodbye and move on to his next conquest when he was done with her.

If she were to give advice to another woman in her situation, she would say to go for it. Keep your eyes wide-open. Keep your heart in the moment. Take advantage of the time limit and let the man make your body happy for a couple of weeks. Then move on. Take the edge off your desperation to find a long-term relationship.

Ethan himself had said he would give her anything she needed to return the favor of pretending to be his bride-to-be. He'd been talking money or gifts.

But J.C. intended to ask him for something much more personal.

Two weeks of bliss.

She was grinning like the Cheshire cat by the time she strode out onto the riverwalk beside the Potomac.

J.C. GRIPPED THE WEIGHTS in her fists and swung them in rhythm with the two-step tune playing on the country music station in her ears. In her mind, she hummed along to the Texas anthem, but she was concentrating on her breathing and elevated heart rate. The breeze off the river was cool, tinged with the greenish scents of the thickening grass and budding cherry trees atop its banks. But beads of perspiration gathered at the small of her back and tickled between her breasts as the springtime sun warmed her muscles with its heated caress.

Oh, yeah. She was large and in charge of her world once more. Fit, fine and ready for fun. She'd brainstormed a more succinct, less personal ending for her article. And she had plenty of time to shower and change before her meeting so that she could drive uptown and find the perfect gown for tonight.

Something elegant and understated, in keeping with Ethan's country-clubbish goals. But something that emphasized her best attributes. Her legs? Cleavage? Let's see, what did Ethan like? J.C. giggled like a naughty schoolgirl. She could hardly emphasize *that* in public! Maybe she should just go for easy access, or—

Suddenly a man's hand clamped around her arm and dragged her out of step.

J.C. screamed as she stumbled against a wiry chest. "Let go of me! Hel—!" A sweaty palm stifled her mouth and the pungent smell of unwashed skin stung her nose.

She stomped on an instep and shoved with her free hand. She heard words of warning, but they were muffled by the earphones and music. She reached for the pepper spray, but the hand at her mouth latched on to her wrist. Trapped in her attacker's painful grip, she twisted her body to angle a knee toward his crotch. "I swear to God, I will—"

Black hair.

Ice chilled her veins and worked her heart into a pounding panic inside her chest. The tattooed bicep, the unshaven face, the bleary black eyes all came into focus. Fear was eclipsed by shock. Anger quickly took its place. She stopped fighting and started thinking. "You again."

The creep from the bar last night. Déjà vu.

He was breathing hard with the exertion of controlling her. The stale smell of hangover breath brushed past her nose. The instant he released her, J.C. put an arm's length of fresh air between them. But she didn't turn her back. He held up his hands in surrender and spoke in what sounded like a whisper. "I tried to get your attention, lady, but you didn't hear me."

She jerked the headphones from her ears and hung them around her neck. She read worry rather than apology in his expression. She rubbed at the pinched skin on her wrists. "Whoever taught you it was okay to grab a woman like that?"

He ignored the question and moved closer, ducking his head to whisper. J.C. backed up the same distance. He muttered a curse as foul as his breath, his voice crystal clear now. "It's Corporal Guerro, ma'am. We met last night."

"I know who you are." She now recognized him as the man who'd been arguing with Norm in the parking lot. "How did you find me?"

"I'm not stalking you," he insisted. "But the guard wouldn't let me up to your apartment."

"I should hope not."

"Look, I don't want to hurt you."

"I don't want to be hurt!"

It was stupid to stand here and argue with this idiot. But when she stepped to the side to move past him, he blocked her path. He wouldn't let her pass on the other side, either. J.C. held her breath to squelch her furious resentment and curled her toes inside her Reeboks to hide her trembling. If she retreated the way she'd come, he'd probably chase her down and grab her again.

This was so not okay.

"How did you find me?" she repeated, keeping her voice as calm and even as when she addressed a client. Whatever reason prompted him to give up a night of sleep and track her down couldn't be good.

"With this." He reached into his pocket and pulled out a small, white cardboard rectangle. She immediately recognized the geometric design and black block print. Oh, no. A business card. *Her* business card.

J.C. lunged for the mini personnel file, but Juan flipped his hand up into the air, holding the card well out of reach. He laughed at her instinctive, foolhardy reaction, fully aware that he had the advantage right now. Regrouping, J.C. rocked back flat on her feet and schooled the panic from her voice. "I didn't give that to you."

He slipped the card deep inside his front jeans pocket, accurately guessing she wouldn't try to retrieve it from there. "Manny found it in your purse and pocketed it before the major clocked him."

Ethan. Yes, Ethan. He'd put this jerk in his place. A surge of adrenaline emboldened her to lie. "Ethan and I are engaged to be married. He won't be pleased to know you're following me. I think he made it clear last night that I'm off-limits to you."

"Yeah, well I'm not interested in your teasing ass, lady. Make a fool out of someone else." His black eyes burned red with the remnants of alcohol and fatigue. "I just want to know what you told him. I already got some black marks against me, and when I report back from leave tomorrow, I don't want to be sent straight to the brig again."

Brig. Military jail. Her father had spent a few nights in one. Not encouraging. "You've been in the brig before?"

Guerro nodded with an arrogant tilt to his chin like, *yeah, so what?* "I got a temper on me. Especially when I've been drinking."

"You were drinking last night." She'd been in bigger danger than she'd suspected.

"Look, lady, what did you tell him?"

"Major McCormick?"

"McCormick, yeah. He's not with my unit, but those officers, they all know each other. Am I screwed for hittin' on his girl?"

Apparently Ethan's charade had been convincing. But she didn't know him well enough to gauge how far he would take last night's incident, or whether he considered the problem handled. J.C. shrugged, seeing traces of her father's personality in Corporal Guerro's loose-cannon desperation. "I don't know if he intends to report you or not."

"Tell him not to."

"I don't think you can give a major an order."

"I'm not. I'm asking for a favor. From you." She owed this man nothing, except, in an indirect way, her introduction to Ethan. "I swear to God I didn't know you were his girl when I moved on you. But you were playin' me and deserved some payback. I can't go back to the brig. They'll strip me all the way down to PFC if I get in trouble again."

With every agitated word, he hunched closer.

J.C. backed away slowly, fighting the urge to run. "I'm sorry. I have to go."

But his fingers dug into her forearm. Shaking her. Stopping her. "Do it, lady. Make it right. You owe me."

"Are you threatening me?" She bit down against the pain and jerked against his bruising grasp. "The major won't like that, either."

He swore in two languages and jumped back, holding his hands up high where she could see them. "Just find out for me, will you? Don't let him make that report. Now that I know you two don't live together, I'll call you."

He knew...? He'd spied...? "You'll call?"

He flashed his teeth in half a grin that she found more threatening than amusing. "I got your card, remember?" He pointed a grubby finger at her. "Make it right."

Guerro backed off, turned and loped down the hill toward a line of parked cars. J.C. watched him, her unblinking eyes stinging with wariness, until he climbed into a battered blue sedan and pulled out into traffic.

She closed her eyes and heaved a sigh of relief. When she opened them again, the world looked normal. But she didn't feel normal. She felt as if some unseen hand had just flipped the switch on a slowly ticking time bomb beneath her feet.

It wasn't just the lingering stench of Juan Guerro's sweat and booze on her clothes that bothered her. It wasn't just the physical force and implied threats he'd surprised her with that hastened her walk into a quick jog back to her apartment.

It was the lie. The necessary deception that allowed her to write one of the fastest-growing editorial-and-advice columns in the country while maintaining what passed for a private life.

She prized her anonymity. It gave her the freedom to speak her mind, the opportunity to say the tough things that needed to be said about living and loving and making love. It gave self-conscious readers the courage to ask delicate questions, to come forward with issues that were just too hard to discuss with someone face-to-face. It distanced her from the crackpots who wanted to bed the sex lady and receive some hands-on therapy.

J.C. unlocked her door and slipped inside. She slid the dead bolt into place, then fastened the chain and locked the doorknob before leaning back against the frame. She was breathing so hard—from stress as much as exertion—that she could barely hear her own thoughts.

Without knowing it, Corporal Guerro had broken through that wall of anonymity. Her business card didn't say she was "Dr. Cyn," but it did bill her as a sex and relationship counselor and listed the number at the paper as well as her cell. If Juan called the work number and got *Woman's Word,* would he be bright enough to connect Ethan's *Dr. Josephine C. Gardner* with the controversial *Dr. Cyn?*

Maybe this would all blow over. After all, *bright* wasn't the first word that came to mind when she thought of Guerro. Ethan had been authoritative enough. He probably saw no need to report Juan and Manny. There would be no mention of brigs or discipline. Juan could stay a corporal and forget all about her.

Sure, it could play that way.

She breathed a little easier. She pushed away from the door and stripped as she headed for the shower.

It had to play that way.

Because J.C. had no doubt that with his act first, think later style, Juan wouldn't hesitate to tell Ethan, his buddies or the tabloids her real identity if it suited his purpose to expose her. Then she could kiss her privacy, her research and two weeks of bliss with Ethan McCormick goodbye.

"I THOUGHT THIS LOOKED like a nice neighborhood. And there's a guard at the gate." Ethan had waited patiently while she unhooked all three locks on her door. "Expecting trouble?"

But threats and deception and preconceived notions were the furthest thing from J.C.'s mind right now.

"Wow." Not her most eloquent moment.

She held her door open and practically drooled over the man standing in the hallway. Ethan cut an impressive figure in his black evening dress uniform with a scarlet cummerbund wrapped at his trim waist and gold braid and buttons accenting the breadth and height of him. The number of colorful ribbons and pins adorning his chest gave him a commanding air of power and authority. He'd tucked his white, flat-topped hat beneath his arm and held a plastic corsage box in one white-gloved hand.

"Right back at you. That dress looks a hell of a lot better on you than it did on the hanger this morning."

"You think?" J.C. twirled around, giving him the full effect of all the skin bared by double spaghetti straps and a modest décolletage. Everything else was demurely covered to her ankles, in deference to the stodgy requirements Ethan said the general and his committee preferred to see at official functions. But the hem flared to give her room to dance, and a touch of sparkle in the sheer overskirt made the outfit fun enough for her rebellious tastes.

"Definitely better than the hanger."

J.C. smiled at the hungry timbre in his voice. "Your sweet talk's improving."

Ethan didn't smile. He was busy assessing her from head to toe, lingering in places that made her toes curl into the carpet and her breasts tingle beneath the fitted bodice of the smoky blue silk. He had that same look in his eyes that he'd had last night at the bar—the look that said he wanted to eat her up. Here. Now. On the chaise. In the bed. Up against the wall. Anywhere he could have her. With his hands and mouth. His body. Would that most masculine part of him be as sleek and toned—and big!—as the rest of him?

An erotic image—sweaty, hot, graphic—leaped into her imagination.

Back off! Back off! Back off! Her brain shouted the warning too late as she suddenly flushed with so much heat that she thought she might faint. Her knuckles turned white as she gripped the door and its frame for support and made a conscious effort to breathe.

In. Out. Left... *Oh, shoot!* Did everything come down to sex with this man? Had she talked and written about sex so much that it was constantly on her mind now? Out. No, in! Out. Was her reaction to Ethan's virility this incendiary because her involuntary abstinence had dragged on for more months than she could count? Despite her training, she might no longer qualify as an expert on the topic. In. Out. He inspired her to do some serious, one-on-one research.

But J.C. couldn't just drag Ethan into her apartment, strip off his uniform and demand his pleasuring skills as payment for pretending to be his fiancée when they were expected across town in an hour. He'd come here early to get their stories straight so it would sound as if they'd known each other longer than twenty hours—not to grab a quickie before the job interview-slash-inquisition began.

She had to cover her bases with the whole Juan Guerro incident first. Protect her alter ego. She'd promised Ethan she'd do whatever she could to help him get that promotion he wanted so badly.

Plus, she didn't want to risk him saying no to her proposition and walking out before she got the chance to study the officers at the ball tonight. How attentive would they be to their wives or dates? How much flirting would they try to get away with? J.C. didn't consider herself a great beauty, but she'd taken extra care with her hair and makeup and choice of accessories tonight. It was pretty shameless to set herself up as bait. But how many men would be like her father and chase after any sexy diversion that came along?

No, she couldn't jeopardize her bet or anything else. Not yet.

She needed to break the charged silence gathering strength between them and get moving before she pulled him down for a kiss that would certainly make them late for the ball. With a teasing smile and a rustle of petticoats, she reached for the corsage. "Is that for me?"

"What?" He swallowed hard, and J.C. wanted to chase the bob of his Adam's apple along the column of his neck with her parched tongue. "Yeah. Here. I wasn't sure what kind of flower would go with your dress. But Captain Black recommended a gardenia for its neutral color, said it would go with everything."

"Who's Captain Black?"

"My aide de camp." She'd heard the term, but he explained it, anyway. "My assistant at the DoD. You'll meet him tonight."

She opened the box and inhaled the waxy flower's heavy, potent scent. She closed it just as quickly, blocking out the sudden image of other things, heavy and potent, triggered by the lush, exotic smell. "Tell him good recommendation. It's beautiful. Thank you." Trying not to breathe any more seductive scents, nor think any erotic thoughts, she ushered him inside and closed the door. The size of her already-tiny apartment shrank even further as Ethan strode into her living room.

"Nice place." He crossed to the set of big double windows she loved. "Great view."

"That's why I chose it. With the river and monument park area to look at, I can almost feel I'm out in the country."

He glanced over his shoulder. "You a small-town girl?"

Boy, they didn't know much about each other, did they. "No. I actually grew up in San Diego. I love everything you can find in the city, but sometimes I just need to see some wide-open space—like the ocean or the mountains."

He nodded toward the window. "Or the park. I can relate."

"Have a seat," she offered, pointing to the purple chaise and contrasting teal-and-lavender-print easy chairs. Ethan's formal attire in the midst her colorful, bohemian decor reminded her of the different worlds they came from and would return to. It was an observation she found reassuring. J.C. was smart enough to know that sharing a sexual attraction didn't mean anything deeper would develop. Their limited time frame should help keep things that way. "What about you? Where do you call home?"

Ethan sat on the edge of one of the lavender chairs, resting his elbows on his knees and leaning forward as if he doubted the delicate piece of furniture could take his entire weight. "Let's see, nine countries on five continents in twelve years—"

"Are you kidding?" J.C. sank into the chair opposite him, cradling the corsage box in her lap. Her father had been transferred every year or two, but she and her mother had always remained cocooned in their own little world in Southern California. She couldn't imagine pulling up roots so often. Of course, maybe Ethan never put down roots in the first place.

"I wanted to see the world. The Corps obliged."

A girl in every port. Had Ethan broken hearts on all five of those continents? Had he found the female company a healthy man like him would crave in each of those countries? J.C. set aside her pending disappointment. This was research, right? "Didn't you ever get…lonely?"

"I missed my family, sure. But they were all on the move, too, until my dad retired and my sister, Caitie, went to college and got married. I had a job to do. A job I loved. I've met people and seen things in this world that most folks never even read about. There's beauty out there, and crazy stuff, and…" His matter-of-fact explanation halted abruptly, as if an unbidden thought had caught him unaware. "I used to love experiencing different cultures firsthand. I couldn't wait to see what challenge the world would throw at me next."

"Used to?"

"Some days I think I've seen more than a man should have to."

His hushed voice and distant focus triggered an unexpected pang of sympathy. It was probably the counselor in her, sensing a troubled soul that needed to talk. But it was the woman in her who leaned forward and touched his knee. "Did something happen?"

Ethan's gray eyes darkened and nailed her as if she'd trespassed into a place she wasn't welcome. It was the first glimpse of strong emotion she'd seen in him, and the depth of it was as powerful as every other part of him. Ethan shot to his feet, breaking contact with her, stalking to the window and staring out toward the sunset. "Is this the get-acquainted part of the evening, where we offer a crash course in each other's lives and share our darkest secrets?"

It was also the first glint of sarcasm she'd heard in his cursed-with-honesty voice.

J.C. rose more slowly and followed him, matching his position but keeping the width of the window between them. "I'm not prying into your secrets, Ethan. But if you need to, I'm willing to listen. I'm actually pretty good at that."

"I fought in a war, Jo." She took note that in this outflux of pain and anger, he'd used a shortened, personalized form of her name. She angled her head to study his profile. That square jaw was set tight, defiant, battling for control over whatever memory had spooked him. "I guarded embassies in countries where Americans weren't exactly popular. I've lost buddies and men whose lives I was responsible for. People took advantage…'' He caught himself and snapped his mouth shut. ''Yeah. Stuff happened.'' He swiveled his head and looked down at her, capturing her with his eyes and holding her prisoner in their shadowy depths. ''I don't know what kind of therapist you are, but that's not what I need from you.''

His solution to handling all that *stuff* was to keep it bottled up inside? Did he detach himself from his personal life so he could survive his professional one? She'd seen things on the news which were disturbing enough to give anyone nightmares. To actually live through the horrors of war, though, to endure the violence and omnipresent threat of danger in a job such as Ethan's, must change a man inside. He would guard his thoughts, turn off his emotions. Trust would be hard to earn. Actions would come more easily than words.

All of which fit Ethan to a T.

Was that where his intense sexual energy came from? Was it the one outlet of free expression he allowed himself?

J.C. chose her next words carefully. ''I wasn't speaking as a therapist, Ethan. I know all you need from me is two weeks of acting like you're the love of my life and pretending I understand what it means to want to marry a Marine and take on this life you're describing to me. Which, to be honest, you're not selling me on.''

The blunt reminder shocked him out of his anger. A muscle in his jaw twitched, then relaxed. ''J.C.… Hell, there's good stuff, too.'' Back to *J.C.* Back on guard. ''Lifelong friendships. A sense of community. The value of self-discipline, the adrenaline rush of meeting tough challenges. Feeling—on most days—like you're doing a good thing.''

''Now you sound like a recruitment brochure.''

He almost laughed at that. Almost, but not quite. "I didn't mean to dump on you like that."

His definition of dumping had barely glossed the surface, she suspected. "I'm sorry if I hit a touchy subject. But, we do need to know something about each other before we meet your general."

"I know. But that's no excuse for snapping at you."

"You're just nervous about tonight."

He nodded. When he turned and faced her, he said something completely unexpected. "*You* make me nervous."

"Me?"

"This is a turning point in my career, a chance to get on the fast track to making top brass, to pass on my wisdom and experience to the next generation of the Corps. But all I can think about is how much I want to kiss you again."

With the tip of one gloved finger, he reached over and toyed with the long filigree earring that dangled against her neck. It was just a whisper of a touch, tickling her earlobe and sending shivers along her neck that danced across her skin and pricked goose bumps. J.C. caught a stuttered breath as he traced the same path with the tip of his finger, grazing her collarbone, then running out across her shoulder until he met a ribbon of strap. It was like drawing silk across all those sensitized nerve endings, only this silk was warm and strong, and the pulse beneath it beat in rapid time with her own.

J.C.'s lips parted, giving herself room to breathe, urging the heat to gather someplace besides the beading tips of her breasts. This was one of those familiar touches that every real couple shared, one of those touches she and Ethan seemed to have no problem faking. Her lips popped in a wishful smack as she forced herself to speak. "Kissing me makes you nervous?"

That white-gloved finger curled into its fist, and Ethan drew his hand back to his side, denying her the magical caress. "Sounds like involvement to me. And I promised there wouldn't be any tie-up's at the end of this arrangement."

J.C. was flattered, flustered, when she turned to face him. "Sounds like hormones to me. And I'm relieved I'm not the only one who can't keep them in line."

"Right. Hormones." Ethan's tongue darted out to moisten the rim of his lips.

J.C. followed the movement with hungry interest but refused to take the action they both craved. "I'll make you a deal. We'll talk about kissing and other...opportunities...later. You said to think about how I wanted to be compensated for helping you, and I've got an idea. If you're up for it." He narrowed his eyes, questioning the double entendre in her tone. J.C. coyly left him hanging. She stepped forward with another one of those proprietary touches and brushed a speck from his sleeve. "This evening, you and I are just going to focus on that promotion of yours."

With that promise, Ethan finally seemed to relax as much as a man with his shoulders perennially arched back at near attention could. "But we *will* talk about those opportunities later?"

J.C. smiled like seduction itself. "Oh, I'll insist on it."

"Did you take a tumble?" Ethan gently snagged her wrist as she pulled away and pointed out the deep, blue-violet bruise on her forearm where Corporal Guerro's thumb had nearly cut off the circulation in her arm that morning.

Though he conveyed nothing but curiosity and a touch

of concern, frissons of alarm cascaded through her, interrupting the fluid heat growing inside her at the hushed, private banter she'd been sharing with Ethan. It was definitely bad karma to think of Guerro right now, in the middle of getting personal with Ethan.

She made light of the injury, pulling away to glance at it as if it was no big deal. "I bumped it against my desk at work."

"That's a mean desk."

Juan Guerro was a mean man when he was drunk, or hungover the next morning. "I taught it a lesson." She made up an amusing cover story. "I tossed my coaster and left a water ring stain on it." She quickly changed the subject, opening the corsage box again and unleashing its scent and all the possibilities it conjured. She pulled the creamy flower out and held it up between them. "Will you do the honors?"

His gaze darted from her shoulders to her breasts and back up to her eyes. "I'm not sure where—"

"Relax, Major. It's a wrist corsage. You just slip it on." *And cover the bruise.* Out of sight, out of mind. And no more questions until the timing was right to broach the subject of Juan and Manny's punishment.

"Shall we?" Ethan turned and offered his arm. "Our limo awaits."

"You splurged on a limousine?"

"Another one of Captain Black's suggestions," Ethan admitted. "Seemed like a good idea at the time."

"Sounds like a great idea." J.C. pulled up her skirt and revealed her bare, painted toes. "But if we're going first class, I'd better go pry my feet into some shoes."

"Ouch." He grimaced in sympathy to her high-heeled plight.

She nudged the jut of his chin as she walked past him. "I'm making the sacrifice for you, big guy."

He grabbed her hand, stopping her in a rustle of silk and organza, and turning her back to face him. "Thank you. For everything."

Good God, if he didn't stop looking at her like that, they would never get out of the apartment. "Maybe you'd better wait and see how I do tonight before you thank me."

7

"GENERAL CRADDOCK, are you flirting with me?" J.C. asked, leaning back against the older gentleman's arm as he swept her around the dance floor in an old-fashioned waltz.

"Now, now, Miss Gardner, I thought I told you to call me Walter."

J.C. batted her eyes with false innocence. "But you make Ethan call you *sir* or *General.*"

"Ethan's just one of the men under my command. You will find out, my dear, that being a Marine Corps spouse has certain privileges." He leaned in for a conspiratorial whisper, never missing a step. "Mrs. Craddock has been reminding me of that for over thirty years."

J.C. laughed as they spun into the crowd of dancers waltzing their way in a counterclockwise circle around the room. Despite pushing sixty, his shiny bald pate and his lovely wife, Brigadier General Walter Craddock considered himself quite the ladies' man. He was light on his feet, quick-witted, and he'd danced with every woman seated at his table at least once. Though Millie, his wife, had had the honor of the first dance, the general seemed more inclined to entertain his guests than to spend time with her or even the four promotion candidates.

This was J.C.'s second dance with the general, and she was honest enough to admit she was enjoying herself. The dinner had been delicious, the dessert decadent, the company interesting, and the orchestra's music—well, she'd already danced with an ambassador, a doctor and, of course, the general. She loved the beat of the music pulsing through her body. She loved the swirl of her petticoats brushing against her legs, and the soft lights glimmering in the iridescent material of her gown. She loved the endorphic high of rhythmic exercise and intelligent conversation.

Amidst all the uniforms and gowns and tuxes, she felt like a regular Cinderella. Except the Prince Charming who'd brought her to the ball in his long, black carriage wasn't dancing with her. Hadn't asked her to. Had turned down her invitation twice and opted to fetch a drink for Millie Craddock and chat with a retired master gunnery sergeant who'd served with his father instead.

Ethan was sending her a message she didn't want to receive. His business with the Corps—scoring points, schmoozing with the top brass—was more important than their personal relationship.

Even though they didn't really have a personal relationship.

J.C. frowned at the tentacles of hurt and disillusionment trying to get a grip around her heart. She and Ethan both had made it very clear that they didn't *want* a relationship. But the sting of disappointment she was feeling couldn't seem to grasp the logic of that.

"…background in the military yourself, Miss Gardner?"

She nearly stumbled as Walter Craddock's question jerked her from her little pity party. But the general's steady arm, as well as his surprising patience, kept the dance moving smoothly. She quickly replayed the words only her subconscious mind had heard and came up with an appropriate response. "Me? Serve in the military? No, thanks. I mean, I'm glad you and your men and women are there to do their job, but it's not for me. I have too hard a time taking orders.''

Craddock laughed at the joke, but grew serious again just as quickly. ''Sometimes, it's a hell of a lot harder to give an order, J.C.''

He nodded toward the banquet tables beyond the edge of the dance floor. Ethan, standing almost a head taller than anyone else in the circle, chatted with a group of officers. *Some days I think I've seen more than a man should have to.*

''Are you talking about Ethan?''

The general nodded. ''A few years back, your fiancé was on a detail guarding an embassy setup crew in the capital of one of our newer Central American allies. Hell, they were a skeleton team just moving in themselves. Rebel forces, backed by a local drug cartel, attacked with a car bomb before dawn and tried to lay siege to the place. Local authorities weren't in a position to help. Armored support was at least twenty-four hours away.

''Being the ranking officer with a crisis on his hands, Ethan ordered a counterattack to rescue injured troops and help the civilians escape. He lost two men to sniper fire before the rest of the team broke through the perimeter and neutralized the enemy.''

This time, J.C. did miss a step. ''Oh, my God.''

The couple dancing behind them bumped into J.C.'s back. Fielding an apology, General Craddock pulled her into his chest and spun her out of the path of the next group of dancers. ''Ethan and his team saved nearly one hundred lives that day. But it's the two you lose who stay with you.''

She stared at the two stars adorning Walter Craddock's shoulders, hearing the melodic strains of music as a distant, discordant noise in the back of her mind. *Stuff happened.* Ethan McCormick, master control freak, was a wizard at understatement.

Despite the press of bodies and almost continuous dancing, a chill crept down J.C.'s spine. She cared that Ethan and the other Marines in his unit had suffered that day. She ached for the families who had lost their loved ones in the line of duty.

Her gaze strayed back to the taut, proud shoulders of the Marine who'd asked her to be his fiancée for the next two weeks. Whatever burdens Ethan carried, he hid them well. He hadn't asked for her help in coping with any of them. Still, she couldn't get past the idea that Ethan needed to talk. That he needed to be held. Or, in his archaic notion that sex was the only way he could express himself freely, he needed to get laid.

The chill of compassion turned into something much less altruistic. A frisson of anticipation. A call to duty. The tingling excitement of destiny waiting to be fulfilled.

She was more determined than ever to offer Ethan all the freedom of expression he could handle. After all, she'd learned that good sex could be a great stress reliever. And if there was any way she could help...

Walter lifted her chin with the tip of his finger. "Sorry. I didn't mean to bring down the mood of the party. I don't suppose Ethan talks much about his heroics."

"No, I'm glad to learn more about him." J.C. held tight to the general's gloved hand and followed along as he urged her to complete the waltz with him. She hoped she hadn't revealed her thoughts with a hungry look or wistful smile. "Ethan's pretty quiet when it comes to talking about himself." She cocked a teasing brow and changed the topic. "But I guess that also makes him the kind of man who can keep a secret for you."

"I have no doubts that Major McCormick is trustworthy and loyal as they come. But then I suspect you already know that."

Her ideas of trust and loyalty had been skewed by her father's self-absorption and infidelities. But, for a military man, she supposed Ethan was about as reliable as they came. "He's the best Marine I know," J.C. answered glibly, pleased that she could tell General Craddock the truth.

"Present company excepted?" he teased.

"Of course." She smiled right back.

"Say, I didn't get a chance to follow up on my original question. What about your family? Any of them in the service?"

Compassion, anticipation and good humor all stalled behind a wall of resentment. Not this topic! But J.C. kept her feet moving and her mouth smiling. "My father was in the Navy. Enlisted out of high school. I'm sure he and my mom never went to any fancy functions like this."

The general surveyed the room, shaking his head. "It is a little over the top, isn't it?" J.C. thought she'd skirted the issue and could steer the conversation back to Ethan and one of the topics they had familiarized themselves with on the limo ride to the ball. Hobbies. Siblings. Favorite foods. Birth dates. Favorite holiday. But General Craddock had a sharp ear for details. "You said *was*. Your father isn't a career man, then?"

"I think he served about twenty years." And dozens of women. "After my parents divorced, he and I sort of lost track—"

The last strains of the music ended in a round of applause, offering J.C. a natural reprieve from delving too deeply into the fact she hadn't heard from Earl Gardner in two whole years, hadn't seen him in five, hadn't hugged him in ten. She and the general separated and added their praise for the orchestra.

The woodwinds trilled the beginning of a modern tune. "This one's definitely not my style. Do you mind?" General Craddock offered her an apologetic smile and escorted her back to their table. "Maybe you could get that major of yours to take you around on this one."

"I'll try," J.C. answered without any real hope of success. She thanked the general and excused herself before he could do any more following up on her personal life. She picked up her water glass and concentrated on polishing off the last of the cool drink, sending off *don't talk to me signals* to any would-be dance partners and buying herself some time to regroup.

Like a slap of reality, the mere mention of her father had banished any Cinderella fantasies and brought back the reason she was here in the first place. To prove a point to Lee Whiteley and her readers. These men might provide stimulating conversation and charming dance partners—they might even get her hormones buzzing—but they weren't marriage material.

Even General Craddock, whom she had to admit had been winning her over to the red, white and blue side, headed straight for a group of officers sitting nearby. He slapped two on the back and said something funny, judging by the laughter that erupted from their table. Then he sat down and joined them in animated conversation, without a touch or word or look to his wife.

Of course, Millie Craddock wasn't exactly alone. Ethan's aide, Captain Black, sat beside her. Angled toward the older woman, his black hair nearly touched her silver-blond curls as they carried on a hushed discussion involving touchy-feely hand gestures and secretive smiles.

Like mother and son or sister and brother—they seemed to be curiously close friends despite the gap in their ages.

J.C. frowned at all the camaraderie surrounding her. Maybe *she* was the was the only one who felt alone. Abandoned. She set down her glass and searched the crowded room until her gaze collided with Ethan's.

Maybe not so alone as she thought.

Above the heads of several official-looking men and women, Ethan's dark gray eyes stared intently into hers, suffusing her with warmth and awareness. How long had he been watching her? Had he sensed her loneliness? Had he felt her longing looks and lustful thoughts from the dance floor? His gaze touched her like a physical caress, lingering on her lips until they pouted, studying her breasts until they thrust against their constrictive binding of shimmering silk. Her arms beaded with goose bumps. Her breath stuttered and caught in her chest.

What that man could do with a look.

Caught in that gray-eyed assault on her senses, J.C. wiggled her toes inside her strappy sandals. She felt flushed and female, and antsy to do something about the simmering heat that threatened to steam through every pore. She wanted to touch him. To talk to him. To feel the weight of him inside her. She wanted him to act on what those eyes were telling her and quit driving her mad with this long-distance, I-want-to-be-a-gentleman-but-I'm-dying-to-do-you torture.

J.C. was moving toward him, drawn like a compass point to its magnetic pole, determined to take this crazy desire into her own hands, when Ethan blinked, breaking the spell. His gaze darted to the left, giving her a split-second warning before a firm grip latched onto her wrist.

"C'mon. Dance with me." If Kyle Black had opened

the bedroom door and caught her buck naked in Ethan's arms, she couldn't have felt more interrupted or exposed.

J.C. jerked self-consciously at the touch, flashing back to her encounter with Juan Guerro. But these were handsome blue eyes, sparkling with mischief, not bleary brown ones filled with menace and fatigue. Ethan's aide. A friend, not a threat. J.C. pressed her free hand over her thumping heart and mustered up a friendly smile. "Captain. You startled me."

"Sorry about that. But I thought I'd seize the moment. And didn't I tell you to call me Kyle?" He was already pulling her toward the dance floor without giving her a chance to accept or refuse his invitation. "My job is to assist the major in whatever way I can. And if that means dancing with a pretty woman when he's too busy to, I'm the man to do it."

A quick glance behind them revealed Ethan watching them serpentine their way through the crowd. His frown might be one of concern or curiosity. But the interpretation made no difference. Without so much as a nod, he dragged his attention back to the conversation at hand. Hmm. J.C. bristled at the easy dismissal. Even if he did think she was in good hands, she needed to have a chat with him about asserting his territorial rights. Passing her off to his second in command didn't make for a very convincing engagement.

For one catty moment, she considered blowing their cover. If Ethan wasn't going to do anything more than introduce her as his fiancée and sit next to her at dinner, then why should she bust her buns to act like a couple? Fortunately her practical streak asserted itself before she shot off her mouth. This was all fodder for her articles. If she abandoned Ethan now, she might as well abandon her bet, too.

Along with two weeks of potential bliss.

When her shoes hit the smooth dance floor, J.C. dug in her heels and tugged Kyle to a halt. "This is above and beyond the call of duty, Kyle. I'll be sure to tell Ethan to write up a commendation for you." She squinched her face up into an apology as she pulled away. "But my feet are screaming at me in these high heels. I really just want to sit out a couple of numbers and spend some time with my sweetie."

Kyle looked beyond her shoulder at Ethan and shrugged. "He's in the middle of a big confab with Colonel Reese and the other candidates. If you want a break, let me buy you a drink, instead." He hooked his arm through hers and steered her toward the refreshment table at the far end of the room. "C'mon, J.C. It'll be bad for troop morale if you say no."

Now *that* was a lame line she would have to print. It was a little too practiced to be original or sincere. But since Ethan showed no interest in rescuing her, she might as well make practical use of her time and see what other flirtatious nuggets she could glean from Kyle.

"Well, if it's for the troops, I suppose I could handle another glass of wine."

They traded the perfunctories about hometowns and tastes in music while they waited in line to be served. "So. It must have been a whirlwind kind of thing between you and the major," Kyle observed.

"I suppose."

Had his fingers brushed against her left hand on purpose?

Kyle's query sounded casual enough, but there was something she didn't quite trust in the sudden change of topic. "Mrs. Craddock wondered why you weren't wearing an engagement ring."

A ring? Duh. Make-believe 101. At least dress the part.

J.C. curled her bare fingers into a fist and said the first plausible thing that popped into her head. "It's in the shop being sized." She expanded with the story she and Ethan had rehearsed. "Everything happened so fast. It was love at first sight, I think. Lust, at least. It didn't take long to figure out the reason we clicked so well so quickly was that we belonged together."

"That would explain why he never mentioned you before today." Kyle had been talking with Millie Craddock. Was it her curiosity or his that had him probing for answers?

She remembered General Craddock's observation and came up with a logical response. "Ethan doesn't talk much about work with me, so I imagine he doesn't talk about me at work, either."

"True. But to be honest, I didn't think the major was even seeing anyone. He works a lot of late nights. Off the clock." Kyle's hand settled at the small of her back to shift her forward in the line. "Where did you say you two met?"

"I didn't." J.C. turned to face him, breaking contact. Somehow, a bar parking lot didn't seem like the most auspicious place for a man of Ethan's reputation to find a wife. Should she make up a story or pretend she hadn't heard the question?

"Look, I work a couple of jobs myself and keep odd hours, so Ethan and I catch time together whenever we can." It wasn't exactly a lie—they'd met in the wee hours of the morning at her car, and before lunch at a clothing boutique. Okay, so maybe those were the *only* times they'd met before tonight. But Kyle Black didn't need to know that. J.C. arched her brow and looked him straight in the eye. "I don't suppose he reports many details to you because he's your commanding officer. Not the other way around. I'd think you'd be doing everything you could to support him and respect his privacy instead of ferreting out information for the gossip mill."

Despite the subtle accusation coloring her tone, Kyle didn't miss a beat. He dropped his voice to a whisper. "I am supporting him. If he gets this job, I could move up, too. Believe me, I'm just asking the questions that Craddock and the others are asking." He cupped her shoulder in his white-gloved hand and brushed his lips against her ear. "If you're helping a friend get a promotion, I'm good with that. I'll do whatever I can to help the act be a little more convincing."

Huffing out an affronted sigh, J.C. pulled away. "This is no act. Ethan asked me to marry him. I said yes."

Kyle put up his hands in surrender. "If that's the case, then put me to work making wedding arrangements. Let me clear the major's calendar, reserve a hall or church, line up the chaplain." His blue eyes darkened with a self-importance that seemed unsettlingly familiar—and as unwelcome as a stern word from her father. "The major counts on me to get the job done. You should, too. I have connections you wouldn't believe."

"I'll keep that in mind." Kyle Black's offer sounded friendly enough, but J.C.'s stomach tensed as if he'd just issued a threat. Maybe it was after midnight and the Cinderella factor that made the ball enjoyable had finally worn off. Or maybe she was right to worry about Kyle's interest in her engagement. Maybe Ethan should worry, too. "You know, on second thought, I think I'll pass on the wine. The orchestra leader just announced the last set and I don't want to miss it."

"So you do want to dance?"

J.C. shook off Kyle's hand and backed away. "Nothing

personal, Captain. But there's someone else I'd rather spend the last few minutes of the evening with. If you'll excuse me.''

Even from the rear, Ethan cut an impressive figure. Though the members of the group had changed from before, he was still holding court, his head bowed to listen to whatever the woman in the long-skirted uniform beside him was saying. He nodded his head sagely and straightened, then turned his attention to a man who wore a turban and spoke with a melodious accent.

For a man who was loathe to talk, Ethan had spent his entire evening in one conversation or another. Either he had a split personality or he was avoiding something. If he was avoiding her, that was about to change.

Fixing a confident smile on her mouth, J.C. linked her arm through Ethan's and pulled herself into the circle. ''Sorry to interrupt, but do you mind if I steal this guy for a little while?''

She didn't wait to respond to the supportive, go-for-it answers. Beneath her fingers, J.C. felt resistance in every corded muscle along Ethan's forearm and biceps. But he let her turn him around and lead him away from the group. ''You've done your duty long enough, Major. It's time to dance with me.''

Like an anchor digging into the ocean floor, Ethan halted. ''I'd rather not.''

The sudden loss of momentum spun her around to face him. J.C. reached up to cup the smooth firmness of his cheek and angle his ear close enough to whisper. ''You *need* to dance with me.'' He frowned in question. Her explanation was brief. ''Captain Black is asking a lot of questions.''

Keeping his face close, he lifted his gaze over the top

of her head. She imagined he was glaring straight at Kyle. "Like what?"

"Like where's my engagement ring? And why hasn't he heard of me before today?"

"It's none of his damn business. Black will do what I tell him."

Feeling more than thinking, she stroked her fingers across the tense muscles that clenched his jaw tight, betraying some of her own alarm as she tried to soothe his. "I don't think he's the only one who needs convincing. Ethan, if we don't make this look good right now, I think the charade will be over."

8

_____

DAMN THE TORPEDOES.

Ethan held tight to J.C.'s fingers and scanned the swirl-ing sea of dancers as she led him to the center of the dance floor. It felt like invading enemy territory. He stood tall and stiff as she curled her hand over his shoulder and twisted her hips to the beat of the music. The poof and swing of her long skirt hid her feet from view, but he gamely tried to match every other step or so.

He'd rather face that bay full of mines with Admiral Farragut than venture onto a dance floor and relive that humiliating night when Ambassador Mead had tapped on Ethan's shoulder and said he was cutting in to dance with his wife. His *wife!*

Surprise!

Did J.C. or anyone else in this crowd know what kind of battle he was facing? But it was too late to back out now. J.C. was right about being the object of unwanted scrutiny. The Craddocks gave him a thumbs-up as they twirled by, and Captain Black toasted him with a drink and watched from the sidelines. Ethan took a steadying breath and shifted from one foot to the next.

Full speed ahead.

Whether he liked it or not.

The music from that night in Cairo beat a loud rhythm inside his head, drowning out the orchestra. It was bad enough that he'd paid twenty American dollars to learn a couple of dance steps from one of the locals. Worse that he'd traded two weeks of the graveyard shift for the night off to attend the cultural festival with Bethany before the ambassador's arrival. But the real kicker had been when she'd giggled as if the joke was on him. *"Sorry, McCormick,"* she'd whispered. *"I guess we're done."* Bethany turned into the arms of a man he would have pegged as her father, planted a not-so-daughterly kiss on him, and left Ethan standing alone in the middle of the crowded dance floor.

He was done, all right.

He'd been screwing a married woman. The young trophy wife of the man he was there to protect.

And her husband, his commanding officer, and most of his unit were there to see his stunning stupidity firsthand. Ethan McCormick—all around tough guy, leader of men—had been duped by a devious woman.

It was enough to turn any man off public dancing and thinking with his pants.

But J.C. thought the solution to proving their engagement was the real deal to a few doubters was to stand out in the middle of this crowd and act as if there was no place else he would rather be. She spun out of his grasp, expecting him to know the steps. She bumped into his chest when he went to retrieve her.

"Oops," she laughed, excusing his incompetence.

"My fault." He reached for her hand again.

Man, it was getting hot in here. Ethan fingered the stiff band of his collar and wished there was some other way to prove his value to the Corps.

J.C. dodged to the side as another couple glided past them, then curled herself around his arm and held on to stay out of the path of the next couple. "Please tell me you know how to dance."

Ethan knew enough to put his hand at the nip of her waist and pull her out of the current of dancers to a relatively empty spot in front of the orchestra podium. "I'm usually asked to guard the door, not take center stage."

Her stricken look of apology was almost worse than a laugh. "That's why you never asked me." Pity quickly gave way to a gleam of determination in her upturned face. "It's not hard. Why didn't you ask me to teach you some basic steps?"

"And when did we have time to do that?"

"How about right now?" She grabbed both his hands and pulled him toward her.

"J.C.—" He crunched her foot beneath his and recoiled, throwing up his hands between them, afraid to touch her. His war with the dance floor continued. "I'm sorry."

"You're not going to start that apology thing all over again, are you? I was okay when you kissed me last night. I'm okay with this." She kept moving closer. He kept looking for a reason to back away. "Don't you want to hold me in your arms?"

Her blue eyes blazed with a challenge he found far more seductive than any of Bethany's come-hither looks had been. Ethan planted his feet and let the other dancers brush past him. He could do this. For J.C. For the promotion. For the Corps.

Hell. He'd been dying for an excuse to take J.C. into his arms and explore those opportunities she'd mentioned back at her apartment. He'd counted seven other men who'd put their hands on her on the dance floor. Seven other men who'd gotten to touch her and hold her and maybe even flirt with her while he tried to distract himself by working the room.

It was his turn. He was going to step up to the challenge and do this for himself.

Still, she should know there might be casualties.

Ethan reached for J.C. His stiff arms held her beyond harm's reach. He raised his voice to be heard over an ominously timed drumroll. "You asked for it. Just remember that you insisted that we dance when your feet are black and blue in the morning."

Her triumphant smile drew his attention to the creamy, coppery curve of her mouth, reminding him there were other things he wanted to do for himself. "I'll take my chances. Now hold me like you mean it." She moved half a step closer, forcing him to bend his elbows and slide his palm behind her back. Her warmth radiated through the silk and stays of her dress, and her hips swayed, lithe and limber beneath his hand. "Just follow my lead."

The fates took pity on his lack of skill and the orchestra eased into a slow tune. "Yes, ma'am."

"One-two-three, one-two-three…" Ethan craned his neck to see down to the floor between them, trying to catch a glimpse of her feet. Okay, so maybe his gaze kept straying to the gentle swells of her breasts rocking like the generous ebb and flow of the tide against the straight neckline of her dress. Man, he'd like to kiss those, too. "One-two-three…"

The swells were gathering, rising above the edge—

"Ow."

"Hell."

He'd stepped on her foot again. *Eyes back to the floor.*

He turned his brain back on and counted the numbers out loud with her. "One-two-three."

Her hand squeezed his. "Is it at all possible for you to relax?"

Better trained men swept by them with their partners.

Ethan raised his head and looked into her upturned eyes. "I warned you."

J.C. was the one to stop this time. "Wait a minute. You know how to march, don't you?"

He raised a *duh* eyebrow. "You know a Marine who doesn't?"

"But you can keep right and left straight, can't you?"

"Of course. We did precision drilling at the Academy."

"Well, this isn't exactly *precision.* But think of dancing in the same way. If you learned those steps, you can learn these." She slipped her hands down to his hips and nudged him back and forth. "Left, right, left. You're just changing the rhythm."

"But my movements have to coordinate with yours, and if I watch my feet, I look like a dope."

She veed her fingers and pointed to her eyes. "Look right here, Major."

The clip of a command in her voice earned his instant cooperation. Possible mistake. That challenge still taunted him from her eyes, daring him to look away, daring him to surrender. Strength flowed in to replace self-conscious doubt. Adrenaline buzzed through his system. *Surrender* wasn't part of his vocabulary. He held his hands out to either side and awaited further instruction. "Then what?"

"I'll do the hard part, like Ginger Rogers. I'll do everything Fred Astaire does, only backward. You just follow my lead, Fred." She arched one eyebrow, silently telling him that she was more than up to handling the task. She slid her hands beneath his jacket and latched on to his waist, guiding his body from side to side. "Left, right, left. Right, left, right.

"No." She turned her palm and splayed her fingers down over the point of his hip. "Do you feel the downbeat of the music? Like this.'' J.C. squeezed, startling him out of step. He grasped her shoulders to right himself and save her feet from his. She patted his hip. Twice. Then squeezed him again.

"What are you reaching for back there, Ginger?''

"Listen.'' Her fingers squeezed. Pat, pat. Squeeze, pat, pat. The soft, mellow thump of a bass filtered into his senses, resonating with the beat of his pulse, matching the teasing rhythm of her hands. "Do you hear it?''

The deafening cadence of that last dance with Bethany faded into a distant echo. This music soothed, seduced. Or maybe it was the teacher who made the cool, melodic strains and low, vibrant beat feel so intimate. His feet began to move in sync with J.C.'s.

"This is dancing?'' It sure wasn't drill marching.

J.C. grinned and his gaze drifted down to the tempting sight. Oh, yeah, he'd never had any rewards like that to motivate him through basic training. Her husky words were as encouraging as that smile. "If you can feel the beat, you can do this.''

His hands were moving up and down her arms now, in time with the guiding rhythm of each squeeze and pat.

Left, right, left.

One, two, three.

Grab, my, ass.

Ethan's groin lurched in response to the coaxing combination of her touch and his success. "Um, J.C.?''

He forced his gaze back to hers, forced it over the top of her head to glimpse the other dancers—all holding each other in a different, more conservative way. The next lieutenant colonel of the Corps had better follow suit.

Ethan plucked her right hand from the warm spot at his hip and cradled it in his palm. He moved her left hand back to the neutral position on his shoulder and offered a rueful smile. "We are out in public."

But the instant he lost contact with her guiding hands, he lost the beat and stumbled across her foot. Ethan huffed his frustration between gritted teeth and swore. "I can field strip an AK-147 blindfolded, but I can't master a damn two-step."

"Three-step," J.C. corrected. Before he could straighten her out on the lousy timing of that amused sparkle in her eyes, she wrapped her arm behind his shoulders and moved in to butt her thighs right up against his. Knee to hip, silk to wool. Left, right, left. Touch, touch, touch. Glued to him like another, suppler layer of his uniform, she moved their bodies as one. "Does this help?"

Oh, yeah. The dancing was better, too.

His little major drifted to attention as his senses absorbed every detail about the woman he held. Beneath the orchestra's melody, he heard the rustle of her dress, a whisper of sound caressing his ear with every graceful step. The friction of her skirt brushing against his pant legs created little tugs of pressure in counterpoint to the thrust of her thighs and hips. The heady scent of her gardenia corsage cocooned them in a tropical, decadent heat that spurred the fire simmering through his veins and pooling behind his zipper.

And that didn't even begin to take in his fascination with the long earrings dangling against her creamy neck, or the silky wisps of chestnut hair that clung to her face and framed those luscious lips. Who wanted to watch his feet now? This view was infinitely more enticing.

That need to kiss her, which was never far from his mind, shouted for action.

Winding his arm behind J.C.'s waist, Ethan pulled her torso flush against his. Her startled breath was a warm caress against his neck. Their whole bodies moved as one now, with the slow, drugging music playing as a pulse beat in the background. "How am I doing?" he asked.

She tipped her head back, putting her lips right there, in reach of his mouth. "Drill instruction paid off."

He saw her lips move, heard the clever compliment. But all he really knew was the firm give of her breasts, pillowing against his chest, and the warm cup of her womanhood, cradling the jutting arousal in his pants. He'd never wanted a woman as badly as he wanted this one. He'd never needed to claim her so quickly.

Dipping his head, he brushed his lips against hers.

She shuddered at the contact, triggering a ripple effect that cascaded throughout his body.

Hitting his stride now, Ethan tongued the arc of her lower lip, then caught the tasty morsel between his own. The kiss assuaged his need like a tiny pinhole in a dam eased the pressure of the water trying to break through behind it.

It wasn't enough. Not nearly enough.

He heard J.C.'s throaty moan, felt her fingers tickling his nape, her palm abrading the back of his head. General Craddock and future plans and bad memories all faded beneath a man's driving need to possess the woman who aroused him so completely. She was strong. Intelligent. Drop-dead sexy.

Judging by this lesson, Ethan needed to rethink his aversion to this dancing thing. It seemed a lot like making love to a woman. Hold her in your arms. Look into her eyes. Let the music create a mood. Then you start to feel the rhythm.

"Left, right, left. Right, left, right." He whispered the mantra like an invitation beside her ear. The answering moan in her throat vibrated against his lips.

One year, four months, two weeks and a handful of days was a whole lot of need to store up inside a man. And this woman was a whole lot of sexy. It was a combustible combination that could provide an embarrassing, unwelcome end to the evening if he couldn't retake control of his body. And, damn, but he didn't want anything to spoil his taste for dancing a second time.

He slid his hand down to her hip, keeping them together as he turned with her. He was smoother than he knew. Instead of tripping over his feet and breaking the spell, the move felt just like rolling over in bed together.

For her, too, apparently.

"Ethan, um…" She licked her lips. He wanted her to lick his. "I think we made our point. Maybe we should—"

"May I cut in?"

Ethan felt the tap on his shoulder like a jolt of gunfire. Captain Black, indispensable aide with a knack for rotten timing, smiled his Tom Cruise smile and expected a shot at J.C.

"No." Ethan said roughly, clutching her tight and trying to recapture the rhythm of the music. Where the hell had Black come from? What was he thinking? "Find your own woman. This one's taken."

It was an outrageously possessive thing to say about someone he'd known for barely twenty-four hours. But he felt the rightness of the claim in every oversensitized cell of his body.

"Nicely played, sir."

This time Ethan did stop. He frowned at the comment and the fact that J.C. was pulling away. "What does that mean?"

But Black was already retreating. "I'll see you in the

office tomorrow at 0-900, sir. Enjoy the rest of your night.'' He nodded to J.C. ''Ma'am.''

''What the hell—?'' He should have made that request an order.

J.C. tugged on Ethan's arm and pulled him out of the circle of dancers. ''I told you he was suspicious of us. Maybe that was his idea of a test. But don't worry. I think you passed.''

''I don't like it.'' Black was up to something.

''Maybe he was just hitting on me.''

Yeah, like that explanation was any better. The instinct to pursue the problem and settle it had him stalking around the perimeter of the dance floor with J.C. in tow. ''If he's got something to say, he needs to say it straight out, or else keep his yap shut. I'm not playing these games with him.''

''Ethan.'' J.C. put on the brakes and he spun around to face her. That utterly expressive, blue-eyed gaze dropped to the tented bulge at the front of his pants. ''Not right now.''

Her arched eyebrow was reminder enough that he wasn't in any shape to accuse Black of trying to pull something. The term *fake fiancée* rang an uncomfortable warning against his conscience. Of course, there was nothing fake about what he'd almost done to J.C. on the dance floor. About what he still wanted to do.

And he was worried about Kyle Black playing games?

Seething with a mix of suspicion and raging sexual frustration, Ethan jumped in his skin when J.C. touched his chin and tilted his face down to hers. ''Is there any reason why we have to stay any later tonight?''

''No.'' They'd said their goodbyes, and he'd gotten the details for their next joint appearance in front of Craddock and the committee. ''Tired?''

"Not really. But I do think it's time you took me home." She stroked her fingers down the column of his neck, adjusted the hook of his collar, then splayed her fingers with suggestive familiarity across his chest. All that crazy hunger came rushing back. She wasn't tired at all. "I'd like to finish that dance."

Despite Bethany Mead and Kyle Black and his own noble intentions, after one year, four months and however the hell many days it had been, it just wasn't in him to resist.

"Yes, ma'am."

"THANK YOU." Ethan's low voice enveloped J.C. with the same sense of intimacy that the limousine's smoke-tinted windows and privacy screen did. Washington, D.C.'s bright lights were but a blur from the world outside as the driver on the other side of that screen took them back to her apartment.

J.C. bent down and unbuckled the straps of her high-heeled sandals. "For what?"

Surely Ethan didn't mean that erotic dance lesson. *She* was the one who'd learned some brand-new steps in the seduction process. Her skin itched beneath the smooth material of her dress and lingerie, as every raw nerve still craved the heat of his body and the imprint of his hard thighs and unmistakable erection. Whatever hang-ups he had about talking and dancing, there was absolutely nothing to complain about when it came to sex.

Unless it was the fact she couldn't get enough of it. She couldn't get enough of him.

Ethan placed his gloves inside his white hat and set them on the black leather seat facing them on the opposite side of the bar console. "You're a hit."

"You think?"

"The candidates are invited to the Craddocks' home near Mount Vernon day after tomorrow. The general warned me not to show up unless I bring you with me." Ethan shifted, searching for a comfortable position on the plush seat. His legs veed open as he adjusted his cummerbund and plucked a crease from his black wool pants. "You must have said something to impress him."

"Walter was easy to talk to."

"Walter?"

She pushed her shoes off her swollen feet and let the painful flood of restored circulation clear her mind so she could concentrate on the conversation instead of the bulge of lingering desire still visible between Ethan's legs.

J.C. quickly glanced away and rubbed the arches of her feet. Ouch. She hated wearing high heels as much as she loved dancing. Too bad tennis shoes weren't better suited for embassy balls.

"He asked me a lot of questions. I think he went with first names to put me at ease. By the way, you and my mom have only spoken on the phone, but she was impressed when you sent her flowers for her birthday last month." She slid Ethan a sideways glance to check his reaction to that whopper. "I made up the story when he asked how we get along with our prospective in-laws, so it would sound as if we'd known each other longer."

"Did you tell him you've met my dad, then?"

"No." J.C. flinched at the cramp forming beneath the toes of her right foot, then explained. "I said your dad invited me to go fishing on his boat this summer, and that I was looking forward to it. I know you don't like lying. But they were plausible little white lies. It's what I came up with off the top of my head. Is that okay?"

Instead of answering, Ethan reached down and grabbed

her ankles. He lifted them, turned her, and pulled her across the seat until her feet rested in his lap. "Let me."

"Is that a yes or—? Oh, God...."

Her whole body convulsed at his touch, and J.C. grabbed the armrest behind her for balance. But just as quickly, she calmed to the permeating scents of buffed leather and fading gardenia. Pain gave way to pleasure, and she rested her cheek against the back of the seat and let him have his way with her feet. Ethan's big hands were warm and rough against her skin, like the rasp of a cat's tongue, yet just as gentle.

As he kneaded away the soreness, the strokes reminded her of the intimate way he'd massaged her last night on the edge of her car. Her kegel muscles clenched in vivid response at the memory, and a warm, moist honey lubricated the slit between her legs.

"Is that better?" he asked, pulling her farther across the smooth leather seat and pushing the layers of her dress up to her knees to rub the tension from her ankles and calves.

"Are you kidding?" Any time he touched her she felt better.

In this position, the backs of her thighs and the slick, swelling heat of her womanhood pressed into his trunk-hard leg. Instinctively J.C. squirmed against the resistance of muscle and bone, seeking relief from the building pressure but finding little satisfaction through all the clothing that separated them.

When she moaned in frustration, he misinterpreted the cause. "Did I hurt you?"

J.C. reached out and fingered the gold braid on his sleeve, not wanting him to stop the tactile favor. "Your hands should be registered as lethal weapons, Major. That feels amazing."

He shrugged off the compliment, missing the suggestive undertones altogether and resumed his handiwork. "I don't know about that. At least they're a little more coordinated than my feet."

J.C. smiled. That was a joke. His control was slipping. About damn time.

Seizing the moment she'd been waiting for all day long, J.C. slipped her fingers inside the cuff of his jacket to tease the crisp, golden hair on his wrist and knead her fingertips into the warm expanses of skin and sinew underneath. "Now that we're alone, there's something I want to discuss with you."

Ethan's hand stilled on her knee beneath the folds of her bunched-up skirt. He looked up and snared her in the endless, knowing depths of his eyes. "Opportunities?"

Taking a steadying breath, J.C. boldly toed his crotch.

"J.C.!" Ethan barked her name like an order, jerking at the purposeful squeeze, expecting her to release him. But she was too fascinated by the uniquely female contrast of pink-painted toes clasping his black wool pants and curling around the masculine bulge inside.

He grabbed her naughty foot and tugged it down on the other side him, unwittingly splitting her legs apart and pulling her halfway across his lap. "I thought you wanted to talk."

Curling the other leg beneath her, J.C. braced a hand on Ethan's shoulder and pushed herself into an eye-level position facing him. He was a solid force beneath her hand—strong, fit, primed with chained-up energy. There was friction at her fingertips, from the starched texture of gabardine and the pervading heat of the man inside the proud, proper uniform.

J.C. touched her finger to the point of his chin and

traced a tremor of tightly coiled tension along his jaw. "Actually I want you to do the talking."

"About what?" His jaw never flexed, his eyes never blinked. He fought her efforts to soothe his discomfort by pressing his mouth into an unyielding line.

J.C. moved her attentions there, stroking the flat, smooth surfaces, coaxing them apart. "Tell me about that last dance tonight, Major. And whether or not you intend to finish what you started."

He snatched her hand from his mouth, but had to release her foot to do it. "Dammit, J.C. It's no secret that I'm attracted to you. That dance lesson just got…" He let go just long enough to scrape his palm over the crown of his head. "Hell. It got way out of hand."

A self-damning curse and ragged sigh rippled down the length of his body and he looked away. J.C. rode the movement of his body, then settled back atop his thigh. Either the big guy couldn't find the right words, or he didn't want to say them.

"You wanted it to go further, didn't you?" She said the words quietly, succinctly.

When his head snapped back to face her, she flinched at the raw desperation that marbled his eyes into a kaleidoscope of silvers and grays. She'd been playing with a live grenade, she now realized, and Ethan was making a heroic effort to keep it from blowing up in her face. "I'm trying to do the right thing here, Dr. Gardner. You're doing me a huge favor already. I'm not going to take advantage of you."

He waited expectantly for her to understand.

She wasted no time in helping him understand.

J.C. pushed herself up onto both knees and straddled Ethan's lap. She slipped her fingers beneath his cummerbund and unhooked the snap of his slacks. "Then I'll have to take advantage of you."

"Jo…" He dragged her hands away and held them out to either side.

"Ethan," she protested, twisting to free herself to resume the seduction. Her unsatisfied hunger hummed along at the same pitch as the limo's tires against the pavement. Her breasts butted against the wall of his chest, jingling the medals pinned there, exciting her with tiny, teasing caresses. Her knees clenched around his thighs, trying to regain some leverage.

His chest expanded in one sharp breath. "Stop it," he warned. "I can't take much more of this."

J.C. went still. Years of study and observation finally gave her an answer. Of course. Ethan was on the brink of giving in to the same desire that consumed her, but fighting his body every step of the way. He would give pleasure, but he wouldn't accept it for himself. It was a classic case of involvement avoidance.

He was the polar opposite of what her father had been. Earl Gardner was a taker. He weaseled out of relationships by selfishly refusing to give anything meaningful back to any of his wives, lovers or daughter. Ethan McCormick was a giver. He would give pleasure, protection—even his life—for another person and not want to be rewarded with anything in return. Because sharing implied a relationship. Friendships, marriages, families thrived on the symbiotic give and take.

A man who didn't want a commitment could either take or he could give. Poor Ethan, with his chivalric principles and old-fashioned ideals, hadn't yet learned that a man and woman *could* share—sex, that is—without committing to anything more than a promise to use a condom.

But she could teach him a new way of thinking.

She'd taught him how to dance. She could teach him this.

J.C. had never felt so wise, so womanly, so sure of what a man wanted.

Who needed hands? With a smile that stemmed from Eve herself, J.C. sank into Ethan's lap. She scooted closer, splayed her legs wider, rocked from buttock to buttock until she found it. Even with a dress and petticoat wedged between them, she felt the prodding knob of his desire push against her.

"J.C...." He released her arms and grabbed her waist. But J.C. had resumed the dance, and now he was the one who seemed to be at her mercy. She rotated her hips one way. "Jo..." His deep voice tried to sound tough, but the uneven catch of his breath betrayed his need. He was strong enough to set her aside, but his hands anchored her in his lap.

A sweet, sweet heat drizzled into her most private places, making her feel heavy, swollen. She dug her fingers into his shoulders and twisted the other way. "Honey..." She brushed against the stiffening rod straining in his pants and played with it, trying to catch it between her nether lips. The groan in his chest vibrated through her palms and skidded along every nerve ending until she whimpered with the need to feel him inside her.

"Ethan, please." She slipped one hand inside his jacket, palmed the hard curve of his pec and flicked the aroused male nipple through the crisp weave of his shirt. His hands tightened convulsively around her waist, holding her in place as he bucked up against her. *Oh, yes. More. No!* "Ethan?"

"We can't." Though his arms trembled with the effort, he lifted her and set her back on his knees. His ragged breaths matched her own. There was no mistaking the stiff peak rising between them. "The driver. I forgot we had an audience."

"He can't hear us, he's playing the radio. And he can't see us through the screen. Since he's not speeding, we have at least thirty minutes left of uninterrupted time while he drives us across town."

Ethan's hands eased their grip. He began rubbing charged circles against her back. When his fingers hit bare skin they jerked and returned to her waist.

"What about—?" He glanced at the door.

J.C. fluffed out her skirt and let the folds float down around them, hiding them both from the waist down. "No one will see a thing."

"But—"

She pressed a finger to his lips to silence him. "Don't be such a straight arrow, Major. We're both adults. You're hot, and I'm hot for you."

Ethan's hands slipped down to cup her bottom. He kissed her finger, then chased it away with a playful nip so he could speak. "I think you're the hottest damn thing on five continents. I want you so bad I can taste it. But this is crazy. We're supposed to be faking it."

"Does this feel fake to you?" She reached beneath the cover of her skirt and cupped him through his pants.

"Jo!" He thrust up into her palm. But with a gut-deep moan he pulled her away. "We shouldn't."

"There's nothing indecorous about sleeping with the woman you're supposedly engaged to. Not in this century. Your reputation's safe, I assure you."

"Mine?" He eyes darkened with the battle between conscience and desire. "I was more concerned about yours. I don't want you to think I'm using you."

"I'm a modern woman, Ethan. I can take care of my-self. I always have." Without further debate, she pulled back her skirt and unzipped him, taking care to protect him as he sprang free.

"You asked me what I wanted. This is it. You. A nice, hot, lusty affair with a guy who really turns me on. Two weeks of fooling around and then we're done. No strings attached. I play your fiancée, we play with each other. I don't expect you to be there for me when it's over. I won't hold you to any promises." She hesitated for an instant, bowing her head and turning away as she heard her bold words. Maybe she was selling something she couldn't really deliver. "I haven't had a lover for a long time. I haven't had one like you...ever."

He nudged a finger beneath her chin and tipped it up. "One like me?"

"You make me crazy with just a look. Imagine what happens when you actually touch me." Okay, now she was sounding desperate. J.C. threw up her hands. "God, Ethan. I'm throwing myself at you. If you're worried about my reputation, then save me from this embarrassment." Was this the kind of rejection she was going to write about in her next column? "Don't you want me?"

He simply looked down at his cock.

J.C. grinned at the proof. "Then take me."

The Marines hadn't stormed Omaha Beach with any more determination than Ethan McCormick making love to a woman.

True to form, he was more a man of action than a talker. In a flurry of hands and lips, he grabbed her bottom and pulled her squarely back onto his lap, bunching her dress up between them. Cocooned in the lush interior of the powerful car, everything was intensified—the scents of leather and flowers and dripping sex—the tastes of salty skin and champagne-kissed tongues—the lambent intensity of dark gray eyes telling her every graphic thing he wanted to do to her an instant before it happened.

While his lips tormented a particularly sensitive bundle of nerves along the side of her neck, Ethan reached behind her and unzipped her dress. "I warn you, it's been a long time for me, too."

He tugged the slim straps of her gown off her shoulders. The rough pads of his fingers left a trail of goose bumps as they slid along her skin.

"Believe me, your skills aren't a bit rusty."

"I might not be able to last." He peeled the bodice down to her waist, exposing her breasts to his feasting eyes.

"Fast works for me, too."

He wrapped his tongue around her engorged nipple and sucked her. Hard.

"Ethan!"

She clutched at his shoulders, dragged her palms up to grasp his head and hold him to her as he drew on her until she was clawing, squirming, throbbing. His hands slipped under her dress and squeezed her bottom through her panties. His erection nudged her thigh. He rubbed himself against her slick cotton crotch and groaned into the pillow of her breast.

"I want to ram it in you right now."

"Wait…" She tipped his mouth up to kiss him, pacifying him as she scooted off his lap. But his hands cinched around her thighs and held her in place against his dancing, distended heat. Laughing breathlessly at his urgency, she leaned over and grabbed her purse. "I have…" He kissed the underside of her breast and she couldn't finish her sentence. She pulled out the foil-wrapped packet and tore it open as she straightened.

"You were planning this?"

"I was hoping." His hands were there to help hers unwrap the condom. "I'm a relationship counselor. I always warn my readers to be prepared and be safe."

A traitorous word slipped out, but she couldn't quite recall what danger would trigger that little niggle of doubt at the back of her mind when every atom of her body was focused on pending orgasmic release.

"Good advice." He palmed her breasts. Played with them, fascinated himself with them—made it nearly impossible for her to focus on placing the protection on his engorged tip and unrolling it down his sleek, hard length. Ethan groaned, thrusting helplessly within her hands. "Hurry."

"I am." J.C. reached beneath her skirt to wiggle out of her panties.

"Jo…I can't wait."

Ethan grabbed the crotch, shoved the material aside and plunged up inside her. He went deep and hard, without any finesse. It was a shock at first—so much man, and it had been so long. But J.C. was wet and ready. She stretched and filled and slipped down around him like a fitted glove.

Just like that, he ground his hips and emptied himself inside her. He tipped back his head and cried out a praise on a panting, low-pitched whisper. "Better…than I remembered."

She was amused, touched, flattered—jealous—of the rapture on his face. "Ethan, I—"

"Not done," he growled. Still joined, he rocked against her. "More."

His face popped back up and he nailed her with a look so dark, so intense, that she trembled in anticipation. Ethan wasn't finished yet.

Not with her.

That storm-filled gaze never left hers as he slipped one thumb between them and rubbed her sensitive nub, coiling her tighter and tighter from inside and out. He tunneled his fingers into the short wisps of hair at her nape and dragged her down for a kiss. He drove his tongue into her mouth, drove himself into her. Rubbed her. Tongued her. Filled her. Look. Thrust. Nip. Stroke. Rub.

The throbbing pressure between her legs swirled in a tornadic spiral and burst. Her thighs clenched. The muscles inside gripped him tight and wept with pleasure. She gasped against his mouth, then arched her back against his clutching hands and savored the aftershocks winging through her body like jolts of pure energy that shot out through the tips of her breasts, her fingers, her toes, leaving her sated and spent in their wake.

"I knew it." J.C. collapsed onto Ethan's chest, almost too tired to catch her breath. His head lolled back on top of the seat and he wrapped his arms loosely around her, as if he, too, had exhausted every last store of strength. Despite the observation that she was half-naked while he was still fully clothed, it had been a perfect mating. In all her days, she would never have expected a Corps-to-the-core man like Ethan McCormick could make her feel this good. She smiled against a sturdy brass button and murmured, "Bliss."

His fingers traced a lazy pattern up and down her spine. "What did you say?"

Corps-to-the-core.

A sudden chill crept in to spoil perfection.

"Nothing important." J.C. snuggled closer, trying to recapture that amazing afterglow.

"Cold?" Ethan misinterpreted her shiver. He pulled her stole from beneath her purse and draped it over her back and shoulders before adjusting her less intimately in his lap, more securely in his arms.

She'd gotten what she wanted, hadn't she? Great sex. Outstanding sex. Thank-God-I'm-a-Woman sex. If her intuition was right, she would be getting it for two whole weeks. And then this fine-bodied Marine would move on.

"No strings attached." Those were her own words. It was the way she wanted it.

So why was she suddenly worried that two weeks in the major's arms wouldn't be nearly long enough?

9

"I SCREWED UP, TRAVIS. I had sex with her last night."

"All right, bro!" His little brother would have slapped him a high five if the width of Ethan's desk wasn't between them. "I knew my training would pay off. Your methods might be outdated, your pickup lines for dummies approach pretty lame…"

"Gee, thanks."

"…but something must be working for you." When he flashed that way-to-go, locker-room smile, Ethan rolled back his chair and stood.

Guilt was a heavy weight for his code of honor to bear. He'd never meant for it to go that far with J.C. The chemistry between them was all well and good—it made the charade more convincing. But he'd intended to be a perfect gentleman for two weeks. He could doff his hat, buy her a nice gift, thank her and walk away. Neither one of them would get hurt. There would be no regrets.

But she'd been so hot, so tight, so damned persuasive. He'd been… "Hell." He started his inevitable pacing, but spared a daunting glare for his brother, as if this whole mess was his fault. "You're not helping."

Travis braced his hands up in surrender. "Hey, I'm just glad to know there's some real McCormick blood still flowing through your veins."

"Fine. So I haven't tarnished the family name. Glad you're happy. But I didn't call to brag." Ethan perched on the corner of his desk and pleaded with the expert. "I need to know how to back this up a notch so it doesn't happen again."

"She wasn't any good?"

She was freaking fantastic. Maybe the year or so he'd sworn off women had... No. He had to be honest here. Josephine C. Gardner had been everything he wanted in a lover. Honest. Funny. Daring. She'd even made dancing a worthwhile risk. She wasn't afraid to go after what she wanted yet was vulnerable all at the same time. She was a healthy handful of temptation with plenty of curves and attitude to grab on to. And those lips. And *those* lips. Hell.

Travis's knowing grin swam back into focus. "Oh. She was *that* good."

Ethan launched himself to his feet and resumed his pacing. "It wasn't supposed to happen. This isn't the right time to indulge any underused body parts. I enlisted her for two weeks to impress Craddock. Period."

"Did she?"

"Big time."

"She sounds like a keeper to me. I don't see a problem." Travis adjusted the rolled-up sleeves of his camouflage shirt around his biceps and stood. "My team's running a rescue drill this afternoon. I could have gone in early to prep for it. I don't understand why I'm here, answering your panicked, crack-of-dawn phone call—"

Ethan stopped. "I wasn't panicked."

Mimicking him in a tone that, minus the cusswords, sounded annoyingly familiar, Travis replayed the call. "'*Can you stop by? We need to talk about this woman plan of yours.*'" He grabbed his cap and shrugged. "My God, Ethan. Who calls picking up chicks a 'woman plan'? I think you're analyzing this thing way too much."

"J.C. isn't just some chick."

"Obviously." Travis strolled to the door, leaving without giving him any answers. "Why can't you just enjoy what's happening? You found a girl who turns you on. She's gettin' the job done you asked her to do, and you're gettin' great sex. Sounds like a sweet deal to me."

Ethan pursued him. "I don't want a relationship. I want that promotion."

"Why can't you have both?"

"Two words. Bethany Mead."

Travis halted, sympathy clear in his voice and expression as he faced him. "All right. So Mrs. Mead screwed you royally—pardon the pun." Ethan wasn't in a mood to laugh. "But from what you've told me, she was a piece of work. Not all women are like that, Ethan. She was looking to make trouble. To make her husband sit up and take notice of her. You were just the poor guy who fell into her trap."

"Yeah. Hook, line and sinker. I got so consumed with her, I couldn't see the big picture." Ethan scrubbed his palm at the tension building in the back of his neck. It didn't take half a second to remember J.C.'s hands there, stroking, grasping—pleasuring herself and demanding more from him. He jerked his hand away from the erotic memory and jabbed it into the pocket of his blue uniform slacks. "I wasn't thinking last night with J.C., either. I can't afford to get blindsided by any surprises until this job is in the bag."

Travis finally took this conversation as seriously as Ethan needed him to. "J.C. isn't married, is she?"

"No." Even if he couldn't trust her word, her apartment had been sized for one person and decorated with funky, female tastes. All the locks on the door indicated she was a woman who defended herself. There wasn't another man in the picture.

"Has she led you on in any way? Done something to make you think she's not being straight with you?"

You asked me what I wanted. Two weeks of fooling around and then we're done.

It didn't get much more straightforward than that.

"No." Ethan wandered back to his desk and mindlessly shuffled through the papers on top. "She says she wants to have an affair during the two weeks we're faking this engagement."

Was that a snort he heard? "Let me get this straight. She wants to have more sex with you, and then let you off the hook when it's done." Travis faced off on the opposite side of the desk. "You're nuts for even debating this."

"There has to be a catch, right? Either we're involved or we're—I'm—in trouble. J.C. and I went from fake to real way too fast for me." Ethan propped his hands on his hips and looked down at his brother, unable to shake the feeling of hidden danger waiting just around the corner. "I'm not like you, Trav. I don't think I can do casual sex."

Travis snapped his shoulders back and folded his arms across his chest, reminding Ethan of when they were kids and his little brother would dig in his heels and threaten to cause trouble if big brother didn't let him tag along. "There's nothing *casual* about it when I go to bed with a woman. I have to feel something before I can hook up with her."

Ethan had never backed down from those challenges growing up. He didn't now. "*Something,* huh? I don't see you engaged or married. As far as I know, you've never even considered it."

Travis laughed as the moment of defending his impugned honor passed. "I get it now." With a sagelike nod of his head, he circled the desk. "We need to have an advanced version of the birds and the bees talk."

"Trav."

He tapped Ethan's shoulder and urged him down into his chair. Then he propped his hip on the edge of the desk and leaned in as if he was sharing the ultimate secret of the female species. "Here's addendum 1-A. No matter what Dad told us in junior high, as adults, you don't have to be in love with a woman to have sex with her. Sure, you gotta care about her on some level—as a friend, someone fun to hang out with, someone you'd like to get to know better—but you don't have to promise the rest of your life to her just to get in the sack."

"I didn't say I was in love with J.C."

Captain Smart-mouth ignored the protest. "Addendum 2-B. Women can have the same attitude about us."

"I didn't say—"

"You've got feelings of some kind, Ethan." Travis's sigh punctuated the allegation and resonated deep in Ethan's conscience. "I think that's what has you spooked. You wanted a business arrangement and you got a relationship instead." He reached out and laid a commiserating hand on Ethan's shoulder. "Maybe if you got laid more often, you'd be a little less uptight about this whole sex thing."

Ethan leaned back and glared at his brother. So he should take J.C. up on her offer and pray to God that whatever he was feeling didn't come back to bite him in the butt when the affair was over? Whether it was his old-fashioned moral code or getting burned by Bethany that made him hesitate, Ethan didn't get a chance to decide.

The sharp rap at his door switched him into business mode and put his personal life on hold. "Come in."

He pushed himself up from his desk as his aide, Kyle

Black, bustled into the office with a stack of reports and newspaper in hand. "Good morning, sir."

Travis slowly stood up and turned, his wary posture suddenly more special forces than kid brother. "Captain Black."

Black acknowledged Travis with a nod. At equal rank, no salute was necessary. But Ethan saw the slight hitch in his aide's step upon recognizing Travis, and sensed an unspoken rivalry of some kind between the two captains.

"You two know each other?" Ethan asked.

Travis nodded. "We went through basic training together. It's been a while."

Whether that was merely a statement of fact or an overture to catch up on old times, Kyle ignored it. He set the memos and correspondence on top of the desk. "How'd it go with J.C. last night after the party, sir?"

Travis squirmed beside him, suppressing a grin at the innocent question. Ethan stayed tough. "That's none of your business, Captain."

"But you two had a good time, right?"

Oh, yeah. The limo ride home had been the highlight of the evening for her. And him. Travis ducked his head to hide his amusement at the unintentional double entendres.

"Dr. Gardner enjoyed her evening." Ethan put an end to the personal questions. He nodded toward the paper in Kyle's hand. "Is there something you needed, Captain?"

"I thought you'd want to see this." Kyle rounded the desk and unfolded the paper on the blotter so that each of them could see. He pointed to the heart and fig-leaf logo marking the column at the top of the page. Ethan groaned inside. With his own screwed-up perception of relationships, he wasn't in any mood to hear how the infamous Dr. Cyn might handle his situation. "Dr. Cyn's started a new series of columns about dating men in uniform. Craddock's pretty steamed about it.''

Ethan snatched up the paper and read the less-than-flattering editorial. *Have your fling. But don't count on a Marine.* "Who the hell does she think she is?"

Travis read the same words over his shoulder and whistled. "She's got balls. Telling it like it is."

Ethan slapped the paper down on the desk. "It's damn near libelous. A fifty-dollar bet to prove we're a bunch of jerks?" He turned to his aide. "Is Craddock doing something about this?"

"He's letting it ride for now. But he wants us to keep an eye out for any negative feedback in the ranks."

"There's positive stuff in there, too," Travis insisted. He pointed to one line in particular. "'Thousands of gorgeous guys in uniforms—all sizes, shapes and colors.' She admits there are exceptions to the love-'em-and-leave-'em reputation, and she welcomes questions and comments from her readers." Ethan steeled himself at the twinkle of challenge in his brother's eyes. "Maybe you ought to go to Dr. Cyn's Web site or write a letter if you feel so strongly about it."

"I'm not going to dignify this woman's misconceptions with any kind of response."

Kyle chimed in, playing devil's advocate, as usual. "Can you imagine what it would do to recruitment if people start believing this stuff? Men will second-guess going into the service if they think it'll cost them a woman. I'll bet that Dr. Cyn is a frustrated old biddy who's not gettin' any."

Ethan wasn't sure he liked the tone of Kyle's humor. But Travis jumped in to defend the unknown writer before he could. "She states flat out that she plans to back up her allegations with research. Sounds to me like she's looking for somebody to prove her wrong.''

Captain Black's chest puffed out, and Ethan quickly asserted his authority to defuse the tension in the room. He rolled up the paper and tossed it into the trash where it belonged. ''It doesn't matter. Nobody will read this. Nobody will buy it.''

''Millie Craddock reads it,'' Kyle stated. ''If Mrs. Craddock thinks it's worth pointing out to the general, then the general's going to expect something to be done about it.''

Ethan grit his teeth. This was not the kind of business he wanted to attend to. But even though public relations wasn't his area of expertise, he'd sworn an oath to protect the integrity of the Corps. ''Put in a call to the general's office,'' he ordered. ''I'll find out how he wants us to handle it. Anything else, Captain?''

Kyle pulled a note from his pocket and handed it across the desk. ''Yes, sir. I ran down those two names you asked for. Guerro and Rodriguez. Both men are stationed at Quantico. Mechanized support unit.''

''And they've been on leave?''

''Yes, sir. But they're due to report back to camp today.''

Ethan nodded, pocketing the names and personnel information Black had gathered. ''Follow up on that. Make sure their unit can account for them.''

''Yes, sir.''

''Then get me Craddock on the phone. That'll be all. Dismissed.''

''Yes, sir.'' Kyle clicked his shiny black shoes together, then turned slightly to acknowledge Travis. ''McCormick.''

Quantico, Virginia was an easy drive from D.C. Was

that far enough away to keep them from pestering J.C. again? She'd had three locks on her apartment door. Did she worry about men like that? Or was she just practicing good common sense for a woman who lived alone? "Captain?"

Kyle turned in the doorway at the summons. "Sir?"

"Put in a call to my fiancée, too. I've got her cell number if you need it."

"Will do, sir."

J.C. could complain all she wanted about his old-fashioned sensibilities. He didn't like her going home alone. Not at night. Especially not until he was sure Guerro and Rodriguez understood that accosting a woman in a dark parking lot was not an option he would allow.

After the door clicked shut, Travis sat on the edge of the desk, leaning into Ethan's line of vision. "Problem?"

"I hope not."

"You sure? You've got that look—like your gut's trying to tell you something. And I trust your gut more than most men's facts when it comes to sensing trouble."

Ethan looked into those silver McCormick eyes that reflected the tension he felt. "You know me, I'm just being thorough."

"Yeah, I know that about you. Well, whatever it is, make sure you include keeping an eye on Captain Black." Travis stood and made his way toward the door again. "There's something about that guy I don't like."

Ethan followed to see him out. "You mean beyond the fact he brownnoses to a fault?"

Travis looked over his shoulder and grinned. "Drives you nuts, too, huh?"

"Totally. But he gets his job done. I can't complain there."

"It just seems like he knows more about things than

he should." Travis stopped with his hand on the door-knob. "I'll bet he could get the lowdown on that Dr. Cyn if you put him to the task."

"Suppress the enemy by any means necessary?" Ethan shook his head. "I'm afraid he'd enjoy it too much." The two men shared a laugh. "Let me talk to Craddock first. Maybe this will all blow over."

Travis agreed. With a couple of playful punches to Ethan's shoulder, he abruptly changed the subject. "Hey, when am I gonna meet this sexy fiancée of yours? I want to welcome her to the family before her two weeks are up."

"Very funny."

"I could give you better advice if I got to know her better."

And expose her to the hipper, handsomer brother who'd had more female conquests than ribbons on his chest? Ethan opened the door for him and gave the smart-ass a well-deserved shove into the outer office. "Not gonna happen."

Until he could figure out where he stood with J.C.—where he wanted to stand—Ethan wouldn't risk the competition.

"CLASSIC DR. CYN!"

With arms open wide, Lee Whiteley greeted J.C. at the elevator doors before she even got to the *Woman's Word* suite of offices. Lee wrapped J.C. up in a hug and danced back and forth, forcing J.C. to either join the excitement or get trampled.

"You're selling papers, girl," Lee praised. "The readers are eating it up!"

When J.C. got a chance to blink her spinning world back into focus, she tugged down the hem of her white blouse and offered her editor a wry smile. "I told you they might be controversial. So you liked the articles I sent in?"

"Liked? Oh, sweetie, your sarcasm's showing."

Lee linked her arm through J.C.'s and strutted through the office doors into the reception area. Today her editor wore a hot-pink velour running suit that clashed with her orange-red hair. The rings on all ten fingers were gold with gaudy cubic zirconia, and her eyes sparkled just as brightly with triumph and pride.

"The phone's been ringing off the hook all morning, and orders for tomorrow's issue have doubled. I knew it when I dreamed it." She splayed her fingers in the air, picturing an imaginary marquee. "*Love with a Military Man.* It was a fantabulous idea, and you've delivered." Lee stopped at the front desk. "Isn't that right, Benjamin?"

"Absolutely." The dark-haired college intern with the chunky build and intelligent gleam behind his thin oval glasses looked up from the note he was writing on his palm data organizer and smiled. "Morning, J.C. Looks like you're a hit."

She'd earned that same compliment last night. But it surprised her to realize she'd taken more pride as J. C. Gardner in pleasing Ethan and the committee than she did in knowing her alter ego had created a media sensation with her outrageous opinions and realistic philosophy about love and relationships.

"Good morning, Ben."

A buzz on the headset phone he was wearing demanded his attention. He doffed her a two-fingered salute to excuse himself and answered the call. "*Woman's Word,* the place where everything women want to talk about gets talked about. This is Ben. How may I help you?"

While Ben chatted with the caller, Lee reached behind the counter and pulled out a metal file basket filled to the brim with phone messages. "Ben's been entering these and printing them out on the computer all morning. These are all for you, lady. Some good, some bad, and—sorry to say—a couple of ugly ones."

"You're kidding." J.C. dropped her purse beside her feet and picked out a handful of messages to sort through. "All these are for me?"

"For Dr. Cyn. I told you military heroes were a hot topic."

They were pretty hot in the back of a limo, too though J.C. wasn't quite ready to share the intimate details of her *engagement* to Ethan. She'd spent a restless night, alternately wishing he'd accepted her invitation to stay the night in her apartment and berating herself for wanting so much from him so fast. Was she no different than the women who'd thrown themselves at her father? Seduced by the striking uniform and fit, able body underneath?

The second-guessing still plagued her. Not just because she might have to concede to Lee's assertion that military men made irresistible lovers. But she would have to rethink the harsh judgment she'd passed against her father. Not that she was ready to forgive him for hurting her mother and abandoning them both once his duplicity was uncovered. But maybe the temptation hadn't all been one-sided. Earl Gardner might not have actively pursued every woman he ran across. Maybe he just hadn't been able to say no if a woman came on to him.

"It's overwhelming, isn't it?" Lee's sympathetic prod brought J.C. firmly back into the moment. "I can't imagine what your e-mail's going to look like. People are a whole lot braver when they can write down a question or opinion and send it over the Internet than they are if they have to talk to a live person like our college wiz kid here.'' She winked at Ben. ''Isn't that right?''

He gave her a thumbs-up and reached for his data pad.

J.C. thumbed through the messages. ''Looks like there's enough information here for a dozen columns.'' She stopped at one. ''Here's a retired Air Force mechanic who says he's been happily married for over forty years. He credits his wife for keeping them together and always giving him a reason to come home. He says he hopes others can learn from their example.''

''Isn't that sweet,'' Lee concurred, her eyes turning a little misty. ''Sounds like my Bobby.'' Just as quickly, a twinkle danced in her eye. ''I think I'm going to win that bet. These readers are calling in to tell you they've had perfectly happy relationships with a military partner.''

''I'm not handing over the money just yet,'' J.C. challenged. She held up another slip. ''Listen to this one. This guy says he's cheated on his girlfriend more than once—every time he gets shipped to a different camp. He wants to know if he should tell her.'' She filed that one in a told-you-so pile. ''He probably expects her to stay faithful at the same time he's out 'getting acquainted' with the new neighbors.''

Lee's jewels glinted in the fluorescent overhead lights as she waved off the lothario with the guilty conscience. ''Pooh on him. He could be a traveling salesman and have a problem keeping it in his pants. The uniform's not an excuse for fooling around on his girl.''

It had been the excuse Earl Gardner had used. *It gets so lonely when I'm away from you, Mary Jo.* was the explanation for his infidelities he'd given J.C.'s mother. *You have to understand a man in my position has needs that have to be satisfied. You can't expect me to do with-*

out for six months and still perform my duties to my ship-mates.

J.C. had once read a quote by an admiral stating that every job on board a ship was vital to the safety and well-being of crew and country. Apparently no one else could fill the cheating jerk-face position on board if Seaman Gardner wasn't *satisfied.*

Clearing the memories with a bone-deep sigh, J.C. quickly moved on to someone else's trouble. Her heart went out to the woman who'd left the next message. "This one's a young mother with three small children who hasn't seen her hubby—or had sex—for over a year. Says I'm right on the money about the loneliness of her relationship." She'd been that small child with an absent father. Her mother had been that virtually single parent "It doesn't seem fair."

"The services all have help groups and counselors she could contact for assistance," Lee argued.

"I know. I looked up sources on the Internet this morning. I even called some of the local recruiting offices. They were happy to give me numbers for area support groups." J.C. arched her brow. "She's staying true to her man, though. She wants to know what kind of sexual aids I'd recommend for a woman in her position. That's definitely something I'll address in my column."

"With three small children I'd settle for a baby-sitter and a nap."

J.C. laughed out loud, along with Lee, until Ben shushed them. He returned his attention to the caller. "No, ma'am. For liability reasons, Dr. Cyn doesn't answer questions over the phone. We encourage you to write a letter or contact her Web site if you'd like to express an opinion or ask for advice. Or I can take a message. Of course."

While Ben worked, Lee took J.C.'s arm and pulled her into her office. Once the door was closed behind them, she urged J.C. into a seat and hurried around the desk to her own overstuffed chair. "Enough about Dr. Cyn. I want to hear about J.C. How's the personal research going?"

"What do you mean?"

"Trolling for military hotties. Did you meet some? Talk? Touch? I told you they had hot asses, didn't I?" Funny. J.C. hadn't gotten around to checking out Ethan's backside, but if it was built anything at all like the front, it would be magnificent. Not knowing made her instantly curious to see him again. In the daylight. From every direction. She considered all the possible visuals just long enough for Lee to get suspicious. "J.C.?"

She allowed herself half a vampish smile. "Well, I did meet someone."

"Aha!" Lee waited several impatient seconds. "And?"

"And we're seeing each other." J.C. put up a protesting hand when Lee clapped. "For a little while," she clarified. "He has no expectations of anything long-term, and neither do I."

Lee sank into her chair with a sigh of dramatized disappointment and clutched at her bosom, jangling rings against necklaces. "Are you giving this thing a chance?"

"A chance to what? He's a Marine—married to the Corps. Don't get me wrong, I appreciate that kind of dedication when it comes to national security. But I want a man who's going to be there for me when I need him. A man whom I can count on to come home to me after work, and trust not to be tempted when his job keeps him away from me."

She sat up straight on the edge of the chair, feigning

confidence that all her training had helped her separate reality from a fantasy life she couldn't have and shouldn't want.

"I'm enjoying the fling for what it is—a little sex, a little research—but I don't expect anything more out of it." She pointed a reprimanding finger at the older woman. "You shouldn't, either."

Lee tutted a mother-hen sound between clenched teeth. "I'd like to meet this guy and see what makes him such a selfish jerk."

"Ethan's not a jerk. I didn't say that." The instantaneous instinct to defend the major was a sobering reminder that she did want that fantasy life. But that didn't mean she believed it was going to happen. She consciously softened her tone. "He's giving me an opportunity to spend a lot of time with other military couples—"

Lee's forehead crinkled with delighted surprise. "Oh?"

"I don't mean like that! He does just fine on his own, thank you very much." Uh-oh. Revealing too much. Lee leaned forward, her hazel eyes sharp, seeking more juicy details. J.C. steadied her reaction with a deep breath. "I mean, it's like going undercover to observe and ask as many questions as I want, but my heart's not going to be broken when he leaves me."

Lee crossed her arms with a huff and sat back in her chair. "Do you hear yourself?"

J.C. shrugged. "What? I'm being realistic."

"'When he *leaves* you'? You don't believe in romance, do you, honey?" Lee came around the desk, sat on the arm of J.C.'s chair and put a comforting hand on her shoulder. "It's plain as the nose on your face that some man hurt you somewhere along the way. I used to think it was all your degrees and unhappy clients that had inured you to the possibility of finding your own man. But now

I see it's nothing clinical at all. You're nursing an old-fashioned broken heart.''

"I am not."

"Then why don't you give this Ethan a chance to win yours?"

Kindness softened Lee's expression beneath her garish makeup. This wasn't about winning a bet. The gentle challenge in her mentor's eyes was about wanting something good for someone she cared about.

But J.C. refused to answer. Giving Lee's hand an appreciative squeeze, she stood and excused herself. "I have a lot of work to do. I'd better finish going through those messages."

"He got under your skin, didn't he?"

J.C. stopped at the door.

And under her dress and into her pants and halfway into her...

J.C. didn't even want to consider the end of that thought. Her heart was off-limits to any man in uniform. She wouldn't be hurt the way her mother was. The way she'd been hurt before.

Maybe if she denied any emotional connection out loud, her brain and heart would wise up and believe it, too. She turned and faced Lee with a conciliatory smile. "I'll admit that Ethan's a great kisser—in a class by himself, even. I'll admit we had sex and that I'd do it again. I'm looking forward to doing it again.

"But physical attraction doesn't mean anything. I won't be sentimental over Ethan McCormick forty years from now the way you are with Bobby Tortelli." She turned the doorknob; she was done defending what she did or didn't feel. She was tired of trying to figure it out. "Now I really do need to get to work."

AN HOUR AND A HALF later, J.C. rolled the kinks from her neck and stood up to stretch behind the walls of her cubicle. She'd finally finished making notes and sorting the messages into three piles—those praising relationships with military hunks, those with complaints, and those with a specific question to address in her column.

But before she tackled the hundred plus e-mails from the Dr. Cyn Web site, she needed coffee. Mocha latte would be nice. Her first date with Ethan had been over mocha latte.

Her last date would be coming sooner than she wanted.

She tipped her head to the ceiling and silently cursed the remorseful thought. As strong and delicious as both could be, she didn't need mocha latte or Ethan McCormick to get through life. Right now, she would settle for something sweet and loaded with caffeine.

J.C. collided with Ben Grant on her way out into the hall. Papers flew into the air and rained down. "Oops. Sorry."

"My fault. I wasn't looking." Ben's stout fingers clung briefly to her shoulders until she regained her balance.

"Don't tell me you brought me more," J.C. teased, squatting down to help gather the scattered notes.

"'Fraid so." Ben handed her the ones he'd retrieved, pushed his glasses back onto the bridge of his nose and stood.

J.C. gladly accepted his outstretched hand and rose beside him. "Thanks. You're a scholar and a gent."

Though he was probably eight or nine years younger than J.C., he blushed at the compliment. "I try to follow a code of honor with the ladies."

"I'm sure they love that." J.C. smiled. "Are these all for Dr. Cyn, or are any of them actually messages I need to return?"

Ben shuffled through the notes and placed one on top of her stack. "You might want to give this guy a call. He said he had some business to discuss with you. He sounded pretty agitated on the phone."

"Agitated?" J.C. immediately thought of Juan Guerro. It might just as well be a client fighting an anxiety attack. But logic couldn't quite reach the panic button to calm her fears. She combed her fingers through her hair, straightened the fringe of her bangs, then raked her fingers through it again. "How do you mean? Agitated about what?"

Ben tunneled his hands into the pockets of his jeans and shrugged an apology. "He didn't say."

"But he asked for J.C.," she clarified, "not Dr. Cyn?"

Ben nodded, shifting nervously on both feet as if picking up on her concerns. "I think so."

She scanned the note from top to bottom, trying to read hidden meanings in Ben's heavy-handed, block letter scrawl. Surely, Corporal Guerro hadn't... "There's no name."

"He said he was someone you knew."

"Someone I know?"

I'll call you. Juan had promised. Threatened.

As if she'd suddenly stepped into a walk-in freezer, J.C.'s blood chilled in her veins. She hugged her arms across her stomach but couldn't find any warmth. Though most of the office had cleared out by lunchtime on a Saturday, she stretched up on tiptoe, her gaze darting to every closed door and shadow, trying to see around corners and over cubicle walls. She couldn't shake the feeling that someone was out there watching her, hating her.

Hating J.C. Not Dr. Cyn.

As she settled back on her heels, she couldn't help but look down at the purpling bruises around her wrist. With the passage of time, the discolorations had risen to the surface and begun to take on the distinct shape of a man's powerful grip.

"J.C.?" She flinched at the touch of Ben's hand on her shoulder. He quickly pulled away. "Is something wrong?"

"I'm sorry." She regretted the worry she'd put in his earnest green eyes.

Was this Juan's promised call to force her to smooth things over with Ethan for him? Unless Ethan already *had* made trouble for him. In that case, she might be facing something much more dangerous than an "agitated" phone call. J.C. clutched at Ben's sleeve, demanding answers. "Did the caller have an accent? Could you tell?"

"An accent?"

"Hispanic, maybe?"

"Naw. He was pretty angry, and I couldn't catch every word he said. But it was all in English."

"You don't have any clue...?"

They both jumped at the chirping sound from beneath her desk. "That's my cell." J.C. hurried back to her desk and reached underneath for her purse. She waved the messages at Ben and apologized. "I didn't mean to grill the messenger."

He took a hesitant step into her cubicle. "You know, maybe you should say something nice about the military in your column tomorrow. Readers might like you better." J.C. pulled out her phone and flipped it open. She didn't recognize the number. Ben was still trying to make a point. "You might get fewer calls."

"I'll keep that in mind, thanks." But if a vengeful corporal was harassing her, a little controversy over Dr. Cyn might be the least of her problems. J.C. tuned out the rest of Ben's suggestions and held her breath as she pressed the talk button. *Don't be him.* "J. C. Gardner."

"It's Ethan."

"Thank God." Her edginess rattled out on a noisy sigh and her entire world shrank down to the sound of that clipped, authoritative voice in her ear.

"You okay? J.C.?"

That impossibly deep voice dropped to a guarded hush. The warm, alert, slightly proprietary tone skittered along her nerves, sank into her bones and reassured her like a protective hug.

"I'm just glad to hear your…"

Reassured her? Whoa. J.C. quickly backtracked from the warm, fuzzy connection. She wanted Ethan for sex and research. Period. She didn't want to depend on him to ease her fears or make her feel a little less alone. She didn't want to start thinking he'd be there for a special word or comforting touch.

After two weeks, he wouldn't be there for anything.

J.C. summoned her composure and a touch of sarcasm. "You're just the man I want to talk to."

He paused for nearly as long as she had. Listening to the long, even sound of his deep breathing, she wondered if he was shifting through mental gears the way she had, trying to get back to friendly yet distant relations after an unplanned emotion had popped through.

"Should I be worried you're going to spring another crazy proposition on me?" he asked.

Indulging their incredible sexual compatibility was crazier than asking a woman he'd rescued in a parking lot to be his fiancée for a couple of weeks? She might have argued that before she'd gotten the anonymous message. But right now her mind was spinning with the possibilities of how to broach the topic without giving too much away.

J.C. was vaguely aware of Ben giving her one of his laid-back salutes and leaving as she curled her leg beneath her and perched on her chair. In the end, she chose the blunt approach. "Do you remember those corporals who got a little too friendly outside Groucho's Pub the other night?"

A beat of dead silence put her instantly on guard. Of course, he'd remember them. "A man forcing himself on a woman isn't my idea of friendly. But don't worry about them—I made sure they reported back to their unit at Quantico."

"You didn't." J.C. shot to her feet and circled her desk. "You contacted them?"

"My aide spoke to their commanding officer. Is there a problem?"

J.C. raked her fingers into her hair and silently cursed the incoherent panic that made a mockery of her level-headed survival instincts. That must have been Juan on the phone. He knew where she lived. Where she worked. He wasn't afraid to take matters into his own hands to save his skin. She had to make this right. She stopped midpace and tried to sound reasonable. "You chewed them out already, Ethan, and gave one of them a bloody nose. Why don't you leave it well enough alone?"

"You brought it up." It was both a fair defense and a subtle question.

One thing she had learned from her father was that the best way to lie was to blend it with a grain of truth. "I was just curious to know how the Marines handle discipline. Would an offense committed off base and out of uniform be punishable by the Corps? Or would the local police handle it? You know that notebook I was writing in at the bar? I'm actually conducting some research for—"

"Is there something you're not telling me?" he asked.

She could hear him up and moving now. Busy and methodical—with a sense of purpose that alarmed her. J.C. crossed her arms and sank into her chair.

"Dammit, J.C. This is what I do. I handle security. I keep people safe. You don't sound safe."

Sound safe? How could he know? Did his ears hear unspoken fears the way his eyes saw every secret desire?

"Talk to me," he insisted.

Those on-the-money instincts and that can't-say-no-to voice stripped the last of her defenses. "I, um, got a phone call that rattled me a little."

"Son of a bitch. He called you?" The movement stopped on the other end of the line, as if the tiny, hesitant admission had appeased his protective anger.

And drawn them closer in a way healthy lust never could.

"Actually he didn't identify himself, and an intern took the message. But after he—" J.C. snapped her mouth shut, catching herself too late. If an anonymous phone call put Ethan on red alert, news of another physical confrontation would probably seal Juan Guerro's fate. And thus, her own. She forced a laughing sound in her throat. "Forget about it. It probably wasn't even him."

"After he what?" The major didn't miss a detail. "An unidentified caller isn't going to scare you unless he made a threat over the phone or he's contacted you before."

She wouldn't answer that one. She'd already made a dangerous mistake by confiding her fear to him in the first place. It wasn't like he'd be there to clean up the mess after two weeks if things got worse. "Was there a reason you called?"

"What the hell is going on?"

J.C. ignored his demand. "Did Walter Craddock invite us to something else tonight? I thought we had a break."

"Just because you don't answer me now doesn't mean I won't still be looking for an answer later." Damn stubborn Marine. But thankfully, he finally moved on. "I wondered if we could meet. Without an audience. Something you said last night got me to thinking, and I want to take care of it."

"The two weeks of wild sex thing?" She had to ask.

He didn't laugh. "I've had some thoughts on that, too."

"So, have you decided to repay my generous contribution to your promotion by giving me thirteen more nights like last night?"

"I don't know. It depends."

"On what?"

A seemingly endless silence baited her curiosity, filled her with doubt, stretched her patience to the limit.

"On whether I kiss you again."

His stark statement touched her soul and awakened her body, giving her a buzz of anticipation that was part hope because she wanted it so much, and part fear…

Because she wanted it so much.

"How about dinner at my place?" she offered. "Around seven. We'll eat whatever falls out of the fridge."

"I'll be there at nineteen hundred hours."

J.C. didn't know whether to look forward to this evening or dread the promised visit. But she got out her lip balm and smoothed it over her lips, just in case.

10

DR. CYN—

My husband is coming home for a forty-eight-hour furlough after being overseas for six months. I want to make the most of our short time together, but I'm worried things will be awkward for us after so much time apart. What's the quickest, most effective way to seduce him?

Signed,

Lonesome for the Lance Corporal

"Lonesome, huh?" J.C. copied the question from her Web site into the text for her next column.

Her reader wasn't the only one anxious about the man showing up at her door. From her spot on the purple chaise, she glanced up at the clock in the kitchen. Quarter to seven. Eighteen forty-five in Ethan talk. He would be here any minute.

She'd alerted Norman, the retired Navy M.P. turned building security guard, that she was expecting a guest and to let him in. But which Ethan would it be? The die-hard Marine, determined to make the world a safer place, who followed a well-structured path whether it meant career advancement or keeping emotions in check? Or the sexy man who muddled through conversations and dance lessons with endearing self-consciousness, and who made love with his eyes almost as well as he did with his body?

She was half-afraid she was falling for the man.

Because that meant she could be hurt by the major.

J.C. shook off the sentimental notions and reprimanded herself. "You're an advice columnist, not a poet." She reread the question on her laptop. "The quickest, surefire way to seduce a man?"

She deliberated for maybe two seconds on her answer. This one was a no-brainer. With a knowing nod of her head, she typed,

Dear Lonesome—

Get naked.

Literally.

Lock up your clothes for the weekend. You won't need them.

Most men are more interested in getting to the goods than in unwrapping the package. If you're pressed for time, don't waste precious seconds fumbling with snaps and hooks. And why throw away money on seductive lingerie that will wind up in a wad on the floor, anyway? Spend it on finger foods, instead. They're a better alternative than a sit-down dinner for locked-in-the-bedroom-style weekends. Cleanup's easy, and a dribble of chocolate fondue or a strategically placed olive can be a creative lead-in to round two—or twelve! Just make sure you have plenty of condoms on hand, and leave the phone off the hook.

Oh, and you might want to take a nice long nap before he gets home.

Good luck!

J.C.'s gaze slid to the clock again. Eighteen-fifty. She wiggled her bare toes in restless anticipation and briefly considered taking her own advice. Maybe she should slip out of her jeans and T-shirt and greet Ethan at the door naked. That would give him more than a hint on how serious she was about having sex with him again.

But a sager, less adventurous voice from her conscience

urged her to keep her clothes on. No sense risking an awkward moment. As much as she knew he was interested, from the tone of his conversation earlier, Ethan might not be planning to take her up on her offer of an affair. Major Do-Right might be coming over to ask her more questions about Juan Guerro. Or worse, he might be having second thoughts about her after that romp in the back of the limo.

Maybe he'd decided she wasn't lady enough to impress General Craddock, that a major's wife-to-be shouldn't be so open about getting it on with the major. It probably wasn't proper officer-club etiquette.

Maybe, like her father, he was already anxious to move on to someone new, someone less complicated, someone who created fewer waves in his life.

A firm knock on her door announced Ethan's arrival.

Maybe she was going to get her answer soon enough.

J.C. put away her laptop, then finger-fluffed her hair as she hurried across the apartment to let him in.

"Don't you ask who it is before you open the door?" Ethan filled the hallway outside, looking equally impressive in jeans and a faded red polo shirt as he had in his evening dress uniform.

"Good evening to you, too."

Ethan marched past instead of greeting her. "At least get a peephole installed so you can see who's on the other side." He shifted the brown paper sack he carried into one arm and poked around her door, inspecting the thickness and design of the wood. "I could install one for you if your super won't do it."

J.C. pulled the door from his grip and closed it, twisting the knob and dead bolt to lock it. "The security around here is fine," she argued gently, needing to believe it herself.

When she turned around, she discovered him still hovering close behind her. Was it her imagination, or did Ethan seem bigger when he was in protective mode like this? Must be her bare feet, she reasoned, that made him seem taller, broader. Tougher. "The outside doors are all locked at eleven," she explained. "Besides, you can't get in unless I leave your name with Norman or I go down to meet you."

"There's always a way to get in." There was nothing ominous in his tone. But spoken so matter-of-factly, it spooked her just the same. Someone *could* get into her apartment if they were determined to.

Warding off a shiver of apprehension, J.C. fixed a smile on her face and moved on to a lighter topic. She pointed to the sack. "You don't have to bring a present every time you come over."

"Where do you want this?" He leaned down and let her glimpse a six-pack of chilled, long-neck beers. "I probably should have brought wine, but I didn't know what went with a 'falling out of the fridge' menu. So I just brought something I like to drink."

"Works for me." It looked yummy, in fact, with beads of condensation gathering on the foreign label and hinting at the rich, tangy flavor of the golden liquid inside.

She ushered him into the tiny space that passed for a dining room and kitchen and pointed to the fridge. There was barely room for Ethan to slide by her between the sink and butcher block console that doubled her counterspace. Though they didn't touch, her pulse revved at the suggestion of his body heat so close to hers. A whiff of his warm, freshly showered skin got her senses buzzing, her nipples tingling and her heart wishing he'd drop that sack, take her in his arms and lose control the way he had last night.

J.C. ignored her body's urgent response and busied her hands opening a can of tomato sauce to add to the hamburger and mushroom mixture she'd already prepared. She wanted Ethan to make the first move tonight. She'd already put herself out there—proposing an affair. If making good on that request wasn't the reason he was here tonight… She had a feeling it wasn't too soon to start distancing herself from him. He was going to leave her—if not tonight, then sometime soon. And she would be damned if she would let another military man hurt her.

"Why don't you open a couple for us and put the others away?" she suggested, pleased with the nonchalant tone she'd managed, in order to hide the antsy concerns inside her. "I've got water boiling on the stove—I hope spaghetti and salads are okay."

"Sounds good to me. What can I do to help?"

She took the beer from his hand and replaced it with a long, crusty loaf of bread and a serrated knife. "You asked."

Cooking and eating dinner turned out to be the most normal time they'd spent together. It was almost like a real first date, filled with questions and gentle teasing and self-conscious laughter. Almost. An underlying current of tension amplified every remotely sexual action—sucking a stray spaghetti noodle through pursed lips, biting down on the elongated tip of the garlic bread—reminding J.C. of the unique, intense, deeper knowledge of each other they shared.

For a short while, J.C. wondered if that had been Ethan's purpose when he suggested they meet—that they simply didn't know enough about each other to pull off the engagement charade. He shared a funny story about his brother, Travis, and told how his sister once worked undercover for the FBI. She talked about her mom and second husband and the goofy things her stepfather did to show how much he adored her mother.

"That's the second time you've mentioned your mom remarrying." Ethan mopped a spot of sauce off his plate with a crust of bread and popped it into his mouth. "Did your father pass away?"

J.C.'s dinner turned into a lump at the bottom of her stomach. Damn. The easy camaraderie vanished and old walls tried to reassert themselves. She hadn't been thinking. If she'd been watching herself, she could have steered the conversation on to a safer topic. But, since they were talking about family, it was a logical question to ask.

She blinked and looked down at her empty plate when she realized how long she'd been staring into those deep gray eyes. Picking at the label on her beer bottle, she tried to answer with the same, logical detachment. "No. But he really wasn't much of a father—definitely not much of a husband to Mom. So when he left, it really wasn't much of a loss."

Ethan reached across table and stilled the nervous movement of her fingers. "I'm sorry to hear that. I can't imagine what that would be like. The five of us were always so close. Dad was always there for us, especially after Mom died."

What? Something didn't compute. J.C. tugged her hand from his comforting grip. "I thought you said your dad was a retired general."

"He is."

A sigh huffed from deep in her chest. "Well, how was he there for you? Wasn't he always traveling somewhere on assignment? Gone for long periods of time?"

"Yeah." Ethan nodded, leaning back in his chair. "But we still knew he loved us. He called and wrote when he could. We spent a lot of time together—camping, fishing, hanging out—when he was home.''

His description of an all-American family didn't jive with her conception of military relationships. ''Didn't you feel abandoned when he was gone?''

''Abandoned?'' Ethan's eyes narrowed and studied her, as if questioning where her curiosity was coming from. He shook his head. ''It was his job.''

''But he must have missed so much of your lives growing up. You must have resented that.''

''It's a way of life, J.C. Sure, there were things he missed. When Travis broke his arm, climbing the tree in our backyard to retrieve his kite. When my sister, Caitie, had her first asthma attack. My high-school graduation. And I know it killed him when Mom passed away in the hospital and he couldn't get home in time to see her that last day.

''But then, I didn't get home to say goodbye, either. Once she got sick, she just went so fast.'' His eyes drifted shut and a look of pain washed over his face. ''There have only been a few times in my life when I thought this job sucked. That day was one of them.''

''I'm sorry.'' Ethan's obvious pain overrode her own. ''I didn't mean to dredge up sad memories.''

She brushed her fingers across the back of his hand where it rested on the table. Instead of startling him, she was the one who jumped when he flipped his hand over and latched on to hers. His eyes popped open and he stared at their clasp of hands for several long, silent moments.

But with just as quick a motion, he snatched his hand away, as if he didn't deserve—or didn't want—her comfort. Or maybe it was just the fact he was talking about things he'd told her he would never share that made him in such a hurry to move on.

He picked up his beer and polished it off with one long swallow, then set it down with a decisive thump. "It wasn't that Dad didn't care. He was away, but he wasn't skipping out on us. We were still his kids, his wife, his family. He was still our dad. He loved us. We loved him. Still do."

"You're lucky to have a family like that," she stated quietly, meaning it.

It seemed impossible to reconcile Ethan's loving description of growing up a military brat with her own childhood. She remembered bracing herself for her father's return, while Ethan and his brother and sister had looked forward to their father's arrival.

But were the McCormicks the exception to the quality of life with a military man in the family? Or was she?

The idea of continuing to press her point for research purposes or personal enlightenment seemed cruel. He'd opened up a crack in his emotional armor, and he needed some time to let the newly exposed scar heal. She could use a little regrouping time herself.

J.C. would willingly listen to him talk about his mother and family and guilt and loss for as long as he needed. But she suspected the time for sharing had ended. Granting him his moody silence, she got up and carried their plates to the sink.

She had the dishes loaded in the dishwasher, and hot water running in the sink for the spaghetti pot when she heard his chair scrape across the tile floor. She felt the heat of him behind her before she heard another sound.

"Sorry." He opened the cabinet beside her hip and dropped their empty bottles into the recycling bin she'd shown him earlier. "Mom always told us that if you didn't cook the meal, you had to help clean up." With his big hand, he palmed her hip and scooted her a step to the right to open the matching cabinet door to dump the crumbs from the bread basket into the trash.

J.C. caught her breath at the burst of kinetic energy that radiated through her from that simple, familiar touch. He was emptying the garbage; she was elbow-deep in soap suds, for gosh sakes! It was hardly the time or setting to justify her body's instinctive tightening and sudden craving for more of his touch.

"I didn't mean to leave you doing all the work," he apologized, closing the door and then scooting her back to her original place. As he spoke, his breath caressed her nape and her nipples puckered. "This goes up here, right?"

She could only nod as he reached over her head to hang the basket from the decorative iron rack she'd mounted above the sink.

"That's okay. You needed some downtime." Was that voice with the husky crackle in it really hers? He was standing right behind her, with more imagination than air separating them. She squeezed her eyes shut and breathed a hungry thought about him moving even closer, trapping her against the counter, pressing that marvelous manhood of his against her rump.

"What else can I do to help?" he asked, his voice at a potent pitch beside her ear.

J.C.'s eyes popped open. What was wrong with her? She should be thinking comfort and compassion. Patience. Not sex. Not now. She gripped the rim of the sink and held on, keeping herself from leaning back into his groin and chest.

"How about opening another couple of beers?" she

suggested. Yes. Icy cold from the fridge. Cold would be nice.

She expelled a pent-up sigh when he moved away from her, and turned her thoughts to the mundane task of rinsing the pot and setting it on the drying tray. Then she unplugged the stopper and drained the sink.

·"Here you go." Ethan twisted the top off one of the beers and held it out to her. "I know for a lot of people, German beer is an acquired taste. I'm glad you like it."

"I don't know if I could ever get into drinking it warm the way you said they did over there." J.C. shook the excess water from her hands, then blotted them on her jeans. She turned to take the bottle. "But I do like the taste. Thanks."

Her damp fingers closed around the slick bottle. Traction just wasn't going to happen. The base of the bottle slipped through her grip. She snatched at the neck with the other hand, but couldn't connect. But Ethan's quick reflexes saved the day. His hand darted out to catch the bottom of the bottle, averting the certain disaster of glass hitting ceramic tile.

But gravity and reflexes and the laws of physics had a funny way of combining to change a mood from polite and somber to shamelessly sexy.

The beer splashed up out of the bottle and soaked the left half of J.C.'s T-shirt.

"Yeesh!" She gasped, jumping back from the frigid slosh of dark gold liquid. But it was too late. The soft pink cotton was plastered to her skin, outlining each floret of lace on the cup of her bra, and the puckered aureole and straining tip beneath.

"Oh, man, another smooth move. I'm sorry." He set both beers on the counter and grabbed the dish towel. The hops-rich scent of fine German beer radiated off her skin and filled the tiny kitchen. She reached to take the towel from his hand, but he'd stopped halfway. The towel dangled from his fist. J.C. tried to pry it open, but it wouldn't budge. Her verbal appeal died in the heat of his transfixed stare. "No, I'm not."

Something hot and urgent rippled through J.C., as if he'd touched her with his hand. She wanted to step back, turn away, find her own towel to cover herself. But that wet breast stood up like a prideful thing, basking in the admiration of his hungry gaze.

"Ethan." It was a token protest. It was a plea for the inevitable.

"I love that beer." Her blood thickened like a warm, rich brew in her veins at the seductive pitch of his voice. "I hate to waste it."

She watched him watch the rise and fall that breast as she gulped in deep, steadying breaths. He watched long enough for her to feel nearly every cell clenching against the cold compress of cloth. Nerves sparked, muscles constricted, things beaded and thrust out beneath the erotic contrast of icy liquid and raw, fiery desire.

"Thirteen more nights of mind-blowing sex, right?" he asked, rethinking her offer from last night out loud.

He seemed tortured. Tempted. Wanting one thing, but struggling to do another.

"I don't know, Ethan. Maybe we shouldn't." She gripped the counter behind her and fought through her own wanton desires to remember the counselor in her. "You were upset. My questions didn't help. You need comforting. I should be giving you a hug or recommending a colleague you could...talk to."

Those gray eyes shifted up to hers and J.C. knew she

was lost. "There's more than one way a man finds comfort."

He picked up his beer and poured it over the other breast.

"ETHAN!"

Hearing his name on those lips in that breathless, about-to-lose-control voice had to be one of the greatest turn-on's of his life.

Ethan skipped the towel and bent his head to lick the liquid caught between her straining breasts. When she instinctively pulled away from the shocking contact, he grabbed her hips and pulled her into his rising heat. Her fists thudded against his shoulders, the last vestige of common sense before the passion consumed them both.

"Oh, Ethan, yes…" He felt her lips in his hair. She clutched up handfuls of his shirt and dug her fingers into the skin and muscle underneath. "…I want this, too."

Reeling with guilt-ridden memories and painful regrets, filled with the need to connect with J.C.'s bold heart and caring soul and thus reclaim a little of his own, Ethan forged ahead, taking what he wanted, asking for what he needed—receiving so much more.

"Oh, Jo." He nuzzled the swell of one breast. "You're so beautiful." He sucked beer from the drenched cotton. "So damn beautiful." He shoved his thigh between her legs, backing her into the sink. The momentum arched her neck back. Her breasts tilted up and Ethan took advantage of the opportunity. "I want everything you can give me."

He closed his mouth over one straining nipple, and J.C. cried out. It was music to his ears. Her hips twisted against his swollen dick and he groaned at the raw pleasure of it.

He slipped his hands beneath the back of her shirt and palmed smooth, feverish skin. It wasn't enough. He swept her shirt off over her head and returned his attentions to the bra-covered breast. He slipped his tongue inside the lacy cup and laved the pebbled tip, relishing her squirming response against his groin. The cloth was cold, but the woman inside was hot to the touch. He found a puddle of beer at the round, heavy base and lapped it up, but the flavor of the dark, rich liquid paled beneath the taste of J.C.'s skin.

He knew a moment of panic, of paradise lost, when she slipped her thumbs in between his lips and urged him away from her breast. "Ethan." Her ragged breath tangled with his own. "Wait."

"Honey..." he begged, lifting his head to tease her lips. She pushed against his chest and stretched her arm out behind her. Pulling away?

He was tightening his hold, pulling her back. "No. Don't. J.C., please."

The tension of her body relaxed an instant before a cascade of bracing, pungent liquid doused his shoulders and back. "What? Damn."

The cold shock jerked him to attention, and the mood was lost in a moment of confusion.

But J.C.'s wicked laughter brought him back to the time and place and woman in his arms. Those gorgeous lips smiled and he knew it was all right.

"I believe in fair play, mister." She softened the teasing with a sweep of her hands across his jaw and a lush, quick kiss against his mouth. Then he raised his arms and helped her peel off his soaking shirt. "Oh, yeah. Much better."

Then she was back in his arms. Skin to skin. Chest to chest. He raked his fingers into her hair angled her mouth beneath his. He kissed her. And kissed her. And kissed.

She explored his body with eager hands, flicking a nipple between her fingers, squeezing a pec, planing her palms along his spine. Each touch was a sweet torture that drew him beyond the limits of his control.

She dipped her fingers into the rigid circle of scar tissue at his shoulder and whimpered. "Ethan," she whispered on a husky breath, tearing her mouth from his to inspect the damage done by a rebel bullet during that hellish battle down in Central America. She kissed the spot, then hugged him tight. She found the schrapnel scars on the back of his hip from the car bomb. "Ethan?"

"I'm okay." With his thumb, he brushed away the mist of tears that clung to her lashes. "Anytime you make it home in one piece, it's okay." Then he kissed her closed lids. Kissed each cheek. Kissed her lips to stop their trembling. She might be realizing for the first time the extent of what he'd done for his country. He didn't just sit behind a desk or train Marines. He could be hurt. He *had* been hurt.

But she caressed each mark and breathed his name and stoked his passion. Her acceptance of his pain eased the pain of his memories.

"Jo…honey." He was as hard as a rock and she was so damn hot. He unhooked the snap of his jeans, fumbled with the snap on hers. He'd never needed Bethany with the same intensity that he needed J.C. Maybe even before that night in Cairo when he'd shut down his heart and put his life on hold, he'd sensed he needed to hold something back, that Bethany would take advantage of any weakness—emotional or libidinous or otherwise—he exposed.

But J.C. was like a breath of fresh air to an oxygen-deprived body. "I want to lose myself inside you. I need to…let go." Of hurts and humiliation. Of guilt and thwarted desires. He brushed his forehead against hers. A powerful backlog of emotional baggage kept in check for far too long surfaced in a soul-baring request. "I need you."

"It's about time you admitted that." She wound her arms around his neck and lifted her hips, wrapping her legs around his waist and aligning herself against his aching shaft. "Quick, Ethan," she breathed against his mouth. "I need you quick."

She didn't know the half of it.

Ethan cupped his hands beneath her butt, his fingers meeting at the seam of her jeans. The denim was wet and warm and in the way. His whole body clenched with the knowledge of how ready she was for him. "J.C.... Jo." He was already rocking against her.

He wanted to carry her to the bedroom, but he knew he couldn't last. So he set her on the nearest flat surface he could find—the butcher block table. He inhaled an uneven breath, trying to pace himself. But the scents of malt-drenched skin, of eager sex, of J.C. herself, made it impossible to slow down.

"Jo..." With rough, needy hands, he unzipped her. He shoved his hand inside her jeans and panties and lifted her out of them, tossing aside the clothes and lowering her to the crotch-high table.

"Ethan..." At the same time, she pushed his jeans down past his hips and let them fall to his knees.

"Honey..."

"Major..."

Together, they stripped his briefs down to his thighs, and in one fluid movement of strength and desire, he pulled her right to the edge of the table and plunged into her. She locked her heels behind his hips, spreading herself wider, taking him deeper.

"I need you," he growled from deep in his throat, leaning her back and driving down into her sweet, hot channel.

"Yes." She arched her back and moaned her delight.

"I need you." It was barely a whisper as he pulled her back up and crushed her to his chest.

"Yes."

"I need…"

They held each other tight as he poured himself into her—pouring out every last shred of guilt and what-if's, ridding himself of burdens and pain, finding hope and emotional courage in the pulsating ribbons of her warm, moist heat that held him, sustained him, set him free.

J.C. WAS EMOTIONALLY drained and physically exhausted.

And ready to do it again.

She smiled against Ethan's warm skin, tempted to lick the tangy flavor of aged hops and honest sweat right off him.

Several minutes had passed since that explosive climax, and J.C. was still wrapped up against the molded strength and abundant heat of Ethan's chest. Good thing, too, she reasoned, feeling the chill of the nighttime air seeping into her quiet apartment and raising goose bumps across her skin.

Across a lot of skin. She was still perched on the edge of the butcher block table, wearing nothing but her bra and a contented smile. Ethan had receded and fallen out of her by now, but he hadn't retreated a step from the vee of her legs. He held her with one gentle hand massaging her nape, the other cupping the flare of her hip.

"It's never been like this for me with anyone else, Jo." He crooned that shortened name against her temple, and she felt humbled, cherished by the admission. "I can't seem to help myself."

"I know." She absently stroked her fingertips up and down his spine. Crisp, golden hair curled against her cheek. The steady rhythm of his heartbeat beneath her ear. There was so much strength to cling to in this man, so much character to admire. "It's the same for me, too."

She wasn't sure exactly when she'd lost control, when two weeks of fun and games in the sack had become something very real, very frightening, very close to things she didn't want to feel.

Maybe it was when he'd poured the beer across her breast and she realized Ethan knew how to have fun, after all. Maybe it was when she'd discovered his scars and nearly wept, thinking back to the story General Craddock had told about Ethan and his men getting ambushed at the embassy in Central America. Maybe it was when he'd uttered those savage words against her throat.

I need you.

Ethan McCormick needed J. C. Gardner.

Not a counselor. Not a fake fiancée. Her.

With a winsome sigh, she snuggled her head beneath his chin and tightened her grip around his shoulders. For a few minutes out of time, she'd felt part of something greater than herself. She hadn't been quite so alone. The wounds inflicted by her father and neglect hadn't pierced quite so sharply.

J. C. Gardner needed Ethan McCormick.

Very frightening, indeed.

"I'm, um, sorry I wasted your last beer."

He pressed his lips to the crown of her head and stepped back to pull up his pants and fasten his jeans. "Not wasted. I don't think a moment I've spent with you has been wasted."

"You said you wanted comfort." She crossed her legs at the ankles and hugged her naked torso, feeling suddenly very exposed. But it was self-doubt, not modesty talking. "Did this…? Did *I* help?"

Ethan leaned in and kissed her. "Oh, yeah. Maybe your style of *listening* is what I needed from you, after all." He stroked his fingers across the curve of her lower lip as he pulled away. Something dark and territorial blazed in his gunmetal eyes. "But I don't want you practicing that particular style of therapy with anybody else."

His words were just possessive enough to reassure her and make her want him all over again. "I won't," she promised.

For two weeks, she was solely and exclusively his.

She didn't want to think beyond that time until she had to.

"I still don't earn much for style points, though, I guess. And I seem to be a little hard on your wardrobe." He scooped up her discarded jeans and panties and laid them in her lap. He dropped both their shirts into the sink and ran water over them. "You know, one of these days I want to see if we can get all our clothes off and actually make it into a bed before we have our next therapy session."

J.C. slipped into her underwear, eager to dress so they'd have the opportunity to undress. "How about tonight?" She nodded toward her bedroom, inviting him to make good on his challenge. "I'll race—"

A horrible thunk outside the living room window startled them both. It was eerie and unnatural, like a bird crashing at full-speed into the pane. "What the—?"

But Ethan recognized the sound. He was already diving toward her by the time she turned to get a better look. She screamed as the picture window exploded into the living room, raining shards of glass and terror into her tiny apartment.

11

ETHAN CINCHED HIS HANDS around J.C.'s waist and dragged her to the floor. The discomfort of the tile's uneven edges digging into various parts of her anatomy seemed a minor inconvenience compared to Ethan's big, solid body lying on top of her, shielding her from head to toe.

Were they under attack? He seemed to think so.

"What's happening?" J.C. asked, fear and the weight of Ethan's body keeping her breathing shallow.

She heard the sounds of a vehicle grinding through its gears, then squealing rubber against the pavement and speeding off into the night. The sound was so clear, she realized, because of the big, gaping hole in her living room where the window used to be.

Ethan heard it, too, judging by the sudden tensing of his muscles. She knew this was Major McCormick in his true element, doing what he'd been trained to do. There was a rigid control about him now. Deep, careful breathing. He charged the air around her with an intimidating sense of hyperawareness—a man on guard to hear or see or sense anything that might put him or his charge in danger. She felt the jerk in his legs, as if he wanted to rise up and give chase. But he stayed with her, sheltering her, protecting her.

"I'm okay," she reassured him. "Go."

But only when it was clear no more missiles were flying

through the window did he roll to the side and let her get up. He immediately crossed toward the disastrous mess, stopping at the line where tile met carpet. He turned over his shoulder and glanced down at her bare feet. "Stay put back there."

The carpet crunched beneath his work boots as he dashed to the side of the window, pressed his back to the wall and peered outside. J.C. scrambled into her jeans and hurried after him. But practicality forced her to obey. The minefield of jagged edges waiting to cut her feet reminded her of the aftermath of the earthquakes she'd experienced in Southern California. Large chunks of glass littered her living room furniture and floor, while a finer layer of glass dust glistened in the moonlight streaming in from outside.

The cool, humid air from outside filtered into the apartment, bringing with it the smells of the river and cherry trees about to bloom. But they weren't comforting smells tonight. They felt invasive, out of sync in her once-safe haven.

She could only stare at the destruction and wonder at its cause. Ethan moved from the safety of the wall and briefly studied the remaining shards hanging along the top of the window. Then he spun around and surveyed the room itself before looking across at her and releasing a deep breath. "There's no movement outside. Whoever did this is gone."

J.C. met his gaze, wanting answers, too. "I heard a car."

He nodded. "Me, too. I want to check with that guard of yours, find out if he saw anything."

"If he did, he'd call the police."

"Not a bad idea." His distant tone told her that something else had distracted him. "We're on the third floor, right?"

"Yes." She dodged from side to side, trying to get a glimpse of whatever had caught his eye.

"You'd need a grenade launcher to do this much damage from that distance."

Grenade launcher? "What are you talking about?"

Using a bandanna from his pocket, he bent down and picked up a jagged, fist-size rock from the center of the debris. He stood and held it out in his open palm. "Old-fashioned but effective."

"*That* broke the window?"

"With enough force behind it, it could shatter anything."

J.C. squinted, assessing it from across the room. "What are those markings on it?"

Ethan turned the rock in his hand. His grim look instantly put her on edge. "Friend of yours?"

He carried it to the kitchen and let her get a good, clear look at the unmistakable threat. Shock pushed the blood to her feet, leaving her feeling light-headed as she read the message a second time. Right there. In her home. Printed in a thick, hasty scrawl.

I know who you are.

ETHAN HOVERED in the background as the two police officers took pictures and statements and told J.C. she could start cleaning up.

He'd already retrieved a clean USMC T-shirt from his truck to put on, and rounded up a piece of plywood and some tools from the building's super. He'd brought her socks, tennis shoes and a gray sweatshirt from her bedroom to put on. He wanted to find her a jacket or pull the blanket from her bed, because even though the spring air kept the temperature in the fifties, she'd been shivering ever since she'd read the words on that rock.

Ethan already knew as much as the cops had found out. Like Ethan, the security guard Norman Flynn had recognized the telltale explosion of heavy gunfire, but hadn't seen the shooter. Norm had caught a glimpse of a small, beat-up car speeding down the street beside the apartment building. But it had been too dark to catch any other detail besides the Virginia license plate.

The rock that had been used as a projectile had striation marks that indicated it had been fired from a large-bore weapon—the kind that anyone outside the military or law enforcement shouldn't legally have their hands on. The message indicated it had been fired on purpose and not as some teenage prank. The pallor of J.C.'s skin told him the message had hit its target.

Despite his concerns for her health and safety, J.C. had hung in there for almost two hours, answering each question the cops asked her. No, she didn't recognize the handwriting. Yes, she supposed she knew someone who might want to scare her. The suspect's name she gave twisted in Ethan's gut.

Corporal Juan Guerro.

The need to take action, to make this right for her—to punish the bastard who'd meant to terrify her and who might damn well have killed her if she'd been standing close to that window—burned inside every bone of his body. The bruises on her arm had come from Guerro, she'd told the officers—he'd stopped her on her morning walk. And that crazy, anonymous phone call had rattled her this afternoon—before she'd made up some flimsy excuse and dismissed it.

All the signs that she was in trouble had been there, and he hadn't seen them. She hadn't wanted him to. Why?

With his connections to both the military and security, wasn't he the obvious resource to turn to for help with

Guerro? And that was just the practical reason for confiding in him. The deeper, less logical, and far more personal reason for letting him in to share her burden and keep her safe was that he was falling in love with her.

Correction. He was there. He was too honest to try to convince himself it was just lust or loneliness talking—though J.C. had sated both those needs in him. Somewhere between class and brains and sirenlike sex appeal, she'd gotten under his skin. Her bold approach to life had struck even deeper. But it was her patient teaching and indulgent praise and insistent need to care about his scars, inside and out, that had sealed the deal.

Yet, by putting a two-week deadline on their relationship, he might have unknowingly encouraged her to place limits on what she would feel, how much she would trust, how much she might share. He didn't know if he possessed the skills to convince a woman he'd be interested in forever with her. She'd been gung ho about having an affair. But did that mean J.C. didn't want anything long-term? She'd admitted she hadn't had a lover for a while. Was that by choice? Had she not found the right guy? Or was she just not a forever kind of woman?

It pained him to think the latter might be true.

Not just for his sake, but for hers.

Even if their fake engagement turned out to be nothing more than two weeks of outrageously satisfying sex, he didn't want her to face whatever this cowardly attack turned out to be on her own. He didn't want her to deal with any of the challenges life threw her way alone.

It was his sworn duty to protect the citizens of the United States.

He made a silent vow of his own to keep this one particular citizen safe. Even if she didn't want him to.

Ethan slipped on a pair of work gloves and headed into

the living room with a double-lined paper sack to begin picking up the debris while J.C. showed the two cops out.

She closed the door with a weary sigh, then methodically fastened each lock—the dead bolt, the knob. Her hand lingered after hooking the chain. ''Seems kind of pointless.'' His own words came back to haunt him as they seemed to rob her of any sense of security. ''There's always a way to get in, right?''

Ethan straightened from his work. ''I'm here. I'm staying. Nobody's going to hurt you.''

Her blue eyes sought out his across the room. She nodded. But it wasn't very convincing. She seemed small and alone and devoid of the fire that had drawn him to her in the first place. She didn't believe his promise.

He set down his bag and closed the distance between them. As he wrapped her up in his hug, her arms circled behind his waist and she nestled her head beneath his chin. She trembled against him and he held on tight. He buried his nose in the silky cap of her hair and tried to let his body tell her what his words could not. His word was as good as his bond. She was protected. Cared for. Loved. Safe.

She breathed a heavy sigh and relaxed against him. But a moment later, she tensed again and pushed away, as if she'd suddenly remembered a forgotten task. She walked straight to the coat closet and pulled out her vacuum.

''I can handle this mess if you want to go lie down for a while,'' Ethan offered.

''Nope.'' She pieced together the equipment and plugged it in before adding, ''I need to stay busy.''

He could relate to that. More than once, he'd taken a long run or attacked a punching bag in the gym when worries and frustrations threatened to get the better of him. He opted to work beside her in silence, keeping a watchful eye on her as she cleaned the chaise lounge and chair that had sustained most of the damage. He hauled the biggest pieces of glass out to the building's Dumpster and came back to find her vacuuming the carpet with a vengeance.

Temper was a better sign than the shock and acceptance she'd shown earlier. She was gathering her energy now, toughening her hide. The spots of color on her cheeks and the determination blazing in her eyes reassured him that she was going to weather this personal attack and come out all the stronger for it.

It also meant she was up to doing a little of that talking she preached so much about.

Ethan fitted the plywood into the empty window frame and reached for a hammer and some nails to anchor it into place. He tried to sound casual and reassuring as he launched his own investigation.

"I already put in a call to Quantico to track down Corporal Guerro. If he can't account for his whereabouts tonight, they have orders to detain him until he can be handed over to D.C.P.D. for questioning." She nodded her comprehension over the roar of the vacuum. Good. She was listening. "Why didn't you tell me about his threats sooner?"

"I thought it would just blow over at first. And then, well…" With a resolute sigh, she flipped off the vacuum switch. Ethan positioned another nail, but paused to listen.

"I'm used to handling my own problems," she explained. "My family's not like yours, Ethan. They're not there for each other when there's a crisis. And let's face it, you're not going to be there for me after a few days, either. I don't want to depend on you. I don't expect that you'll come running if I need you."

He turned and faced her, genuinely confused by the

idea that she thought she couldn't depend on him. "I know our relationship started out as a lie, but I think we've gotten closer than either of us expected. Why wouldn't I be there for you?"

She almost laughed, but he didn't detect any humor. "Because you're a Marine."

"What?" He pounded in the nail with a single blow. He sure as hell hadn't expected that answer. Breathing deeply to steady his knee-jerk response to any attack on the Corps, he set down his hammer and demanded an explanation. "Why does my job mean you can't trust me?"

Her eyes darkened with some kind of hurt, but her mouth stayed set in a stubborn line. "Because you're going to ship out of my life. Your loyalty is to your job, your country—the next continent you're assigned to protect—not to me."

"I can do both. I have done both. A lot of men take care of their duty *and* the people they care about."

"And a lot of men don't."

He ignored the admission that he cared about her and advanced a step closer. "Are you comparing me to a bully like Guerro?"

"No."

He kept advancing. "Do you think a man like General Craddock doesn't take care of his own family as well as he takes care of his men?"

"I didn't say—"

"Do you think my father, who was married to the woman he loved for twenty-six years, didn't ache inside every time he had to leave us? Didn't bust his buttons with pride and joy every time he came home?" She was retreating now. "What is it you don't like about the Corps, J.C.?"

To her credit, when she backed into the chaise, she planted her feet and stood up to his verbal attack. "I have a hard time knowing that you might not come home to me—and I'm not just talking about the danger of your job. I'm talking about trust. About how a man handles himself when he's not with his wife and family or girlfriend or fake fiancée. Men like you have needs—"

"Men like me?" That sounded like an insult waiting to happen. "Let me get this straight. You didn't want to tell me about a guy who assaulted you and threatened you because you think I'm going to skip town and get with some other chick just when you need me most?"

Her bravado misfired. Hell. That *is* what she thought. Her gaze dropped to the floor, then darted around the room as if searching for an ally. Her tone was less convincing when she looked him in the eye again. "I don't need you. Not for anything more than sex. I don't need anyone. I can handle this all on my own."

Ethan's anger evaporated on one long breath. Not even her sarcasm rang true. She was truly dealing with something here. Something he'd glimpsed before but had paid no mind to because she always seemed so cocky. Confident. Strong. "Where is this coming from?"

Damn. Now he could see her backpedaling, coming up with a lie to stall his compassion and divert suspicion. "I told you I was doing research on military relationships. That's why I was in that bar Thursday night."

"That's the biggest crock—"

"I can show you my notebook. I have documented evidence about the unreliability of men in uniform."

My God, she was serious!

"Let me see this evidence." Reaching down into that big red bag that carried her laptop and what looked to be enough supplies to sustain a small platoon, she fished out a spiral binder and handed it to him.

Ethan tugged off his gloves and stuffed them into his back pocket, taking his time to thumb through the pages of notes she'd collected. From the corner of his eye he could see J.C. hug her arms across her stomach. She stared at the book, then his face, then the book again, impatiently waiting for him to analyze her proof.

He read some amusing things that didn't speak well to male intelligence when it came to picking up women. He read some truths he could agree with—courtship wasn't necessarily easy for either gender. He read a couple of items that alarmed him to the danger she'd put herself in by conducting this "research." And he read some of the insulting things that no doubt justified her low opinion on the reliability of fighting men.

"Well?" she prompted, as he turned to a blank page.

"Any man in any bar can be a jerk like some of these guys. I'm sorry that you—that any woman—has to deal with that. But the uniform isn't what makes them behave that way. The uniform doesn't determine whether or not the man has character." He snapped the book shut and held it out to her. "That comes from something he already has inside—something he's born with, something he's raised with. You're making generalizations here that just aren't fair."

She snatched the book out of his hand and pointed it at his face. "Do you deny that you'll be leaving me in a few days?"

Ethan hesitated. "That's what we agreed to, yes. But—"

"Then why should I count on you? Why should I count on anything but my own brains and my own two hands? Why should I care about someone who's going to hurt

me? I don't need any more failed promises in my life."
She stuffed the notebook into her bag, then picked up the
whole thing and stormed off toward her bedroom.

"J.C.!"

She stopped at his command, but didn't turn around.
He was torn with the need to shake some sense into her—
to kiss an understanding of who he was and what she
meant to him out of her—and to simply let her go and
have her space until she could be reasonable again.

He wasn't just defending the Corps.

He was defending his own honor.

He was defending her right to believe in forever.

"Just because you've never had anyone you could
count on, doesn't mean you don't need anyone." He
pulled out his gloves and picked up his hammer to finish
the job at hand. "And it doesn't mean you can't count on
me."

SEVERAL HOURS LATER, J.C. kicked off the sheets that had
twisted around her bare legs and rolled over to stare at
the faded family portrait lying on her bedside table. Her
puffy eyes still burned from the good, old-fashioned cry
that she'd muffled with her pillow so that Ethan wouldn't
hear her from where he slept in the living room.

Despite every argument to the contrary, he'd informed
her that she was either a, going home with him or b, he
was staying here. Juan Guerro's vengeance was his responsibility, he'd insisted. *She* was his responsibility.
Ethan was probably just protecting his investment in her
as his ticket to becoming a lieutenant colonel.

So when he plunked himself down on her chaise couch,
she'd slammed the bedroom door.

She wished she could shut him out of her thoughts just
as easily.

Just because you've never had anyone you could count on, doesn't mean you don't need anyone.

She did need someone. To keep her safe. To make her crazy with desire. To come home to. To care. To take her love and trust and treat it like a prize. Respect it. Protect it.

She just didn't want that someone to be a Corps-to-the-core Marine like Ethan McCormick.

Not even for one night.

But if he wanted to play the noble sentinel, standing guard over a broken window, she'd let him. Let him play his role as doting fiancé to the hilt, even though it meant protecting the neurotic woman who'd turned out to be completely wrong for the part of his would-be wife. Imagine, trying to impress the brass with a woman who had such a built-in prejudice to men in uniform.

It might not take him two weeks to dump her independent, paranoid, antimilitary ass.

That would sure prove her point and win her the fifty-dollar bet.

J.C. sat up against the headboard and hugged a pillow to her chest. It would also leave her desperately alone. Because she knew that every time Ethan talked a little more, every time they made love, every time he held her in his arms, he was digging his way a little farther inside the fortress that guarded her heart.

Oh, this was so gonna hurt when the time came to leave her. When his job took him away to something bigger and more exciting. Or he met another woman—to confound and intrigue, to protect and make crazy love to—to fill in the next time he needed a two-week fiancée to impress a general.

J.C. reached over and picked up the picture again, to

remind herself of all the reasons she shouldn't care about Ethan McCormick.

She'd pulled the photo from an album at the back of her closet. She wanted a clear picture of her father; she needed a stark reminder of all the pain he'd caused. A pain she'd tried desperately to outgrow, but that still clung to her insecurities with the tenacity of a…Marine.

"Oh, damn." Bad metaphor. She rolled onto her side, wrapping herself around the pillow, wishing it had arms to wrap around her.

This was the last picture she and her parents had taken together. The full moon streamed in through her bedroom window, offering enough illumination to highlight every painful detail. On a casual glance, they looked like any normal family. Earl stood in the back, dressed in his white Navy uniform. He had one hand on his wife Mary Jo's shoulder, one hand on J.C. She'd just turned fourteen and, despite the recent, rock-star haircut she'd been so proud of, she'd fixed her hair in pigtails the way her dad said he liked it. The way she'd worn it back in elementary school! Sure. He'd paid real close attention to her growing up. Not.

Mary Jo Gardner wasn't smiling in the picture, either. J.C. vividly remembered the morning the picture was taken. Because it had signaled the end to any effort at pretending they were a happy, loving family. Mary Jo wore the beautiful silk dress Earl had brought her from the Philippines. In her hand she clutched the gift tag that read, "For my adoring wife—Ling. Love, Earl."

"Good times," she whispered sarcastically.

She never wanted another man like her father in her life.

No woman needed that kind of heartbreak and humiliation.

Every woman deserved a man who was honest and reliable, even if he was a little square around the edges. He should be hot for her. Devoted. Trustworthy.

All of which sounded a lot like…Ethan.

"Oh, God."

A whole new feeling swept through J.C., leaving her edgy and restless and downright ashamed of herself.

She crawled out of bed and pulled the oversize T-shirt she wore down to her thighs. Ethan was out there in her living room, sleeping on a couch that was probably too small for his big body, sticking by her because she'd been scared. Because she'd been in danger.

He might be here out of duty. He might be here out of guilt.

But he was here.

She couldn't say the same for her father.

J.C. pulled the cotton throw from the foot of her bed and tucked it over her arm. She quietly opened her door and peeked into the main room. With the picture window boarded up, she had to wait a minute for her eyes to adjust to the darkness. The place was still as a tomb, the air just as cold. Maybe it was her trepidation and imagination that made it seem so chilly.

But she wouldn't let any errant flights of fancy dissuade her from her purpose. With just enough light filtering in through the kitchen window and her familiarity with the room to guide her, J.C. tiptoed across the carpet. She spotted the silhouette of Ethan's head sticking up beyond the back of the chaise. As she noiselessly drew closer, she could distinguish the curve of his bare shoulder from the stack of pillows. She could hear the soft, even whisper of his breath as he dozed.

As she circled around to the side of the chaise lounge, she could make out the length of denim-clad legs with bare toes sticking beyond the end of the chaise. The moonlight created tiny, curlicue shadows amongst the sprinkling of gold across his chest. The gossamer-like contrasts of light and shadow narrowed across his flat stomach and trailed into a thin line that ran straight to his belly button. Beckoning like an invitation, the line disappeared beneath the open snap of his jeans. Inside those jeans she'd find a pair of trim white jockey shorts, another thatch of golden hair, and the potent evidence of a virile, sexy man. A remembered heat chased away the chill as she stood and admired his big, well-made body.

She jumped at a stray noise from outside, a single smack of metal on metal. Goose bumps prickled across her skin. She caught her breath and tensed, but even her untrained ear could tell the difference between weapon fire and the slam of a car door. She forced herself to breathe evenly, quietly, in and out through her nose. No more rocks were coming through her window tonight.

But the sound was enough of a distraction to remind her that she'd come out here to make amends, not ogle the stuff of her fantasies.

She looked up at Ethan's face, his jaw square as ever, refusing to relax even in sleep. His hair wasn't even long enough to have a lock out of place. Still, she reached out to draw a finger across his brow in a gentle effort to ease some of the guarded tension from his body.

He shivered in his sleep and J.C. snatched her finger back into her fist. With only a couple hours left until sunrise, she needed to complete her mission and then try to get some sleep herself.

J.C. unfolded the cotton throw and draped it over Ethan. She quickly realized she could either cover his toes or his chest. She couldn't help smiling as she shook her head. The big lug. Even in his sleep, he proved a stubborn son of a gun. Ultimately she opted for maximum coverage and pulled the throw over his chest and tucked it around his shoulders.

"Good night, Major," she whispered, resisting the urge to bend down and kiss his cheek.

Before she turned away, one sleepy gray eye slit open. "Does this mean we're on speaking terms again?"

J.C. gasped, startled by the succinct, low-pitched voice. She pressed her hand to her chest to soothe the rapid thump of her heart. "Sorry. I didn't mean to wake you."

The second eye opened. "You didn't. I wasn't sure where the whole hover over me and stare at my body thing was going, but—"

"You were watching me?" Her indignant surprise quickly petered out. Of course. Those eyes noticed everything.

He reached out and brushed his fingers across the back of her hand. "Everything okay?"

"I didn't want you to think I was completely rude." She pulled her hand away from the comforting touch and hugged her arms around her waist. "I do appreciate you fixing the window and hanging around. I mean, I could have done that." She thumbed over her shoulder at the plywood. "But I'm glad I didn't have to think about it right then. I was a little…" She tucked a wisp of hair behind each ear, hating how nervous she felt—knowing she wouldn't be nervous if she didn't have feelings for this man.

But nervous just wasn't her way. "Could I sit down? I need to talk."

"Ah, more talking." He seemed amused by her direct approach. But he pulled up the cover to invite her in beside him. "It'll be a pretty snug fit."

"I don't mind if you don't."

His answer was to turn onto his side and scoot to the far edge of the chaise to make room for her. J.C. sat down with her back to him and leaned into the pillows at the top of the chaise, resting her cheek on his left arm and pulling her legs up to match his position.

But it was pointless to try to hang on to the edge and keep a suggestion of polite distance between them. Ethan looped his arm around her waist and pulled her beneath the cover with him. He cradled her against his chest, her bottom snugging in the cup of his pelvis, their legs entwining. Denim and muscle brushed against soft, bare skin, and his palm rested with confident familiarity beneath the weight of her left breast.

His lips brushed a delicate kiss at her nape and she shivered. "You're cold."

She wouldn't be for long. Wrapped up in his arms and body, cocooned in the moonlit darkness of her apartment, J.C. released a sigh that mixed contentment with relief, and she settled into Ethan's heat.

Maybe talking wasn't really what she wanted, after all.

"You must think I'm a total flake. To say those things and then to come back and ask you to…"

His hand rubbed soothing circles against her rib cage. His knuckles gently lifted her breast with each caress. His low voice was a whisper against her neck. "I said I'd be there for you. You were scared."

Ethan's subtle teasing coaxed the beginning of a smile. "Yeah." She covered his hand with her own and urged it upward to include the full breast in his massage. "I was a little rattled by the whole window exploding, personal message thing."

"It's hard to filter thoughts and emotions when you feel threatened like that." He slipped his palm up over her T-shirt and squeezed, catching her nipple between cotton and muscle and tenderly tweaking it to life. "I imagine you were being very honest. I don't agree with you. And I wonder why you have such a low opinion of the military, but I can't hold an honest expression of emotion against you."

"It's not the military…" J.C. closed her eyes against the sweetly honeyed sensation that lazed its way down to the juncture between her legs and swelled those lips with an almost painful gathering of heat and pressure. "It's the separation. The opportunity to cheat." She thrust herself into his palm and moaned deep in her throat with pleasure. "It's knowing how easy it is to forget what you've left behind."

He tongued the bare skin at her nape, building up an easy rhythm between his hand and mouth. "Somebody must have hurt you something awful."

She felt his interest swelling against her bottom. She confirmed his words with a nod. "When my dad was in the Navy…" Tears burned in her eyes, but in the comfort of darkness and Ethan's hands, she wasn't afraid to let them fall. "…he was gone almost all the time. He cheated on my mom with several women. He—" She sniffed away the sting in her sinuses. "He had another family overseas. I think he knows those children better than he ever knew me."

Ethan's whole body hugged tightly around hers. A tear ran down and dripped onto his arm where it rested beneath her cheek. She swiped the salty track away from her own face, then kissed the spot where he'd absorbed that drop of her pain.

"I'm sorry, honey. I'm so sorry." His hand stilled its sensual massage on her breast. "Do you want me to stop?"

"No." She lifted his hand to her mouth and kissed each

fingertip. Then she placed his hand back on her breast, welcoming him, conceding to his earlier assertion. "I do need you for this. Please. I don't want to be alone. Not tonight."

"I'm right here with you, Jo. I'm here all night long."

Ethan didn't stop at her breast. He slid his hand down her body, and with a helpful kick of her feet, removed her panties and tossed them onto the floor. His knuckles brushed along her bottom as he unzipped his jeans and freed himself from his briefs.

Then his hand came back, under her shirt. He cupped the weight of one breast, then the other, in his palm. He pinched the nipples between his fingers and plucked and rolled them until she was squirming against the wall of his chest.

While his gentle, callused hands worked her body, his soft words drizzled against her ear and meandered into her heart. "Most of the men and women I serve with *can't* forget the families and homes they leave behind. We learn how to turn off our emotions so we can get the job done and focus on staying alive. Sometimes, thinking about home and what we're fighting for can tear a man up inside."

His lips lingered in an openmouthed kiss near the top of her spine. The stubble of his beard grazed the delicate skin and J.C.'s own mouth parted open in a stuttered breath, releasing a surge of heat. "If we give in to worrying about who's paying the bills, or we imagine who a lonely girlfriend might turn to for companionship, or we wonder who our children will adopt as a father figure in our place, we'll lose it. We count on the people at home to be just as strong as you expect us to be."

"But Mom and me, we were always there for my father. We always waited for him to—" He flattened his palm against her stomach and held her still as he rubbed his groin against her bottom. "Oh!"

She gasped for breath as the sweetness between her legs thickened and grew heavy. "Your father did you a disservice. You give the right man that kind of loyalty, and he'll sacrifice damn near everything to be faithful to you."

His hand sank lower, until his fingers tangled in the triangle of hair between her thighs. He cupped her swollen labia and squeezed the sensitive nub in between. Her insides were slowly turning into a liquid heat, as sweet and thick as sugar turning into warm candy. "Ethan."

He dipped a finger inside her slick folds, then two, as if testing the candy's consistency for himself. He pulled his fingers out and she felt her own sticky wetness against her thigh. The scent of her readiness filled the still air around them.

"Damn near anything," he breathed with an open kiss against her nape. "I wish..." His hard, hot penis nudged her between her cheeks and tried to slip between her legs. "I wish I'd been able to trust the woman I once..." He pulled her thigh up over his, and wedged her open. His stomach pushed against her back and rump as his diaphragm muscle jerked to control his breathing. "God, Jo. Do you have any idea what kind of faith I've put in you? Not just with Craddock, but with my past. With this." He nipped at her shoulder. "We have to trust each other, babe. We have to."

His hand skimmed back over her aching, weeping clit and dragged her back into his helpless thrust. "Ethan. Please."

J.C. arched her back, granting him the right angle to slip inside her. Slowly he stretched her, filled her, inch by tantalizing inch. He was long and thick and touched that one magic spot almost immediately. As her inner ring of muscles clutched convulsively around him, he retreated half an inch, creating a delicious friction, prolonging her pleasure.

Prolonging her torture. "Mmm..." she gasped. "Ethan?" She begged him to finish her.

"Not yet, baby, not yet." Her whole body was focused on the incredible pressure between her legs. Big man. Tight fit. His fingers teased her mercilessly. She writhed against him, skewered on the brink of ecstasy. "I want you to say it. Say you believe that I'm here for you. That you believe in me. That you need me for more than sex. Say it."

"Tonight. Yes, I believe in tonight."

"Not just tonight." He was sliding back in. "Forever. Say it—"

But it was too much for both of them. The candy pot boiled over.

Her release was as sweet and drawn out and complete as the buildup had been, leaving her utterly relaxed and drifting toward a secure, dreamless slumber wrapped tight in Ethan's arms.

When he pulled out, he made no effort to re-dress either one of them and break the skin-to-skin connection.

"You awake, Jo?" he whispered.

She shut her eyes without responding. She was too content, too physically and emotionally drained to risk spoiling the perfect moment.

J.C. was surprised she could feel this close to Ethan without feeling him inside her.

But she never said the words he wanted to hear.

She couldn't believe in forever.

12

PARKS AND MONUMENTS and crowded streets gave way to green, rolling farms and tree-studded hills as Ethan and J.C. drove out of the D.C. metro area into the Virginia countryside. A command performance at the Craddocks' picnic awaited them.

"I never got around to the reason I wanted to see you last night." Ethan glanced across the cab of his tan truck, lifted the rims of his sunglasses and winked at her. "Well, besides that."

She grinned. "I'm glad you came over for *that,* too."

J.C. went syrupy and warm inside, remembering those last few hours they'd spent together before grabbing a quick shower and changing for the Craddocks' picnic. They'd cuddled, slept, talked and made love on her purple chaise lounge.

Fast and furious or slow and thorough, every time she and Ethan were together amazed her. That karmic connection that had spoken to each other across the distance of that smoky bar intensified with each passing moment. Suddenly J.C. felt those promised two weeks together ticking past with the ominous finality of a time bomb.

Because somewhere along the way, if not at that very first kiss, she'd foolishly given him her heart.

And she couldn't quite seem to find a way to snatch it back unscathed.

If his job didn't tear them apart, her doubts and deception would. The healing that had taken place last night—each sharing past hurts and doubts, hopes and fears—was still a tenuous thing between them. Open wounds, though recently tended, could still leave nasty scars if the same kind of hurts were reinflicted. As a therapist, J.C. knew that emotional healing could be a long process with setbacks that had to be dealt with and nurtured over time. But with the built-in obsolescence of their relationship, time might be the one thing they didn't have.

"There was a detail about the charade you wanted to work out?" she questioned lightly. Talking would be easier than stewing in silence and obsessing over regrets.

"Yeah. Something you said Kyle Black had pointed out to you." He pushed himself up on the seat and reached inside the front pocket of his jeans. He pulled out a small, white box and dropped it into her lap. "Here. I want you to put this on."

On closer inspection, she identified the box's design and function. A ring box. An antique, judging by the hard plastic celluloid it was crafted from. A mixture of guilt and anticipation twisted J.C.'s stomach into a knot. But he'd relaxed behind the wheel, his masked eyes focused on the highway. "Ethan, what have you done?"

"Go ahead. Open it."

She squeezed her eyes shut and propped open the hinged lid.

"You like it?"

She slowly opened her eyes, knowing what to expect, never expecting it to be so simplistically elegant. The early-afternoon sunshine glinted off a crystal clear solitaire mounted on a plain white-gold band. "Please tell me this is a cubic zirconia."

"Nah, it's real."

A real diamond? Ho, boy. She shrugged, not knowing

what to say. Not knowing what he was asking. "It's beautiful."

"Good. Then you can wear it when we meet with the others today. I don't want anyone hassling either of us about why I'm too chintzy to get my girl a ring. I don't want to give anyone any reason to doubt how serious we are about each other."

"You really want that promotion, don't you?" J.C. closed the box and tried to laugh. But she ended up sounding more nervous than amused. Not a proposal. Not even a gift. Just a prop. "You shouldn't keep spending money on me like this."

He slowed the truck and exited onto a smaller county highway. "Didn't cost me a thing. It was my mother's ring."

The knot inside nearly strangled her.

"I can't take this." She pushed the box back across the seat. "It's a family heirloom. I'm sure it means a lot to your father. He wouldn't want you giving it away to a stranger."

He pushed it back her direction. "I hardly think that with everything we've gone through the past few days—everything we've done—we qualify as strangers."

J.C. adjusted her seat belt and turned to face him dead-on. She refused to touch the box. "You know what I mean. We're not really getting married. It'd be a sacrilege to wear it."

"Getting this out of the lock box yesterday morning isn't a decision I made lightly. Think of it as a gesture of trust, a tangible thank-you of how much I appreciate what you've done for me."

"I'm not going to take your mother's ring."

He hit the brake and pulled off onto the shoulder of the road. Once he set the truck in Park, he tossed his sunglasses on the dashboard and turned the full power of those battleship-gray eyes on her. "Until you and I are done, I want you to keep it."

Uttered as succinctly as a command, she bristled at the order. Then she heard what his words were saying. J.C. breathed a little easier, seizing on that one morsel of common sense. "So it's just a loan? Easy access for you? Easy on the budget?"

Easy on her conscience?

Instead of answering, he picked up the box and opened it, lifting the ring out between his finger and thumb. He held it up to the light and studied the facets reflecting a prism of colors. "Dad gave it to me after Mom died. He said it was her wish that I have it to give to a woman who was special to me."

With a deft maneuver, the ring disappeared inside his fist. He shifted in his seat to mirror her position. She looked up into those eyes and read the fervent vow stamped there. "You're special to me, J.C. It was like I'd been asleep to the stuff that really matters in life. I'd shut off my memories and desires. You reawakened me."

"It must be the counselor in me," she reasoned. Then she tried to joke. "I'll send you a bill."

But Ethan wasn't laughing. He slid his hand along the back of the seat to tease the fringe of her hair at her temple. "To be honest, I'd kind of given up on wanting to be with a woman again. My last relationship had all the bells and whistles a man could want. But I was too blind to see the substance wasn't there. Bethany—that was her name—lied to me at every turn. But you're bold. Honest." Oh, Lord. "For whatever reason possessed you, you're in this thing because you want to be with me. For two weeks, maybe a little longer, I don't know. But you're not using me to make a point with some other guy."

This Bethany person had used Ethan to make some other guy jealous? She hadn't appreciated how strong, how fiercely protective, how endearingly tender and downright sexy he was? *Missing the point!* J.C. screamed the warning inside her head. She switched off her emotions and listened to her conscience.

"Ethan, I'm not—"

"I'm not putting any pressure on you." He pulled his hand away and offered a reasonable argument. "The ring doesn't mean anything you don't want it to. Think of it as costume jewelry to make our engagement more convincing. Think of it as a thank-you for all the help you've given me. Whatever works for you. But I want you to wear it."

Right. Make the charade more convincing. After last night—from the protection to the listening to the loving—she supposed she owed him that much.

"Okay. But I'm giving it back," she promised with a resolute sigh.

"Not until you and I are done," he repeated. He reached for her left hand and slipped it on to her third finger. Then he kissed the ring and leaned over and kissed her. It was a quick, perfunctory kiss, sealing a business deal, nothing more.

As Ethan put on his sunglasses and drove the truck back onto the road, J.C. looked down into her lap and studied the ring gleaming on her left hand. It fit as if it had been made for her. More karma. But was it a good omen? Or a cruel, ironic trick?

J.C. ROLLED OVER on top of Ethan, laughing so hard she couldn't catch her breath. He was laughing, too, making her words a garbled croak of elation as she bounced up and down on his chest. "Oh, God, I haven't done that in years!"

"Semper Fi, J.C.," he whooped in victory, slapping her a high five. "Semper Fi."

God, he was dazzling decked out in boyish exuberance. It was a dimension of Ethan she hadn't seen before. It was another reason to love him. Another reason she should be more on guard than ever.

A round of applause and shouts from the wooden deck above them drowned out her labored breathing. As she sat up to take note of the cheering section, four more couples tumbled over the finish line behind them.

"Pay up, Black," Ethan taunted, rising up on one elbow, his hand raised in a victorious fist. "We smoked you!"

Kyle Black seemed less thrilled to have come in second and lost the bet. But he was grinning as he sat up to untie his leg from the tall, striking blonde he'd brought as his date to the Craddocks' barbecue picnic. "Considering you carried your partner halfway across the yard..."

"He did not!" J.C. protested. "I had to work twice as hard as he did, to keep up with his long legs. And believe me, when this guy falls on top of you, you'd better be tough or you'd better wear body armor." She had the grass stain and ache on her backside to prove it.

"Excuses, excuses." Kyle's blue eyes sparkled with emotion. But even though he was smiling, she couldn' quite make out the humor in his expression. "I demand a rematch on the croquet field."

"*I?*" The blonde, Darla something or other, showed more backbone than J.C. had originally given her credit for. She tugged on Kyle's sleeve. "Don't you mean *we?* As in 'we're a team'?"

"Of course, baby." He tunneled his fingers into Darla'.

shimmering locks and kissed her full on the mouth, earning a fair number of teasing catcalls from his fellow officers. Even Ethan razzed him for showing off. By the time they came up for air, Darla was blushing. But J.C. got the feeling that Kyle enjoyed being the center of attention more than he wanted to please his lady. "*We* will kick their butts in croquet," he vowed.

"After we eat," General Craddock announced, waving a pair of giant chef's tongs toward the grills he'd set up in the side yard. "The steaks, hamburgers and hot dogs are ready."

The announcement that the meats were prepared to go along with Millie Craddock's gourmet spread earned an even bigger round of cheers than the silliness of the three-legged race or Kyle and Darla's kiss had.

As the crowd of twenty or so guests thinned to go inside and fill their plates at the buffet, J.C. and Ethan went to work freeing themselves from the two ropes that bound them at ankle and knee. When their fingers brushed together, Ethan caught her hand and held it up, letting the late-afternoon sunlight play off the sparkle of her ring. Oh, gosh. If he said something mushy…

J.C. tensed, and hurried to speak first. "I'm having a lot of fun today. Thanks for inviting me."

Ethan released her and removed the last rope. "Thanks for helping *me* have fun. I thought I'd be more uptight with Craddock and the others watching over my shoulder, but I'm actually enjoying myself."

"Good." J.C. stood and brushed off the bits of dirt and grass clinging to her jeans. She reached out in a token offer to help him stand. "Sometimes I think you're too serious. It's okay to let loose and do something crazy every once in a while."

His eyes warmed with suggestion. "I seem to be doing

a lot of *crazy* things these past few days since I met you. I never knew I was such a stick-in-the-mud.''

J.C. shushed him, in case anyone was still close enough to eavesdrop. She gave his hand a reassuring squeeze. ''Walter will promote you because you're the best man for the job, not because you can follow rules better than the next guy.''

''That's right, boss.'' J.C. started at the sound of Kyle Black's voice behind her shoulder. Ethan tightened his grip and pulled her to his side, apparently as unsettled by his aide's skulking about as she was. ''You're the best man for that T.I. job, and I think you selected the best fiancée to help you get it.''

''You're out of line, Captain.'' Boyish exuberance was now a thing of the past. Authority oozed out of Ethan's every pore.

''No offense intended, sir. You know you've got my vote.'' He glanced down at their clasped hands. ''Nice ring, by the way.''

Kyle joined Darla on the deck and went inside, leaving J.C. and Ethan alone in the yard.

Ethan's heavy sigh said everything necessary about the festive mood being spoiled. ''Why do I get the feeling he's spying on me all the time?''

''You don't think he's helping one of the other candidates, do you?'' After the other couple had disappeared inside, J.C. decided it was all right to follow. ''Or maybe he's like a mole, checking on everyone for the review board.''

''He reports to me, not Craddock or anyone else.'' Ethan reached around her to open up the screen door, but paused with his hand on the frame. He whispered into her ear. ''He's got some agenda of his own that I just don't understand. I hate to ask this but...'' His hand slipped to her shoulder. "Maybe it's not me he's so curious about. You didn't know him before we met, did you?"

She turned and looked up at him, stunned by what he was suggesting. Was he considering Kyle as suspect in terrorizing her?

"No. I met him for the first time at the ball. You don't really think he's the one who shot out my window, do you?" She clutched at the front of his shirt, soothing her own anxiety by soothing him. "That had to be Guerro."

"He'd have access to the kind of weapon that was used last night."

"But for what reason? We're practically strangers. He doesn't *know* me."

"I'm not ruling out anything yet." He covered her hands with his own to still her nervous petting. Then he tucked a wisp of hair behind her ear and ushered her inside. "Let's just go enjoy the food. I'll keep an eye on Black."

BY THE TIME EVENING set in, J.C. knew she was never going to recapture the fun she and Ethan had had earlier in the day.

Everyone had gathered on lawn chairs or benches on the Craddocks' deck and patio to enjoy the warm spring night and sip coffee or beer. But somehow, the conversation about full stomachs and favorite recipes had morphed into a nightmarish discussion about Dr. Cyn's latest advice columns.

Since sinking through the floor wasn't an option, and the kitchen had been thoroughly cleaned—and she'd already visited the ladies' room twice—J.C. was forced to sit in the corner and study the liquid in her coffee mug, praying the men would either lose interest in the topic or she'd get struck by lightning.

No such luck.

"No, wait. Read this one." One of the other promotion candidates, Major Doug Sampson, grabbed one of the newspapers the guests had been passing around. He scrolled down the page, then snapped his fingers when he found the quote he wanted. "Listen.

"I don't want to give too glowing a recommendation because readers might interpret it as a guarantee of happiness. Men in uniform would unfairly become sexual targets for needy women. The pressure to deliver time and again could prove embarrassing, even debilitating to the man's sexual performance."

Doug laughed, amidst a chorus of "woo-hoo's" and "yeah, baby's." He rubbed the top of his bald head. "Can you see me as a *sexual target?* Bring it on, I say. Now there's a battle I want to fight."

Doug's wife, Kay, smacked him in the arm and snatched the paper away. "Down, Target Boy. I think Dr. Cyn makes a valid point. I hate to break it to you, Dougie dear, but you guys aren't larger than life gods. God love ya, but you're men. That means you have all the same quirks and hang-ups as any other guy."

Millie Craddock chimed in. "The uniform doesn't make egos go away." She looked across the circle at her gray-haired husband and winked. "I've been waiting thirty-five years for that to happen." She left a dramatic pause. "I'm still waiting."

The group took their cue from General Craddock's laughter and joined in. Clearly the only person in this assembly who could criticize the general and get away with it—and even earn an indulgent smile—was Millie. Walter blew his wife a kiss. "All right. I'll grant you she's on the money with some of her advice. But when she talks about soldiers and Marines getting it on with a different woman every time they go on furlough, I gotta wonder if I'm serving in the wrong branch of the service.''

''I haven't seen that kind of action since Kosovo,'' someone chimed in.

He was quickly razzed. ''You've never seen that kind of action anywhere.''

There was more laughter. J.C. hid her face behind a long drink of her tepid coffee. The hand at her knee startled her and she nearly spilled her drink. But she recovered quickly enough to see Ethan's somber eyes glance her way. He squeezed her leg, offering mute support for her discomfort, though she suspected he'd misjudged the cause. He probably thought talk of military infidelities had triggered painful memories of her father.

But the real pain came in seeing the error of her judgment. These couples interacted in a normal, healthy way, unlike anything she'd seen between her mother and father. Whatever misgivings she'd had about men like Earl Gardner and Juan Guerro were being challenged by men like Walter Craddock and Ethan McCormick. These were good men—more than Marines—loyal and devoted, anxious to make the most of their precious time together with their spouses and families and friends. As far as she could tell, these weren't men with hidden lives on foreign continents. These were men who loved their country and the people back home with all their heart.

She searched deep into the compassion in Ethan's honest eyes and felt the need to confess the truth, to apologize for the furor her opinions had caused. ''There's something I should tell you about Dr. Cyn.''

''You read her, too?'' He gave her knee a forgiving pat and leaned in to share a conspiratorial whisper. ''Don't worry. Apparently I'm the only square peg here tonight who doesn't follow her column regularly. All I know is that her articles got the general pretty hot under the collar yesterday.''

"No." She grabbed his arm and held him close when he shifted to pull away. "I'm a relationship therapist, remember? *I'm* Dr. Cyn."

Millie Craddock's sharp ears picked up on their side conversation. "I believe that's true of a lot of women, J.C. We're all Dr. Cyn."

Oh, no. Ethan would think she was talking symbolically now, not sharing the facts. But it did remind her that her confession, and the probable blowup that would result, was best saved for a private time and place.

She looked over at the older woman and forced a smile onto her face. "You think we're all advice columnists?"

Millie waved her joke aside. She was serious. "I'm older than all of you young ladies, and wasn't raised to talk about such things as sex and relationship problems. I had a couple of friends, when Walter and I were first married, whose husbands cheated on them while they were away on assignment. But they just sucked it up and accepted it because that's the way things were done then."

Mary Jo Gardner had been part of that same generation. She'd sucked it up for as long as she could. Maybe if she'd sought help instead of isolating herself and her daughter, maybe if she'd stood up to her husband sooner, neither she nor J.C. might have suffered as much.

The general tried to interrupt. "Honey, this is a party."

"No, Walter, I want to finish this." The mood of the group quieted, and everyone listened. J.C. especially wanted to know what positive twist Millie would spin on this topic. "I think Dr. Cyn has her finger on the pulse of the way women need to think today. She's not afraid to tackle tough issues. She's smart about taking care of herself and what she wants. She preaches healthy relationships, not one-night stands. Women could learn a lot from her. Men, too.''

J.C. was glad to hear someone supporting her alter ego for a change, but couldn't exactly bask in the praise.

"No offense, Millie," Walter argued. "But I don't agree with everything she's teaching. There have been times when I'd like to put my hands around the doctor's neck and strangle her. I have good men under my command. It's bad for business and troop morale when she advises women to guard their hearts and their chastity belts around us.''

A chorus of low-pitched "hear-hear's" chimed in with their support.

J.C. jumped in to argue, needing to defend herself, even though she couldn't admit it was herself who needed defending. "I think Dr. Cyn does a fair job of presenting the pros and cons of military relationships. Besides, isn't her freedom of speech one of the things that you fight for?''

"Of course. But it's a lot harder to defend someone who kicks you in the teeth than someone who pats you on the back." The general softened his disagreement by adding, "Now don't go all feminist on me. I'm expressing an opinion, same as her. I just wish her opinions weren't so widely read.''

As J.C. suspected was usually the case, Millie Craddock jumped in to have the last word. "You have to admit, Walter, that we both liked some of her suggestions on how to make the most of a couple's short time together. It might be worth recommending a few columns to your newlywed officers and recruits. She takes off the rose-colored glasses and gives a reality check about the stresses a new couple can face when a spouse is deployed for the first time.'' She stood, putting a blessed end to the double-edged conversation. The men in the circle rose politely as she crossed over to her husband and linked her arm through Walter's. ''You know, if you play your cards right, I might try a couple of her suggestions for a welcome home celebration on you tonight.''

The general blushed, but not as hotly as J.C. Oh, God. The Craddocks were using her ideas in bed? Probably not the selling point Ethan had been looking for when he'd asked for her help.

''Not in front of the men, dear,'' he scolded, dropping a kiss onto her cheek. ''But I'd definitely like to discuss that later.''

J.C. was beginning to see that the apparent cold shoulder Walter had given his wife at the ball had more to do with practicality than any emotional snub. With the sheer number of guests at the ball, they'd had to split up to work the room. But here, with the relaxed gathering in their own home, they could indulge themselves in each other's company.

''Now let's look into dessert,'' Walter ordered with a smile. ''Cherry pie and chocolate cake for anyone who's hungry again. I know I am.''

With the offer of sweets and calories to distract everyone, Dr. Cyn and the debate she'd triggered were quickly forgotten. But J.C.'s guilt wasn't. She needed to tell Ethan that she *was* the cause of all the controversy. And she needed to tell him sooner rather than later.

Because if Ethan ever did start reading her columns regularly, he was smart enough to figure out that her insecurities and life experiences resonated in every opinion Dr. Cyn had to offer. And Major Honesty—who'd been pissed off when she hadn't told him about the threats she'd received from Guerro—would be doubly angry to learn that her secret identity was the woman the general wanted to strangle with his bare hands.

If his connection to Dr. Cyn was revealed, however unintentional, it might cost him his promotion.

A lie was one thing. He might even be able to forgive her that.

But cost him his status in the Corps?

She didn't think *forgive* would be part of his vocabulary anymore.

"WAKE UP, SLEEPYHEAD."

"Hmm?" J.C. stirred in the cocoon of her warm, snug bed, responding more to the vibration beneath her cheek than to the softly spoken words.

"I need you to wake up, honey."

That was Ethan's voice. *He* was her bed of sorts. She'd fallen asleep on the ride home. The vibration tickled her cheek again, and her drowsy brain filled with all sorts of naughty ideas about where that vibrator might be better served. "Uh-uh," she refused, with a tease in her voice. "This is more fun."

"J.C." Ooh. That wasn't a fun voice.

With the darkness outside and the monotonous drone of the pavement beneath the tires, it hadn't taken much to coax her to stretch out across the seat and rest her head on Ethan's thigh. After her late night and full day, she'd zonked out. Now, as she opened her eyes, she could see the stars had disappeared above the lights of the city.

With a groggy sense of awareness she blinked away the erotic images and pushed herself up to a sitting position. "Are we there yet?"

"Just about." He grinned, reaching across the seat to brush her bangs out of her eyes. "My phone was ringing. I couldn't reach it with you there."

She eyed the pocket where he kept his cell. "Oh, so that's what that was. In my dreams it was something more…interesting."

He laughed and stuck his hand into his pocket. "There'll be time for interesting stuff later, I promise."

Ethan McCormick talking double entendre with her. Laughing. Promising sex. She liked that. "I'll hold you to that, Major."

He was grinning as he opened his phone and pressed the talk button. "McCormick."

The lights from the dash and the streets outside were bright enough to illuminate his expression. In a matter of seconds, his smile flatlined, his posture stiffened. And just like that, the intimate mood vanished and J.C. gripped the armrest, feeling suddenly as tense and concerned as the urgent message Ethan's body language transmitted.

"When?" She didn't know who was calling, but it sounded serious. She could hear snippets of an equally deep, efficient voice in the background. "How badly is he hurt?" Ethan's expression turned grim. J.C. was wide-awake now, wanting information, wanting to help. "I see. They're operating now?"

"Operating on who?" she whispered.

Ethan glanced her way, but his focus was still on the phone. "I'll be there as soon as I can, Dad. Did you call Caitlin? Good." They'd reached her building. J.C. waved to Norman, who opened the gate and let them into the parking lot. "If he wakes up, tell that jackass I love him." He swung into a parking space and braked to a jolting stop. Something his father said triggered a bit of a laugh. "Yeah. Love ya, Dad. Bye."

He disconnected the call and shut off the engine without even looking her way. J.C. was worried for him, but she wasn't sure whether he'd welcome her touch, or if he needed his space for a minute. The silence scared her. "Ethan?"

With a sudden move, he spun around and reached for her hand. He cradled it between both of his. "It's my brother, Travis. There was some kind of explosion on the training mission he was on this weekend. He's in the hospital down at Quantico. He's got burns and lacerations, and it shattered one of his legs."

"Oh, Ethan." His hand squeezed around hers and she held on tight. "Is he going to be all right?"

"Dad says he's stabilized. They're operating on him now, but they don't know if they can save his leg." He rubbed and plucked at her hand as if inspecting the details of every minute line and curve. J.C. let him, knowing it was an outlet for his pent-up fears and anger. "He loves his special forces assignment. If he winds up crippled, he'll be discharged or put behind a desk. Dad said Travis told the surgeon to let him die on the table if he couldn't save the leg."

Tears stung J.C.'s eyes at the anguish she heard in Ethan's voice, at the sense of doom Travis must be feeling. She reached up and cradled Ethan's cheek, absorbing some of his pain, offering compassion. J.C. pushed his hand away and reached behind her to unlock the door. "Then he needs his big brother there to talk some sense into him. He's hurt right now. Maybe he doesn't even realize it, but he's afraid because he doesn't know what's going to happen to him. You have to go. Right now. You need to be there for your family."

Ethan nodded, reaching for his door. "I'll walk you up."

"No, you won't. If he's in surgery now, you need to hit the road. I think I can find my way upstairs by myself from here."

He grabbed her arm and stopped her from climbing out the door. His tone was as firm as his grip. "I will see you to your door, check your apartment and make sure everything's locked up tight before I leave you here alone. You may have forgotten about those threats you received, but I haven't."

"I assure you, I haven't forgotten, either. But don't worry. I promise I'll be careful."

"If you want me to leave with a clear conscience..."

"All right, then." She could see she wasn't going to win this argument, so she conceded. "But let's hurry."

With his guiding hand at the small of her back each step of the way, Ethan walked her up the stairs. Then he warned her to stay put while he inspected every corner of her apartment, from testing the security of the boarded up window to looking under her bed and behind the shower curtain. He verified that her answering machine was empty, and laid a business card with his cell and office numbers right beside the phone.

"Time's wasting," she urged him as he propped his hands on his hips and surveyed the main room again.

Though his body was primed for action, his eyes were dark with regret. "I was looking forward to spending the night."

"Me, too." She walked over to him, braced her hands on his chest and rose up on tiptoe to kiss him. His head bobbed after hers, wanting to linger when she quickly pulled away. She slipped her hands down to fold around his, and led him toward the door. "Stop by when you get back. Take all the time you need for your family, of course."

He dipped his mouth and claimed her lips again. "You'll be my first stop, I promise. And call me if something happens. If you get another message, anything. All right?''

''I'll be fine. Now go.''

He looked hard into her eyes, demanding guarantees. ''I mean it, Jo. I'm not bailing on you. On us. If you need something, you call.''

She smoothed the front of his shirt, let her palm rest against the powerful beat of his heart. ''Your brother's your priority right now. I can take care of myself.''

He tipped his face to the ceiling and muttered a curse. He faced her again, the tension in him radiating with such force that she snatched her hand away. ''I wish you'd stop saying that. It makes it sound as if you want to be alone.''

''I just want to reassure you so you don't worry about me. I'll keep all my doors locked.'' An inevitable tension of another kind sparked between them, but J.C. chose to ignore it. ''Call me when you find out about your brother's status.''

''I will.'' Ethan stroked her cheek, brushed his fingers across her lips, feeling the same yin and yang of duty and desire calling them in different directions. ''And I'll be back. I want you to believe that.''

She pulled his tantalizing fingers away before she gave in to the answering heat spiraling through her and did something totally foolish and poorly timed. ''Go. Hopefully Travis is out of surgery now and cursing the fact you're not there to see him.''

''Yeah.''

And then his arms were around her, his fingers tangled in her hair. Her back was against the door and her hips were crushed beneath his. Ethan's mouth covered hers in a hungry, helpless, desperate kiss that felt like a bigger goodbye than it should have. J.C. held on and poured out her love, her compassion. Her regret.

Their lips smacked when he abruptly ended the kiss. He stepped back, holding up his hands as if warding off temptation itself. "I have to go."

"I know." J.C. held on to the doorknob, wondering if her weak knees and fearful heart could sustain her. "Drive safely. Give your family my best. Don't worry about me."

"I'm coming back," he reiterated, opening the door and backing out into the hallway. He waited on the other side until she'd fastened all three locks. "I'm coming back."

And then he was gone.

13

FEELING THE SAME vague sense of loss she used to feel whenever her father left for his next Naval appointment, J.C. returned to work the next day and buried herself in the stack of e-mails waiting for her. The readers who'd gone to her Web site loved her or hated her, but there was certainly no shortage of questions and opinions for Dr. Cyn to address.

That had kept her busy all morning. But as evening approached, she was running out of work to keep her mind off Ethan.

With no word yet from him regarding his brother's injuries, she worried that the damage was more severe than his father had reported. The surgery had failed or, God forbid, Travis had died. Alive or dead, healthy or crippled, there would be a lot to deal with. And for a man like Ethan, who liked to maintain control, it would be a hellish vigil to keep. She wanted to call him, just to see that he was okay.

But his mother's diamond ring, winking in the fluorescent office lights as she typed the final paragraphs of her next column, sat like a heavy burden on her finger. It reminded her that their relationship was all about sex and masquerades. It was about playing a wife-to-be and a heroic protector. It was about impressing the brass and scaring away the shadowy menace.

It wasn't about love. It wasn't real.

It was for two weeks, not forever.

Still, the impracticality of her feelings shaded the tone of her column.

There's a certain heartache of separation built into a military romance. That's why it's not for the faint of heart.

A man in uniform has to fight a lot of different battles. Not just enemy gunfire. Not just dealing with niggling comments about the lack of hair on his handsome head.

There's the physical and mental exertion of training. The war within himself to juggle the vastly different roles he faces—warrior, family man, lover. He has to handle the mental game of sending men into danger, the emotional challenge of healing his mind and body from injury, the occasional doubts of wondering if he's needed at home as much as he is on the front line.

The soldier's significant other has to miss him, support him, love him, seduce him, get tough with him. She has to give him a reason to come home every time, give him a reason to fight every day, warn him to watch his back without preaching to him as if he's a child.

Can you handle that?

If the answer is yes, then I might be losing my bet. There's a smorgasbord of men out there who can be just as hot out of uniform as they are fully dressed.

If the answer is no, then steer clear of anything in epaulets or army boots. You'll find more heartbreak than happiness.

In my next—and last—column on romancing your favorite branch of the service, I'll give you my final assessment on the personal research I've gathered.

But until then, keep it safe and casual, ladies. Don't invest your feelings in a soldier boy—unless you're prepared to enlist yourself—body, heart, mind and soul.

"That's depressing. I don't know whether to salute or cry."

J.C. jumped in her chair at the flame-haired woman peeking over her shoulder. "Jeez, Lee!" Pressing a hand over her thumping heart, J.C. made a conscious effort to breathe normally again. How long had her editor been lurking inside her cubicle? "You startled the hell out of me."

Lee hiked up the hem of her leopard-print caftan and perched on the corner of J.C.'s desk. "So. What did he do to you?"

J.C. executed the save command on her laptop and feigned innocence. "What did who do to me?"

"Your *research project* who's so good in the sack." J.C.'s fake engagement ring paled in comparison to Lee's gaudy display of gold and gems as she pointed out J.C.'s left hand. "And who I'm guessing gave you this trinket as some kind of bribe or consolation prize?"

For a flake with gray roots, Lee Whiteley could be annoyingly perceptive. J.C. rolled her chair away from the desk and looked up at the concern her boss's eyes. "A, it's not a trinket. This was his mother's engagement ring so its value is priceless." She hastily put up her hands to ward off the instant glee. "And, no, we're not engaged. It's complicated."

"Must be." Lee was clearly intrigued and showed no signs of moving on.

"Major McCormick didn't do anything to me. I'm the one who's hurting him."

"So he gave you an engagement ring that's not an engagement ring because you hurt him?" She tutted her tongue against her teeth. "My God, the rumors are true. Men don't make any sense."

"Lee."

"I'm sorry." She tapped the edge of J.C.'s laptop. "From what I just read, that major's gotten into more than your pants. Am I going to have to pay you fifty bucks? Did this guy break your heart?"

J.C. reluctantly smiled at the maternal tone in Lee's voice. "Ethan's a good guy. Don't blame him. I think I'm the one who's screwed things up between us."

Lee crossed her arms, settling in for an explanation. "The place has cleared out for the day. You want to tell me about it here or over Cosmopolitans at Tiki's?"

"I'd better avoid any bars." J.C. sighed. "I need to think this through."

"You've got it bad for your soldier boy, don't you?"

"He's a Marine, not a soldier."

"Pardon me." J.C. weathered Lee's teasing without a smile.

Confession *was* good for the soul. And if Ethan wouldn't listen… "He doesn't know I'm Dr. Cyn. And apparently, Dr. Cyn has stirred up enough controversy with his superior officers that it could cause him trouble with his job. He doesn't deal well with deception and the Corps means everything to him."

"I'll bet not everything." Despite her flashy exterior, Lee had a wise, kind soul inside. "You know, there's an old-fashioned trick for dealing with deception in a relationship. I'm surprised you didn't study it in college."

"What's that?"

"Tell him the truth."

J.C. pushed out of her chair and circled the desk. "I tried, Lee. He blew it off. I think the idea of him seeing someone who could wreck his whole career was too ludicrous to even consider being true."

"Try again. Make him believe."

"How?"

"You're the one who has a way with words. I'll leave that up to you."

With her thumb, J.C. toyed with the engagement ring. "He's out of town right now with a family emergency. Calling him up to tell him I lied and I'm sorry sounds trivial and selfish." She fisted her hand and held the ring down at her side, out of sight. "Maybe I should just let it go and stick with our original two-week plan. Let the affair run its course. He can walk away none the wiser, and Dr. Cyn never has to hurt him or his career."

"How fair is that to either one of you?"

"Lee—"

"Honey, if he makes you blush the way you did the other morning, and makes you hurt the way you do tonight—then he might be the one." Lee was on her feet, wagging her finger at J.C. "Now I'm all for a good romp in the hay and walking away with both parties satisfied. But if you've found someone you want to romp with the rest of your life, I'd say go for it."

In her own colorful way, Lee had touched on everything J.C. was feeling—everything she was fearing could be lost. "But what if I'm not what he wants for the rest of his life?"

"Do I really have to say this?" Lee jingled as she hugged an arm around J.C.'s shoulders. "This is a relationship, right? What would Dr. Cyn advise you to do?"

J.C. READ THROUGH her final column one last time, adjusted a couple of typos, then took a deep breath and forwarded it to Lee's computer.

Passing up Lee's offer to buy her dinner and talk some more, J.C. had been motivated to sit down and write. Baring her soul and risking her heart seemed a fair enough trade-off, considering everything Ethan had been asked to endure on behalf of his country. Surviving rebel attacks. Missing the end of his mother's life. Learning to dance.

By the time the column came out, she would have had time to sit down with Ethan and talk this out. She could show him the columns on her laptop, the piles of phone messages and e-mails addressed to Dr. Cyn. She would tell him her fifty-dollar bet was a mistake, and she would gladly pay up. She would tell him that, luckily for her, her research project had turned into something she thought was very special. She would tell him that he had proven her wrong about getting involved with a military man.

Would he please forgive her? Judge her as J. C. Gardner, and not Dr. Cyn? And if the deception was too much to forgive, if he didn't think she was the right kind of woman for the man he needed to be, then…

She squeezed her eyes shut and sank back into the chair. "Oh, God, Ethan, where are you?"

Her voice echoed in the empty suite of offices. She was weary. She was lonesome. And she was desperately afraid he'd leave her for good the way her father had.

"No," she argued with herself, closing her laptop and straightening her notes. "He said he was coming back. He'll be back."

The next time she saw Ethan, she would tell him everything.

When he called, she would tell him that they needed to talk. He would probably beg to be shot instead. But maybe if she promised him his whole sweet, square—completely hot—totally naked and actually in the bed fantasy, he would be willing to listen to her explanation and apology.

When he called.

J.C. stared at the cell phone she'd left sitting on her desk for easy access.

Ethan still hadn't called.

The achy growl in her stomach reminded her it was well past dinnertime and she'd barely touched her lunch. She paper-clipped her Web site printouts and carried the stack over to her file cabinet to put them away.

With his brother in the hospital, worried about his future, Ethan was probably busy being strong for his family. Or there was some insurance snafu that his practical mind was taking care of. Or he'd lost her number. Any of those or a dozen other excuses could explain why he hadn't yet called.

It couldn't be "out of sight, out of mind"—that he'd forgotten his promise to her. That he'd forgotten her.

She slammed the file drawer shut, trying to clear the thought from her head. Her father had worked that way, not Ethan. But once the idea had been planted, all those old hurts dug their sharp little claws into the back of her mind and refused to let go. J.C. could only mute them by busying her hands with packing up her laptop and her bag, and digging out her keys to walk down to the parking garage.

When her cell phone chirped, she jumped in her shoes. But her startled response quickly gave way to a silly joy that started in her smile and cascaded all the way down her body until it curled her toes.

The Out Of Area message on the dial only broadened her smile. She pressed the talk button. "Ethan?"

Dead silence.

A blip of unease sobered her giddy feeling of relief.

Something was terribly wrong. "Ethan…" How did she say this delicately? "Is Travis going to be all right?"

"Ethan? Travis?" A garbled, unfamiliar voice turned her blood to ice. "It's a wonder you can get any man to call you, Dr. Cyn, the way you trash us in your column."

J.C. shut the phone and dropped it onto her desk. She

shook her fingers loose as if she'd been zapped with an electric shock.

Her heart raced in her chest. Her breath came in stuttered gasps. She turned a jerky circle, scanning each darkened desk and corridor for any sign of a friend.

I know who you are.

He had her card. He knew where she lived, knew where she worked, knew her real name. Did he know she was by herself right now?

The phone chirped again and she wondered why the hell she hadn't turned the thing off. She watched it on her desk. Two rings. Three. Four.

What if it was Ethan calling?

Yes. Ethan.

Adrenaline poured through her body, sparking hope, giving strength.

She picked up the phone and answered. "Hello?"

"That wasn't very nice."

Fear crept in, creating imaginary movement in the shadows around her, sharpening her hearing to detect every noise—from the whirring of the water fountain to the distant sounds of traffic outside to her own heartbeat pounding in her ears.

But she fought to hold on to rational thought. She tried desperately to connect the voice to her memory of Juan Guerro's threats. The pitch seemed lower, but the words were too muffled to be sure.

"Who is this?" she asked, her voice more of a tremor than a demand. "I didn't get you into trouble, you know. You did that yourself. What are you trying to accomplish? Why are you doing this to me?"

"Shut up, bitch! I'm talking."

J.C. retreated a step, as if he'd shouted the order in her face. "I'm sorry."

''That's better. Now I'm going to talk, and you're going to listen. And if you hang up again, we'll have this conversation in person.''

She thought she heard a metallic click in the background on the phone. Was it the cocking of a gun? The unlatching of a door lock? Whatever it might have been, it was ominous enough to get J.C. to toss her bag over her shoulder and head out of her cubicle to the bank of light switches behind Ben Grant's desk. She flipped on every switch until the entire floor was flooded with light. Thankfully she was alone.

Any sense of security was fleeting. She was *alone*.

''I'm one of those military heroes you've been bad-mouthing. I'm a lean, mean fighting machine, and women love me.''

Not every woman. ''And?''

''I want you to print a retraction.'' Even muffled by the static on the phone, she could hear the suggestive catch in his voice. ''I want you to say I know how to please a woman. Any woman. Every woman. We train harder, we *are* harder—''

''I get the picture.'' She squelched the urge to gag at the crude topic of conversation. ''You want me to write something about how good you are in bed.''

''I want every woman who reads your column to look at me and say she wants me. I don't want to read any more of your crappy advice about avoiding me.''

''It's not personal—''

''The hell it isn't! You write it right, Doc, or I'm going to tell that boyfriend of yours who he's really screwin'. I'll tell the world who you are. Then every sap on the street will stop you and tell you his pathetic story about how he can't get it up and how you have to fix it for him. Won't that be fun?'' J.C. cringed at the image of total strangers walking up to her on a street corner or stopping her at restaurants or knocking on her front door to share every lurid, personal detail about their sex lives. "I want to see it in tomorrow morning's paper. Got that?"

This went from creepy bad to impossibly worse. "I have columns coming out all week. Three of them have already gone to press. I can't stop them."

Logistics didn't matter to this guy. Saving his studly reputation by shutting up Dr. Cyn did.

"One more bad word about me and I'll find a way to stop *you*."

For a stunned second, she couldn't believe he'd hung up on her. By the time the silence registered, she was dumping her bag out on Ben's desk and rifling through all the junk she carried to find her card wallet. She flipped through the pages. Ethan's number… There! She dialed her cell and waited.

Terror, shock and anger had boiled down to the desperate need to hear Ethan's voice. To feel his protection. To know his steady strength was a contagious thing that gave her courage.

If he was there for her.

"Please answer," she prayed. She hugged her arms tightly around herself and paced, two short steps to the left, three back to the right. His phone kept ringing. "Ethan, where are you?"

He wasn't there.

Click. "Ethan?"

Panic puffed out in an audible breath as his voice-mail message kicked in.

"It's J.C. I need you. He called me. Just now. At work. I mean, I'm by myself at the office and he got my cell number and he…" No, no. Too much. Too hysterical. She swallowed hard and tried to control the rambling outpouring of fear. "He said if I didn't…he would tell you…I can't stop the…"

The hope drained out of her on a long, waning sigh.

She took stock of her surroundings and grabbed hold of some common sense. Ethan was miles away. What could he do to help, even if he did hear her plea?

Her voice was clipped, almost businesslike now as she steeled herself to fight her own battle. "I'm sorry. Forget all that. I know you must be needed there. I hope Travis is okay. I'm sure you're busy. Tired. Worried. I've been thinking about you all day. I didn't mean to freak out. It's just late. I'm going home to get some sleep. Don't worry. I can take care of myself."

She severed the connection, then turned off the phone completely. She didn't want to deal with any other calls right now. Not from her stalker. Not from Ethan. She couldn't handle the drama.

Instead she stuffed everything back into her bag. She probably ought to take her own advice and go get some sleep. Norman would be on duty. He could walk her up to her apartment and check for intruders before she locked herself in.

She picked up the armed forces recruitment brochures from Ben's desk. There was no need to stuff these back into her bag. She was done gathering information for her articles. Besides, the man pictured on the cover, with his dark blue dress coat and nickel-plated sword, reminded her of another tall, broad, well-postured Marine whom she didn't want to be missing any more than she had to tonight.

With a quick glance around the offices, she hurried back to her file cabinet and opened the middle drawer. She quickly thumbed through the folders, "M. Military."

She pulled out the folder to drop the brochures inside

and paused. J.C. peeked over her shoulder as the creeping sense of being watched kicked in again. She looked back at the open folder.

The same brochures were already inside.

She normally asked Ben to assist with her research, but why was he duplicating her efforts? Or had her columns triggered an interest in signing up for the military? With Ben's interest in computers and other sorts of electronic gadgets, there was bound to be some sort of program that would pay him to get the education he wanted in exchange for serving a few years in the service.

Maybe it was just a freaky coincidence. Chunky Ben with the thick glasses and sweet demeanor certainly didn't seem the military type.

She shook her head, wondering why she was debating this at all.

"Go home, J.C.," she advised herself. "Just go home."

She tossed the brochures back on to Ben's desk, grabbed her bag and headed for the elevator.

After that phone call, anything and everything was going to look suspicious to her.

ETHAN MARKED OFF the entire length of the hospital corridor as he listened to J.C.'s message a second time. Her fear, her pigheaded strength—her lack of faith in him—all came through loud and clear in her voice.

He spun a neat 180 and paced back toward Travis's private room.

I need you.

He needed her, too. He needed her to be safe. *I've been thinking about you all day.* He needed to hear those words again. He needed her to believe he was there for her, even though they were miles apart.

But, damn, she was a hard sell. The last line of her message said it all.

"No, you cannot take care of this yourself. Stop saying that!" He quickly dialed her number. "Answer the damn phone!"

Of course. He couldn't blame her for turning off her cell if that bastard had called her and made some kind of threat. And what office was she talking about? Where did she meet with and advise her clients? She'd never said.

Ultimately he had to settle for the same frustrating means of communication she had. He left a message. "I'll be there as soon as I can, honey. Keep your doors locked and don't let yourself be alone with anyone, anywhere. Especially after dark. Hell, don't go out after dark. Double hell. I'll be there before dark. I will be there."

"Is there a problem, son?"

Retired Brigadier General Hal McCormick met Ethan in the doorway to Travis's room. He still wore his blond hair as short as the day he'd received his commission, though there was considerably more gray on top now.

Ethan looked into his father's weary eyes. "No, sir."

"Then why are you cussing out your phone?"

"I'm not." He made sure it was turned on and slipped it into his pocket. "I was trying to reach J.C. But there's no answer."

"And J.C. would be…?"

"She's a girl. Josephine Gardner." Ethan let the door close behind him and dropped the volume of his voice so as not to disturb the conversation Travis was having with their younger sister, Caitlin. "A woman I've been seeing. She's, um—"

Travis might never be too far out of it to offer up a smart remark. "She's that hot chick he met in the bar and gave Mom's ring to."

"What?" Hal was justifiably shocked by the news. "Your mother's ring?"

Ethan strode to the foot of the bed and glared at his brother. Travis wore bandages along his jaw, on both arms, his torso and his right leg. His left leg was encased in a cast, sewn together with more than a dozen steel pins, and elevated with a complex set of cords and pulleys.

But the son of a gun was smiling. So whether it was painkillers or positive attitude talking, he deserved a little ribbing for opening his trap. "Excuse me, but the doctor said you're supposed to take it easy, not poke your nose into my business."

"Hey, my leg's busted up, not my hearing. You shouldn't have confessed how you feel about her when I was in the recovery room if you didn't want me to hear."

"You were still under the effects of the anesthesia. I was talking to pass the time."

"It was entertaining to hear you trying to make sense of something that makes no sense."

Ignoring the argument, Hal joined them, his tension visibly relieved. "So you're serious about this girl."

"Ethan, that's wonderful." Caitlin unfolded her long legs from the seat beside the bed and gave her oldest brother a hug. "It's about time you decided to have a personal life."

Travis grinned from ear to ear. Apparently focusing on someone else's problem was good therapy for him. "Oh, he's serious enough. Been spending all his free time with her from what I hear. He just doesn't want to rush things because, despite her impulsiveness, J.C. isn't the type of woman who can be rushed. Seems she has some pretty stubborn opinions."

Now Caitlin was getting into it. She winked at Ethan. "Gee. Who does that sound like?"

Ethan would have laid Travis out if he wasn't already stuck in a bed. "Did you get *any* sleep last night?"

Travis shrugged, then winced in pain. "What are you still doing here, big brother? She needs you."

I need you. Ethan felt a siren call to get back to J.C. as quickly as he could. Not just to put an end to those messages meant to intimidate her. But to love her. To make love to her. To prove to her once and for all that the reason they were so good in bed together was because… they were good together.

But he had a responsibility to his family, too. "I thought I was looking out for you."

"I've got the finest doctors in the country looking out for me now. And if they can't cut it, these two will keep me in line." Travis's expression got surprisingly serious. "I panicked when they first brought me in. I was hurtin' so bad I couldn't see beyond the moment. I needed that ass-whippin' you promised me to get my head on straight."

Travis hadn't listened to sympathetic pleas, but like a true Marine, he'd responded to Ethan's stern reminder about duty to his country, his family and himself. His positive attitude could make the difference in his recovery, according to the surgeons who'd pieced him back together.

"You'd have come around soon enough," Ethan assured him.

His brother waved aside the support. "I'm going to do more than walk again, Ethan," he vowed. "I'm going to make it back to special forces. You'll see."

Ethan's heart pounded a little harder in his chest at Travis's determined attitude. His bold confidence reminded Ethan of J.C. His feet shifted, as antsy as the rest of him to get back to her before she got the idea she really could get through life without him.

Some of that emotion must have gotten out and shone on his face. Travis grinned. "What are you still doing here? Go."

Fine. He was going already. "You sure you'll be okay?"

"Nothing a few months of physical therapy won't cure. Don't worry, bro. I'll be back in action."

Ethan hugged his way around Caitlin to stand by Travis's side. "Don't push it too hard too soon. I like having you around. Even if you are a pain in the butt." They shook hands. Even with an IV stuck in it, Travis's grip was as firm as he remembered. "Take care." The handshake became a hug.

Then Travis pushed him away. "You know I will. Now go on, get out of here. Dismissed."

"I outrank you. You can't dismiss me."

Hal McCormick wisely knew when to step in and stop his sons' bickering. "I can. Dismissed, Marine. We'll hold down the fort without you."

"Yes, sir." The two men hugged. "Love you, Dad."

"Love you, son."

After one more round of goodbyes and assurances that Travis was in the clear for now, Ethan hurried out the door toward the parking lot.

He was only vaguely aware of his father dashing out the door and calling down the hall after him. "Say, does this girl of yours like to fish? Your mother liked to fish."

"Dad!" He heard Caitlin dragging Hal back into the room. "You can't stop him now."

No one could.

Ethan McCormick was a man on a mission.

QUANTICO, VIRGINIA, was a major training base for the United States Marine Corps, the FBI and other security agencies. With the huge number of recruits, training classes and working units to negotiate, it had taken him a lot longer than he'd anticipated to secure clearance and track down the man he was looking for.

Corporal Juan Guerro.

Ethan hadn't taken time to put on his uniform or even shave. But there was no mistaking the rank and authority in his posture when the M.P. brought Guerro into the brig's interrogation room.

The black-haired man sported a pair of handcuffs, a split lip and a deer-in-the-headlights stare when he saw who was waiting for him. He charged the door as the M.P. closed it behind him. "Hey, you can't leave me in here with this guy!"

Ethan fully intended to take the cocky son of a bitch down a notch before he was through with him. Step one was making him understand he was a weasly coward.

"Sit down, Corporal," he ordered.

With Ethan towering over him in both size and attitude, Guerro decided it was smarter to comply. "Yes, sir."

He nodded at Guerro's lip. "I see somebody tried to bully you the same way you bullied my fiancée."

"I was just trying to reason with her, sir." Beads of sweat dotted his forehead as Ethan circled behind him. "I thought you were going to bust me. But she could make you see that that kiss was all just a misunderstanding."

Ethan snapped down beside Guerro's ear. "You left bruises on her arm. I don't understand that at all."

"I did? I'm sorry." He was squirming now. "I didn't mean to. I'm…sorry."

Straightening, Ethan continued slowly pacing around the table. He intended to stop J.C.'s troubles right here.

"You will be. I've reported you to D.C.P.D. as well as the military police. Assault. Making terroristic threats. Willful destruction of property. Illegal possession and discharge of a firearm within the city limits—"

"Whoa, whoa, whoa. What are you talking about?" Guerro danced in his chair, his bound wrists pleading for mercy. "I didn't do half that stuff."

Ethan grabbed the opposite chair and flung it aside. Guerro jumped. Good. "Do you deny threatening J. C. Gardner so I wouldn't make any trouble for you?"

"No, sir."

"You haven't seen trouble yet, believe me."

"But I didn't shoot anybody."

"You fired a flippin' rock through the window of her apartment. I was there."

"No."

Ethan shoved the table out of the way. "You called her last night and threatened her."

Guerro lurched to his feet, knocked over his chair, backed into the wall. "No, sir. I didn't. I swear." Ethan kept coming. "*Madre Dios,* I didn't call anybody. I got arrested for drunk and disorderly two nights ago. I haven't been anywhere but my cell since then."

Ethan halted. He could smell Guerro's fear. The man would be a fool to lie to his face. "You didn't make any calls from the brig last night?"

"No, sir. You can check with the guard. I did stop your fiancée that morning by the river. But that was the last time I talked to her. Hell, I've been locked up pretty much since I got back to the base."

"But if you didn't…" Ethan barely voiced the thought out loud. "Son of a bitch."

"Sir?"

But Ethan was already moving. He pounded on the

door, alerting the officer outside before barging through. Guerro's story checked out. His damn story checked out!

Ethan cleared the gates and ran to his truck. He intended to make the drive into D.C. in`record time. He intended to put his arms around J.C. and hold her as close as she'd let him.

Because if Guerro wasn't stalking J.C., that meant someone else was. Someone she'd never even suspect.

Someone who was probably a lot closer to home.

"NORMAN?"

J.C. sat in her Camaro outside the gate to her apartment parking lot, wondering where the trusty watchdog who guarded her building so diligently had disappeared to. She'd honked her horn once, but didn't want to raise too big a ruckus at this late hour.

She could park on the street easily enough and walk in. But what was the point of having a secure building if she didn't take advantage of it? Even if Norman was taking a break, he'd still be in the guardhouse. And if he'd gone inside to use the facilities, well, he wouldn't be gone from his post this long.

Unless something was wrong.

J.C. killed the engine but left her headlights on to check outside. She'd worn a short-sleeved blouse with her slacks. But despite the sunny day, night had brought with it heavy cloud cover and ozone-scented air that threatened rain. The chilly breeze blowing off the river brushed across her bare arms and raised goose bumps.

She rubbed at her chilled skin, wishing it wasn't so late, wishing it wasn't so damp, wishing she wasn't so alone.

Tonight she'd let Lee take her out after work, just to have the company. Ethan hadn't called; he hadn't come to see her. She'd jumped through hoops today, trying to stop the presses to delete or alter her columns. But she'd only been able to pull one. No doubt this morning's exposé about how big a turnoff giving orders in the bedroom could be was less flattering than her caller wanted to see. But she'd run out of reasons to keep Lee up past her bedtime and had finally driven home.

To an abandoned guardhouse and shadowy parking lot.

She knocked on the door before peeking inside. "Norman?"

Empty. Her breathing deepened in counterpoint to her quickening pulse. What if he'd taken ill or had a heart attack? What if he'd been mugged on his rounds? Was he lying unconscious between a couple of parked cars?

J.C. went back to retrieve her phone and a flashlight. Then she shimmied under the locked gate and began her search. She checked the utility bathroom first. Empty and dark. Norman's prolonged absence was reason enough to call the super. Maybe even the police.

Flipping open her phone, she finally turned it on. Her voice mail was completely filled with Out of Area messages. She didn't want to hear that voice again. Not here in the shadows. Not anywhere.

But what if one of them was Ethan?

Taking a chance, seizing a tiny shred of hope, she pushed the button to let them play while she searched the lot with her flashlight, keeping well to the center of each row.

"You stupid bitch. I warned you—"

She deleted the message.

"I tried to do this nice, but—"

She hit delete.

"I know where you live. You can't—"

Delete.

"Where the hell are you, Norman?" She'd reached the

far side of the lot, without so much as a candy wrapper to leave a trail to his whereabouts.

She'd go back to her car. Park it on the street. Go inside and wake the super.

"Dammit, J.C., pick up!" She stopped and pressed her knuckles to her mouth, squelching the ridiculous urge to laugh with joy or cry out with relief at the sound of Ethan's stern voice. Stern. She frowned. More like angry. Desperate. And what was the whooshing sound of wind in the background of the recording? *"Do not go out alone. Lock yourself in your car or your apartment or your office—wherever the hell that is. I'm coming for you. If anything happens before I get there, call the police. I did some investigating on my own. I talked with Guerro. He's not the man who called you."*

She'd had twenty messages on her phone. Someone had called.

J.C. stumbled as adrenaline jerked through her body. Thunder rumbled in the distant sky, an ominous portent that shaded the warning in Ethan's voice. She hurried toward her car, looking for something more in the shadows than her old pal Norm.

"It's nine o'clock. I'll be at your apartment in an hour, tops. Be careful, Jo. And don't be scared, honey. I'm coming."

The first drop of rain hit J.C.'s skin and she screamed as if someone had grabbed her.

Ethan's next message had been recorded a few minutes later. It repeated the warning. *"I'm in the city now, hon. I'm coming."*

Forget the phone. She was running now. Lightning split open the sky and the rain poured down. She turned the corner around the last car and ran for the gate. Straight into the headlights, sloshing in puddles. Goose bumps tightened her skin beneath a tense assault of lightning-charged air; cold, wet cotton and fear.

She jammed her phone into one pocket, pulled her keys from another. Should she dive under the gate or climb over the top? She was there. She was safe. She…

A large, black figure stepped from behind the guard-house and crossed in front of her car, silhouetting himself in the blinding headlights. J.C. slammed into the gate, crashing to a stop. The flashlight flew from her hand.

"Who are you?" The figure moved. J.C. backpedaled. "Stay away from me!"

"I told you you'd be sorry." Tires squealed in the background, an engine roared. But the sounds were lost in her stopped-up ears as her eyes strained to bring the man into focus. "I warned you and you wouldn't listen. I guess I'll just have to show you what a real soldier can do."

He stepped out of the lights and she could make out the pattern of a camouflage uniform. Black, calf-high boots. But his face. She couldn't see his face. "I'll scream my head off," she warned, feeling no advantage now that she could make out the bulk of a knife belted at his waist—and the barrel of a gun pointed at her stomach. "There are sixty apartments in that building. Someone will hear."

"Scream away, bitch. I've rewritten your columns the way they should be. All I have to do is get rid of you and no one will ever know who Dr. Cyn really is."

Lightning flashed, giving her a split-second glimpse of the green and black greasepaint that distorted the features on his face. And the glasses. This sicko wore glasses. She knew this sicko.

"Ben?" Chunky brainiac with the sweet personality and the enlistment brochures? "My God, Ben, why?"

Her hips hit the fender of a car. She was out of room to retreat, but he kept advancing. She jumped at the thunder smacking the sky overhead, or maybe it was the roar of an engine. It didn't matter. Ben snatched her arm above the elbow and dragged her into step beside him. He jabbed the gun into her ribs and marched her toward the river.

"You give soldiers a bad name, J.C. I tried to tell you to stop. Now I have to do this."

"But you're not a soldier." She jerked against his arm. He nearly jerked hers out of its socket, forcing her back beside him. For an out of shape computer nerd, he was surprisingly strong. "Why are you dressed like that? Where did you get that gun?"

"Do you know how many women give a four-eyed fat guy a second look?"

She imagined she heard her name on a rumble of thunder.

"But you're cute. You're funny. Nice. Smart." *Psycho*.

"I tell them I'm a soldier and they're all over me." He laughed. At his own cleverness? At her imminent demise? "You can buy anything you want over the Internet. I got the costume, the weapons—"

"It's not a costume," she argued, feeling an odd sense of pride overriding her fear. "It's something you earn the right to wear."

"Why the hell couldn't you say *that* in your column, Dr. Cyn? What is that about, anyway? *Sin*ful? Even your nickname's lame, Dr. Josephine Cynthia Gardner."

"J.C.!"

She turned along with Ben to see a golden-haired tank of a man hurtling toward them.

"He has a gun!"

But the warning was a moot point. Ethan McCormick

plowed into Ben. J.C. sailed out of harm's way. The struggle was one-sided and brief. She saw a fist, heard a grunt.

Then Ethan was on his feet, tucking the gun and the knife into the back of his jeans. Ben was out cold on the asphalt and J.C. was flying into Ethan's waiting arms. He scooped her up off the ground. Kissed her hard, muttered a curse, then set her down and stepped away as he pulled out his phone and called the police.

"Are you hurt?" he asked between deep, ragged breaths.

"No. Ethan, you came back. I needed you and you were there." She clutched at his shirt, wondering why he was shielding her from an unconscious man, wishing he'd hold her in his arms again. "I couldn't find Norman, though. He might be hurt."

"I found your security guard knocked out in a car parked on the street. I saw your abandoned Camaro. I heard what that bastard said to you. What he called you. *Dr. Cyn.*"

And now she understood why he hadn't kept her in his arms.

The cold night soaked into her very soul.

"I tried to tell you, Ethan. At the Craddocks'. I tried to explain, but you wouldn't listen. Can we sit down and talk about this?"

"Talk?" No emotion whatsoever registered on his rain-streaked face when he looked down at her. "I don't consort with the enemy, Dr. Cyn."

14

"McCormick!"

Ethan snapped to attention in General Craddock's outer office. "Yes, sir."

"What the hell took you so long?"

With a nod from the general's aide de camp, he strode into the roomy Pentagon office and resumed his ramrod straight posture. He stared straight ahead, not looking at the general until given permission to do so. "You called my office five minutes ago, sir. I came down as soon as I got your message."

"We have a situation, McCormick."

"Situation, sir?"

Ethan's whole life was a situation. It had been since that night a week ago when he'd learned the truth about J.C.'s duplicity. He'd gone and done the same stupid thing he had with Bethany Mead. He'd fallen in love with a woman who was using him. Hell, yeah, he'd been using J.C., too. But at least he'd been up-front about it.

But then J.C. had complicated things by insisting on pursuing that inexplicable sexual chemistry between them. He still thirsted for the taste of her lips, still hungered for the feel of her firm, responsive body against his. Then she'd gotten him all mixed up by tapping into his heart, sensing his fears and regrets—convincing him to share what he hid deep inside him, healing the rawness with funny words and luscious kisses and the hot, ready welcome of her body.

Bethany's betrayal had stung his ego, damaged his career. But J.C.'s lie had cut his heart straight in two. He'd been so scared he wouldn't get to her in time, that he couldn't keep her safe. And then she'd stabbed him in the back.

He had a situation, all right.

Dr. Cyn, not J.C., had been the target of Benjamin Grant's delusional wrath. The crazy kid had tried to enlist in three different branches of the service and been turned down each time because he couldn't pass the physical. So he'd created, armed and defended his own little army of one against the advice columnist he blamed for giving him a bad rap with the women he wanted to date. Crazy.

Hell. Like wearing the uniform made meeting the right woman any easier. He sure knew how to pick them. He'd fallen in love with a traitor to the Corps.

General Craddock was looking through his window blinds, searching for something at ground level outside. "Damn," he muttered. "Too late."

Ethan dragged his thoughts back to the job that had always been there for him. "Is there a problem, sir?"

Craddock turned away from the window and propped his hands behind his back. "I'll say. Your fiancée was just in here."

Ethan nearly jerked from his attentive posture. "Sorry, sir. She shouldn't have bothered you. She's not really my fiancée."

"I know the whole story. She seems as miserable as you."

His gaze darted to the general. "Sir?"

Craddock swore and crossed to his desk. "Romance is wasted on the young. Too much plotting and contriving.

I swear to God, if you like the girl, just say so, and give up all these stupid games.''

"I don't understand what you're saying, sir.''

"At ease, McCormick. Sit.'' With a steadying breath, Ethan perched on the edge of a chair. "Do you love J.C.?''

"I don't think my personal—''

"Well, I like her. A lot. She'd make a damn fine addition to the Corps.''

Ethan flat out stared at his superior officer. "Sir?''

"You know the story about her father, don't you? Damn bastards like that give all of us a bad name.''

Bigamy, cheating on her mother, abandoning her—Earl Gardner's choices had all played a factor in J.C.'s unwillingness to trust him with either her heart or the truth. Hearing it from a third party helped Ethan understand just how far J.C. had to come to feel anything for him at all. Wait a minute. A third party? "She came here to tell you about her father?''

"She was here to make a formal apology to the Corps and show me her final Dr. Cyn column about military relationships.''

There it was. She'd taken a final parting shot at the Corps because of him. "I didn't know that's who she was, sir. When she said she was a relationship therapist, I thought—''

The general picked up the newspaper and tossed it across the desk. "Good stuff, McCormick. I like her style. Tells it like it is and isn't afraid to admit when she's wrong.''

Ethan scanned the article. *This* was Dr. Cyn? Writing how her firsthand education with a certain Marine changed her mind about loving a man in uniform. Loving?

Craddock continued. "She said that you're a man of

character and integrity—that you stuck by her when she had that imposter stalking her. She made a very convincing argument about why I should give you that lieutenant colonel promotion.''

"She had no right to, sir.''

But he kept reading, hearing her voice in the words. *Don't prejudge a military lover the way I did, ladies. It's the man that makes the uniform—not the other way around.*

Good God, what had he done? What could he do to make this right? Bethany had cast him aside without so much as batting an eyelash. But J.C. was fighting for him. With her words and actions, she was trying to do right by him. She'd made the tough choice he hadn't been able to make. Until now.

Ethan laid the paper on desk and stood. "J. C. Gardner is the kind of woman who says what she thinks and means what she says. She's got a good heart, and she's not afraid to use it to help others. If that kind of honesty has been a black mark on the Corps, I won't apologize for it. For what it's worth, I like her style, too.''

"So what are we going to do about this situation, Major? An advocate like this would be an asset to the Corps. And I have a feeling she could go a long way toward improving the morale in this office if we can get her back on the team.''

Get her back.

Ethan snapped to attention. "Request permission to take care of the situation myself, sir.''

"Permission granted.'' General Craddock grinned. "I just saw her leave the parking lot. She said she was headed home. If you hurry, you can catch her.''

"Is that an order, sir?''

"Does it have to be?''

J.C.'S HEART LURCHED in her chest when she opened her apartment door. Ethan stood there in his blue and khaki uniform—tall, proud, strong—intense as always. But the message in those gray eyes confused her.

She held tight to the door, desperately wanting to believe what those eyes promised. Forgiveness. Trust. Forever.

"May I come in?" he asked.

Once she realized how hard she'd been staring, she blinked and backed aside. "Of course. Sorry."

He strode in, closed the door for her and fastened all three locks. "Don't apologize to me," he said, tucking his flat white hat beneath his arm. "I'm the one who owes you an apology."

"For what?" She crossed into the living room, trying to warm herself in the light shining through her replacement picture window. "I'm the one who lied to you about Dr. Cyn and got you into trouble."

"The only trouble was in my own stubborn head." He set down his hat and followed her to the purple chaise lounge. "Craddock loves you. The Corps loves you.

"I love you."

J.C. snapped her head around. He meant that metaphorically, right? But those eyes said it was the real thing. A nervous swarm of bees buzzed in her stomach. "What?"

Not her snappiest comeback.

He snatched her left hand up between them and frowned. "Where's my mother's ring?"

"Oh." It was a metaphoric *I love you.* She hurried into the kitchen and retrieved the ring in its box from her purse. "Here." She handed it over, feeling as if she was handing over the best part of her life. "I didn't think you wanted me to continue the charade. I talked to General

Craddock this morning and explained everything. The fake engagement, my research, Ben Grant, Dr. Cyn.''

He opened the box and pulled out the ring. "I talked to Craddock, too. I explained that I was an idiot to judge you by what some other woman did to me. You didn't betray me—I betrayed us by not giving you and me a real chance. And I'm sorry. Here.''

He lifted at her left hand and slipped the ring onto the tip of her third finger. "I said I'd take it back when you and I were done." She watched his eyes as he slid the ring down into place. He *did* love her. "I hope you'll always keep it.''

The chill vanished from her heart and sunshine flooded her soul. Smiling with her whole body, she launched herself into Ethan's arms. "Oh, yes, Ethan. Yes. Yes." She hugged her arms around his neck, kissed his ear, his shoulder, whatever she could reach. "I love you, too.''

His hands slid down to cup her bottom through her jeans and lift her. He split her legs around his hips, spun, and plopped down onto the chaise with her straddling his lap. "You make me crazy, Jo. You make me happy. You make me feel alive.''

His fingers combed through her hair, cradled her head. And he kissed her. Wildly. Wetly. Long and deep. She hugged his swelling heat and kissed him back. "You make me crazy." Their fingers fumbled for shirt buttons together. "You make me happy." She arched her back as he swept her blouse and bra off her arms. He shrugged those massive shoulders as she pushed his shirt down to his waist. And then they were holding each other tightly, chest to chest, skin to skin. And kissing. Oh, God, she loved kissing this man! "You make me believe in us.''

Ethan leaned back into the chaise's cushions, pulling her on top of him. He was kissing her breasts now, rolling the tips beneath his tongue and stoking the heat at her most feminine core.

"I was so scared when I saw that crazy kid dragging you along to the river. When I saw his gun." He unzipped her jeans and slipped his hands inside to squeeze her bottom. "Hell, J.C., the minute I heard your voice on my phone saying you needed me, I wanted to be here with you. I thought I could settle it with Guerro, but it wasn't him. By then I was scared I couldn't get to you in time."

J.C. pulled his mouth back to hers and kissed his deeply, apologizing for the fear she heard in his voice. Sitting atop the jutting ridge of his desire, she pulled back just far enough to frame his square jaw between her hands. The love shining from his eyes amazed her. "That wasn't fair of me to put that kind of pressure on you. I understand now that it's as hard for a Marine to be away from the people he cares about as it is for us to miss you."

She dropped a humble kiss to his lips. "I can take care of myself." She felt him shift beneath her, sensed the protest on his lips. She pressed two fingers over his mouth and shushed him. "If I have to." Searching his eyes, she saw that he could reluctantly accept this truth. Then she arched one eyebrow and smiled wickedly. "But I love it when you're here to save the day."

He rewarded her for that one with a swat on the rump that thrust her against every delicious part of him. She was more than game to try something a tad on the kinky side with this man. But she had a better idea for right now. Something just for him.

Hushing his questions with a reassuring kiss, J.C. climbed off Ethan and shed her jeans. Then she backed toward her bedroom, slipping two fingers beneath the elastic of her panties. She teased him as she touched herself, and found her lips swollen and wet and ready for him as always. He sat up, definitely interested in her invitation. She turned around, wiggled her bottom at him, then slipped the panties off and tossed them into his lap.

"Lose the uniform, Major," she ordered. "And follow me."

She led him to the bed where they tumbled onto the sheets together, completely naked, completely happy, completely in love.

And when he filled the heart of her with the gift of himself, and carried them both to that place of infinite joy and release, she knew she finally understood what it was about a military man that made him so irresistible. The knowledge was well worth losing that fifty-dollar bet.

Some time later, lying in the center of her bed, covered with a little bit of sheet, a lot of man and utter contentment, J.C. sighed. "Wow. Naked in the bed, missionary style. I like trying new things." She trailed her fingers along the back of Ethan's neck and felt him shiver in response. "I don't think sex with you will ever be boring."

He trailed his fingers along the inside of her thigh and cooed with drowsy anticipation as he slipped them inside her. "I don't think life with you will ever be boring."

And just like that, it started again. A kiss. A touch. A word.

A phone rang, leaving J.C. gasping for breath and satisfaction as Ethan left the bed to retrieve both their cells. "Yours or mine?" she called after him when his big, gloriously naked body disappeared from sight.

He came back, his phone to his ear, a smile on his face, and his eyes promising everything her aching body wanted from him. "Yes, sir. Thank you, sir." He climbed back into bed, straddled her hips and knelt above her, giving her something to play with while he finished the call. "I'll be there first thing in the morning. Yes, sir."

He disconnected the call, dropped the phone on the bedside table and slipped inside her. "Now. Where were we?"

"I love you, Major."

He gathered her into his arms and claimed her lips in a long, drugging kiss. But then he pulled back, smoothing aside the wisps of hair that clung to her cheeks and forehead. His eyes glinted with a hint of mischief she wasn't used to seeing. "That's not quite right."

"What do you mean? Of course, I love you."

"Love me all you want," he teased. He was moving inside her, leaning in to kiss her again. Taking her to blissful heights and showing her the love and devotion and security she'd always craved.

"But it's Lieutenant Colonel."

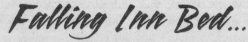

HARLEQUIN® *Blaze*™
Cover Model Contest Update

We asked you to send us pictures of your hot, gorgeous *and* romantic guys, and you did!

From all of the entries, we finally selected
the winner and put him right where he
deserves to be: on one of our covers.

Check him out on the front of
VERY TRULY SEXY
by Dawn Atkins
Harlequin Blaze #155
October 2004

**Don't miss this story that's every bit as
hot and romantic as the guy on the cover!**

Look for this book at your favorite retail outlet.

If you enjoyed what you just read,
then we've got an offer you can't resist!

Take 2 bestselling love stories FREE!

Plus get a FREE surprise gift!